W9-COG-601

PENELOPE'S IRISH

EXPERIENCES

BY

KATE DOUGLAS WIGGIN

BOSTON AND NEW YORK

HOUGHTON, MIFFLIN AND COMPANY

The Riverside Press, Cambridge

1901

TO MY FIRST IRISH FRIEND

JANE BARLOW

New York, March 25, 1901

CONTENTS

PART FIRST

LEINSTER

PENELOPE'S IRISH EXPERIENCES

PART FIRST. LEINSTER

I

WE EMULATE THE ROLLO BOOKS

" Sure a terrible time I was out o' the way,
    Over the sea, over the sea,
Till I come to Ireland one sunny day, —
    Betther for me, betther for me :
The first time me fut got the feel o' the ground
I was strollin' along in an Irish city
That has n't its aquil the world around,
    For the air that is sweet an' the girls that are pretty."
                                    Moira O'Neill.

DUBLIN, O'Carolan's Private Hotel.

IT is the most absurd thing in the world that
Salemina, Francesca, and I should be in Ireland
together.

That any three spinsters should be fellow-trav-
elers is not in itself extraordinary, and so our
former journeyings in England and Scotland
could hardly be described as eccentric in any
way ; but now that I am a matron and Francesca
is shortly to be married, it is odd, to say the least,
to see us cosily ensconced in a private sitting-room

of a Dublin hotel, the table laid for three, and not a vestige of a man anywhere to be seen. Where, one might ask, if he knew the antecedent circumstances, are Miss Hamilton's American spouse and Miss Monroe's Scottish lover?

Francesca had passed most of the winter in Scotland. Her indulgent parent had given his consent to her marriage with a Scotsman, but insisted that she take a year to make up her mind as to which particular one. Memories of her past flirtations, divagations, plans for a life of single blessedness, all conspired to make him incredulous, and the loyal Salemina, feeling some responsibility in the matter, had elected to remain by Francesca's side during the time when her affections were supposed to be crystallizing into some permanent form.

It was natural enough that my husband and I should spend the first summer of our married life abroad, for we had been accustomed to do this before we met, a period that we always allude to as the Dark Ages ; but no sooner had we arrived in Edinburgh, and no sooner had my husband persuaded our two friends to join us in a long, delicious Irish holiday, than he was compelled to return to America for a month or so.

I think you must number among your acquaintances such a man as Mr. William Beresford, whose wife I have the honor to be. Physically the type is vigorous, or has the appearance and gives the impression of being vigorous, because it has never the time to be otherwise, since it is always engaged in nursing its ailing or decrepit relatives. Intellectually it is full of vitality; any mind grows when it is exercised, and the brain that has to settle all its own affairs and all the affairs of its friends and acquaintances could never lack energy. Spiritually it is almost too good for earth, and any woman who lives in the house with it has moments of despondency and self-chastisement, in which she fears that heaven may prove all too small to contain the perfect being and its unregenerate family as well.

Financially it has at least a moderate bank account; that is, it is never penniless, indeed it can never afford to be, because it is peremptory that it should possess funds in order to disburse them to needier brothers. There is never an hour when Mr. William Beresford is not signing notes and bonds and drafts for less fortunate men; giving small loans just to " help a fellow over a hard place; " educating friends' children, starting them in business, or securing appointments for them. The widow and the fatherless have worn such an obvious path to his office and residence that no bereaved person could possibly lose his way, and as a matter of fact no one of them ever does. This special journey of his to America has been made necessary because, first, his cousin's widow has been defrauded of a large sum by her man of business; and second, his college chum and dearest friend has just died in Chicago after appointing him executor of his estate and guardian of his only child. The wording of the will is, " as a sacred charge and with full power." Incidentally, as it were, one of his junior partners has been ordered a long sea voyage, and another has to go somewhere for mud baths. The junior partners were my idea, and were suggested solely that their senior might be left more or less free from business care, but it was impossible that Willie should have selected sound, robust partners — his tastes do not incline him in the direction of selfish ease ; accordingly he chose two delightful, estimable, frail gentlemen who needed comfortable incomes in conjunction with light duties.

I am railing at my husband for all this, but I love him for it just the same, and it shows why the table is laid for three.

" Salemina," I said, extending my slipper toe to the glowing peat, which by extraordinary effort had been brought up from the hotel kitchen, as a bit of local color, " it is ridiculous that we three women should be in Ireland together ; it's the sort of thing that happens in a book, and of which we say that it could never occur in real life. Three persons do not spend successive seasons in England, Scotland, and Ireland unless they are writing an Itinerary of the British Isles.

The situation is possible, certainly, but it is n't simple, or natural, or probable. We are behaving precisely like characters in fiction, who, having been popular in the first volume, are exploited again and again until their popularity wanes. We are like the Trotty books or the Elsie Dinsmore series. England was our first volume, Scotland our second, and here we are, if you please, about to live a third volume in Ireland. We fall in love, we marry and are given in marriage, we promote and take part in international alliances, but when the curtain goes up again, our accumulations, acquisitions — whatever you choose to call them — have disappeared. We are not to the superficial eye the spinster-philanthropist, the bride to be, the wife of a year ; we are 'the same old Salemina, Francesca, and Penelope. It is so dramatic that my husband should be called to America ; as a woman I miss him and need him ; as a character I am much better single. I don't suppose publishers like married heroines any more than managers like married leading ladies. Then how entirely proper it is that Ronald Macdonald cannot leave his new parish in the Highlands. The one, my husband, belongs to the first volume ; Francesca's lover to the second; and good gracious, Salemina, don't you see the inference ? "

" I may be dull," she replied, " but I confess I do not."

" We are three."

" Who is three ? "

" That is not good English, but I repeat with different emphasis *we* are three. I fell in love in England, Francesca fell in love in Scotland " — And here I paused, watching the blush mount rosily to Salemina's gray hair ; pink is very becoming to gray, and that, we always say, accounts more satisfactorily for Salemina's frequent blushes than her modesty, which is about of the usual sort.

" Your argument is interesting and even ingenious," she replied, "but I fail to see my responsibility. If you persist in thinking of me as a character in fiction, I shall rebel. I am not the stuff of which heroines are made ; besides, I would never appear in anything so cheap and obvious as a series, and the three-volume novel is as much out of fashion as the Rollo books."

" But we are unconscious heroines, you understand," I explained. " While we were experiencing our experiences we did not notice them, but they have attained by degrees a sufficient bulk so that they are visible to the naked eye. We can look back now and perceive the path we have traveled."

" It is n't retrospect I object to, but anticipation," she retorted ; " not history, but prophecy. It is one thing to gaze sentimentally at the road you have traveled, quite another to conjure up impossible pictures of the future."

Salemina calls herself a trifle over forty, but I am not certain of her age, and think perhaps that she is uncertain herself. She has good reason to forget it, and so have we. Of course she could consult the Bible family record daily, but if she consulted her looking-glass afterward the one impression would always nullify the other. Her hair is silvered, it is true, but that is so clearly a trick of Nature that it makes her look younger rather than older.

Francesca came into the room just here. I said a moment ago that she was the same old Francesca, but I was wrong; she is softening, sweetening, expanding; in a word, blooming. Not only this, but Ronald Macdonald's likeness has been stamped upon her in some magical way, so that, although she has not lost her own personality, she seems to have added a reflection of his. In the glimpses of herself, her views, feelings, opinions, convictions, which she gives us in a kind of solution, as it were, there are always traces of Ronald Macdonald ; or, to be more poetical, he seems to have bent over the crystal pool, and his image is reflected there.

You remember in New England they allude to a bride as " she that was " a so and so. In my private interviews with Salemina I now habitually allude to Francesca as " she that was a Monroe ;" it is so significant of her present state of absorption. Several times this week I have been

obliged to inquire, " Was I, by any chance, as
absent-minded and dull in Pettybaw as Francesca
is under the same circumstances in Dublin ? "

" Quite."

" Duller if anything."

These candid replies being uttered in cheerful
unison I change the subject, but cannot resist
telling them both casually that the building of
the Royal Dublin Society is in Kildare Street,
just three minutes' walk from O'Carolan's, and
that I have noticed it is for the promotion of
Husbandry and other useful arts and sciences.

II

> " And I will make my journey, if life and health but stand,
>   Unto that pleasant country, that fresh and fragrant strand,
>   And leave your boasted braveries, your wealth and high com-
>   mand,
> For the fair hills of holy Ireland."
>
> *Sir Samuel Ferguson.*

OUR mutual relations have changed little, not-withstanding that betrothals and marriages have intervened, and in spite of the fact that Salemina has grown a year younger ; a mysterious feat that she has accomplished on each anniversary of her birth since the forming of our alliance.

It is many months since we traveled together in Scotland, but on entering this very room in Dublin, the other day, we proceeded to show our several individualities as usual, — I going to the window to see the view, Francesca consulting the placard on the door for hours of table d'hôte, and Salemina walking to the grate and lifting the ugly little paper screen to say, "There is a fire laid ; how nice ! " As the matron I have been promoted to a nominal charge of the traveling arrangements. Therefore, while the others drive

or sail, read or write, I am buried in Murray's
Handbook, or immersed in maps. When I sleep,
my dreams are spotted, starred, notched, and
lined with hieroglyphics, circles, horizontal
dashes, long lines, and black dots,

signifying hotels, coach and rail routes, and
tramways.

All this would have been done by Himself with
the greatest ease in the world. In the humbler
walks of Irish life the head of the house, if he
is of the proper sort, is called Himself, and it is
in the shadow of this stately title that my Ulysses
will appear in this chronicle.

I am quite sure I do not believe in the inferi-
ority of woman, but I have a feeling that a man
is a trifle superior in practical affairs. If I am
in doubt, and there is no husband, brother, or
cousin near, from whom to seek advice, I instinctively ask the butler or the coachman rather than
a female friend ; also, when a female friend has
consulted the Bradshaw in my behalf, I slip out
and seek confirmation from the butcher's boy or
the milkman. Himself would have laid out all
our journeying for us, and we should have gone
placidly along in well-ordered paths. As it is,
we are already pledged to do the most absurd and

unusual things, and Ireland bids fair to be seen in the most topsy-turvy, helter-skelter fashion imaginable.

Francesca's propositions are especially nonsensical, being provocative of fruitless discussion, and adding absolutely nothing to the sum of human intelligence.

"Why not start without any special route in view, and visit the towns with which we already have familiar associations?" she asked. "We should have all sorts of experiences by the way, and be free from the blighting influences of a definite purpose. Who that has ever traveled fails to call to mind certain images when the names of cities come up in general conversation? If Bologna, Brussels, or Lima is mentioned, I think at once of sausages, sprouts, and beans, and it gives me a feeling of friendly intimacy. I remember Neufchâtel and Cheddar by their cheeses, Dorking and Cochin China by their hens, Whitby by its jet, or York by its hams, so that I am never wholly ignorant of places and their subtle associations."

"That method appeals strongly to the fancy," said Salemina dryly. "What subtle associations have you already established in Ireland?"

"Let me see," she responded thoughtfully; "the list is not a long one. Limerick and Carrickmacross for lace, Shandon for the bells, Blarney and Donnybrook for the Stone and the Fair,

Kilkenny for the cats, and Balbriggan for the stockings."

" You are sordid this morning," reproved Salemina ; " it would be better if you remembered Limerick by the famous siege, and Balbriggan as the place where King William encamped with his army after the battle of the Boyne."

" I 've studied the song writers more than the histories and geographies," I said, " so I should like to go to Bray and look up the Vicar, then to Coleraine to see where Kitty broke the famous pitcher ; or to Tara where the Harp that Once, or to Athlone where dwelt the Widow Malone, Ochone, and so on ; just start with an armful of Tom Moore's poems and Lover's and Ferguson's, and yes," I added generously, " some of the nice moderns, and visit the scenes they 've written about."

" And be disappointed," quoth Francesca cynically. " Poets see everything by the light that never was on sea or land ; still I won't deny that they help the blind, and I should rather like to know if there are still any Nora Creinas and Sweet Peggies and Pretty Girls Milking their Cows."

" I am very anxious to visit as many of the Round Towers as possible," said Salemina. " When I was a girl of seventeen I had a very dear friend, a young Irishman, who has since become a well-known antiquary and archæologist.

He was a student, and afterwards, I think, a professor here in Trinity College, but I have not heard from him for many years."

" Don't look him up, darling," pleaded Francesca. " You are so much our superior now that we positively must protect you from all elevating influences."

" I won't insist on the Round Towers," smiled Salemina, " and I think Penelope's idea a delightful one ; we might add to it a sort of literary pilgrimage to the homes and haunts of Ireland's famous writers."

" I did n't know that she had any," interrupted Francesca.

This is a favorite method of conversation with that spoiled young person ; it seems to appeal to her in three different ways : she likes to belittle herself, she likes to shock Salemina, and she likes to have information given her on the spot in some succinct, portable, convenient form.

" Oh," she continued apologetically, " of course there are Dean Swift and Thomas Moore and Charles Lever."

" And," I added, " certain minor authors named Goldsmith, Sterne, Steele, and Samuel Lover."

" And Bishop Berkeley, and Brinsley Sheridan, and Maria Edgeworth, and Father Prout," continued Salemina, " and certain great speech-makers like Burke and Grattan and Curran ; and how

delightful to visit all the places connected with
Stella and Vanessa, and the spot where Spenser
wrote the Faerie Queene."

> " Nor own a land on earth but one,
>   We're Paddies, and no more,"

sang Francesca. " You will be telling me in a
moment that Thomas Carlyle was born in Ske-
reenarinka, and that Shakespeare wrote Romeo
and Juliet in Coolagarranoe," for she had drawn
the guidebook toward her and made good use of
it. " Let us do the literary pilgrimage, certainly,
before we leave Ireland, but suppose we begin with
something less intellectual. This is the most pug-
nacious map I ever gazed upon. All the names
seem to begin or end with kill, bally, whack,
shock, or knock ; no wonder the Irish make good
soldiers ! Suppose we start with a sanguinary
trip to the Kill places, so that I can tell any
timid Americans I meet in traveling that I have
been to Kilmacow and to Kilmacthomas, and am
going to-morrow to Kilmore, and next day to
Kilumaule."

" I think that must have been said before," I
objected.

" It is so obvious that it's not unlikely," she
rejoined ; " then let us simply agree to go afterwards to see all the Bally places from Ballydehob
on the south to Ballycastle or Ballymoney on the
north, and from Ballynahinch or Ballywilliam on

the east to Ballyvaughan or Ballybunnion on the west, and passing through, in transit,

> Ballyragget,
> Ballysadare,
> Ballybrophy,
> Ballinasloe,
> Ballyhooley,
> Ballycumber,
> Ballyduff,
> Ballynashee,
> Ballywhack.

Don't they all sound jolly and grotesque ? "

"They do indeed," we agreed, " and the plan is quite worthy of you ; we can say no more."

We had now developed so many more ideas than we could possibly use that the labor of deciding among them was the next thing to be done. Each of us stood out boldly for her own project, — even Francesca clinging, from sheer willfulness, to her worthless and absurd itineraries, — until, in order to bring the matter to any sort of decision, somebody suggested that we consult Benella ; which reminds me that you have not yet the pleasure of Benella's acquaintance.

III

" O bay of Dublin, my heart you 're troublin',
Your beauty haunts me like a fever dream."

Lady Dufferin.

To perform the introduction properly I must go back a day or two. We had elected to cross to Dublin directly from Scotland, an easy night journey. Accordingly we embarked in a steamer called the Prince or the King of something or other, the name being many degrees more princely or kingly than the craft itself.

We had intended, too, to make our own comparison of the bay of Dublin and the bay of Naples, because every traveler, from Charles Lever's Jack Hinton down to Thackeray and Mr. Alfred Austin, has always made it a point of honor to do so. We were balked in our conscientious endeavor, because we arrived at the North Wall forty minutes earlier than the hour set by the steamship company. It is quite impossible for anything in Ireland to be done strictly on the minute, and in struggling not to be hopelessly behind time, a " disthressful counthry " will occasionally be ahead of it. We had been told that we should arrive in a drizzling rain, and that no one but Lady Dufferin had ever on approaching Ireland seen the " sweet faces of the Wicklow mountains reflected in a smooth and silver sea." The grumblers were right on this special occasion, although we have proved them false more than once since.

I was in a fever of fear that Ireland would not be as Irish as we wished it to be. It seemed probable that processions of prosperous aldermen, school directors, contractors, mayors, and ward politicians, returning to their native land to see how Herself was getting on, the crathur, might have deposited on the soil successive layers of Irish-American virtues, such as punctuality, thrift, and cleanliness, until they had quite obscured fair Erin's peculiar and pathetic charm. We longed for the new Ireland as fervently as any of her own patriots, but we wished to see the old Ireland before it passed. There is plenty of it left (alas! the patriots would say), and Dublin was as dear and as dirty as when Lady Morgan first called it so, long years ago. The boat was met by a crowd of ragged gossoons, most of them barefooted, some of them stockingless and in men's shoes, and several of them with flowers in their unspeakable hats and caps. There were no cabs or jaunting cars because we had not been expected so early, and the jarveys were in attend-

ance on the Holyhead steamer. It was while I
was searching for a piece of lost luggage that I
saw the stewardess assisting a young woman off
the gang plank, and leading her toward a pile of
wool bags on the dock. She sank helplessly on
one of them, and leaned her head on another.
As the night had been one calculated to disturb
the physical equilibrium of a poor sailor, and the
breakfast of a character to discourage the stout-
est stomach, I gave her a careless thought of pity
and speedily forgot her. Two trunks, a hold-all,
a hatbox, — in which reposed, in solitary gran-
deur, Francesca's picture hat, intended for the
further undoing of the Irish gentry, — a guitar
case, two bags, three umbrellas; all were safe
but Salemina's large Vuitton trunk and my valise,
which had been last seen at Edinburgh station.
Salemina returned to the boat, while Francesca
and I wended our way among the heaps of luggage, followed by crowds of ragamuffins, who offered to run for a car, run for a cab, run for a
porter, carry our luggage up the street to the cab
stand, carry our wraps, carry us, "do any mortial
thing for a penny, melady, an' there is no cars
here, melady, God bless me sowl, and that He be
good to us all if I 'm tellin' you a word of a lie !"

Entirely unused to this flow of conversation, we
were obliged to stop every few seconds to recount
our luggage and try to remember what we were
looking for. We all met finally, and I rescued

Salemina from the voluble thanks of an old woman to whom she had thoughtlessly given a threepenny bit. This mother of a "long wake family"
was wishing that Salemina might live to "ate the
hin" that scratched over her grave, and invoking
many other uncommon and picturesque blessings,
but we were obliged to ask her to desist and let
us attend to our own business.

"Will I clane the whole of thim off for you for
a penny, your ladyship's honor ma'am?" asked the
oldest of the ragamuffins, and I gladly assented
to the novel proposition. He did it, too, and
there seemed to be no hurt feelings in the company.

Just then there was a rattle of cabs and side
cars, and our self-constituted major-domo engaged two of them to await our pleasure. At the
same moment our eyes lighted upon Salemina's
huge Vuitton, which had been dragged behind
the pile of wool sacks. It was no wonder it had
escaped our notice, for it was mostly covered by
the person of the seasick maiden whom I had
seen on the arm of the stewardess. She was
seated on it, exhaustion in every line of her figure, her head upon my traveling bag, her feet
dangling over the edge until they just touched
the "S. P., Salem, Mass., U. S. A." painted in
large red letters on the end. She was too ill to
respond to our questions, but there was no mis-
taking her nationality. Her dress, hat, shoes,

gloves, face, figure were American. We sent for
the stewardess, who told us that she had arrived
in Glasgow on the day previous, and had been
very ill all the way coming from Boston.

"Boston!" exclaimed Salemina. "Do you say
she is from Boston, poor thing?"

("I did n't know that a person living in Boston
could ever, under any circumstances, be a 'poor
thing,'" whispered Francesca to me.)

"She was not fit to be crossing last night, and
the doctor on the American ship told her so, and
advised her to stay in bed for three days before
coming to Ireland; but it seems as if she were
determined to get to her journey's end."

"We must have our trunk," I interposed.
"Can't we move her carefully over to the wool
sacks, and won't you stay with her until her
friends come?"

"She has no friends in this country, ma'am.
She's just traveling for pleasure like."

"Good gracious! what a position for her to be
in," said Salemina. "Can't you take her back to
the steamer and put her to bed?"

"I could ask the captain, certainly, miss,
though of course it's something we never do, and
besides, we have to set the ship to rights and go
across again this evening."

"Ask her what hotel she is going to, Salemina,"
we suggested, "and let us drop her there, and
put her in charge of the housekeeper; of course

if it is only seasickness she will be all right in the morning."

The girl's eyes were closed, but she opened them languidly as Salemina chafed her cold hands, and asked gently if we could not drive her to a hotel.

" Is — this — your — baggage ? " she whispered.

" It is," Salemina answered, somewhat puzzled.

" Then don't — leave me here, I am from Salem — myself," whereupon without any more warning she promptly fainted away on the trunk.

The situation was becoming embarrassing. The assemblage grew larger, and a more interested and sympathetic audience I never saw. To an Irish crowd, always warm-hearted and kindly, willing to take any trouble for friend or stranger, and with a positive terror of loneliness, or separation from kith and kin, the helpless creature appealed in every way. One and another joined the group with a " Holy Biddy ! what's this at all ? "

" The saints presarve us, is it dyin' she is ? "

" Look at the iligant duds she do be wearin'."

" Call the docthor is it ? God give you sinse ! Sure the docthors is only a flock of omadhauns."

" Is it your daughter she is, ma'am ? " (This to Salemina.)

" She 's from Ameriky, the poor mischancy crathur."

"Give her a toothful of whiskey, your ladyship. Sure it's nayther bite nor sup she's had the morn, and belike she's as impty as a quarry-hole."

When this last expression from the mother of the long weak family fell upon Salemina's cultured ears she looked desperate.

We could not leave a fellow countrywoman, least of all could Salemina forsake a fellow citizen, in such a hapless plight.

"Take one cab with Francesca and the luggage, Penelope," she whispered. "I will bring the girl with me, put her to bed, find her friends, and see that she starts on her journey safely; it's very awkward, but there's nothing else to be done."

So we departed in a chorus of popular approval.

"Sure it's you that have the good hearts!"

"May the heavens be your bed!"

"May the journey thrive wid her, the crathur!"

Francesca and I arrived first at the hotel where our rooms were already engaged, and there proved to be a comfortable little dressing, or maid's, room just off Salemina's.

Here the Derelict was presently ensconced, and there she lay, in a sort of profound exhaustion, all day, without once absolutely regaining her consciousness. Instead of visiting the National Gallery as I had intended, I returned to the dock to see if I could find the girl's luggage, or get any further information from the stewardess before she left Dublin.

"I'll send the doctor at once, but we must learn all possible particulars now," I said maliciously to poor Salemina. "It would be so awkward, you know, if you should be arrested for abduction."

The doctor thought it was probably nothing more than the complete prostration that might follow eight days of seasickness, but the patient's heart was certainly a little weak, and she needed the utmost quiet. His fee was a guinea for the first visit, and he would drop in again in the course of the afternoon to relieve our anxiety. We took turns in watching by her bedside, but the two unemployed ones lingered forlornly near, and had no heart for sight-seeing. Francesca did, however, purchase opera tickets for the evening, and secretly engaged the housemaid to act as head nurse in our absence.

As we were dining at seven, we heard a faint voice in the little room beyond. Salemina left her dinner and went in to find her charge slightly better. We had been able thus far only to take off her dress, shoes, and such garments as made her uncomfortable ; Salemina now managed to slip on a nightdress and put her under the bed covers, returning then to her cold mutton cutlet.

"She's an extraordinary person," she said,

absently playing with her knife and fork. " She
did n't ask me where she was, or show any interest in her surroundings ; perhaps she is still too
weak. She said she was better, and when I had
made her ready for bed she whispered, ' I 've
got to say my prayers.'

" ' Say them by all means,' I replied.

" ' But I must get up and kneel down,' she
said.

" I told her she must do nothing of the sort ;
that she was far too ill.

" ' But I must,' she urged. ' I never go to bed
without saying my prayers on my knees.'

" I forbade her doing it ; she closed her eyes,
and I came away. Is n't she quaint ? "

At this juncture we heard the thud of a soft falling body, and rushing in we found that the Derelict had crept from her bed to her knees, and had
probably not prayed more than two minutes
before she fainted for the fifth or sixth time in
twenty-four hours. Salemina was vexed, angel
and philanthropist though she is. Francesca and
I were so helpless with laughter that we could
hardly lift the too conscientious maiden into bed.
The situation may have been pathetic ; to the
truly pious mind it would indeed have been in-
describably touching, but for the moment the
humorous side of it was too much for our self-
control. Salemina, in rushing for stimulants and
smelling salts, broke her only comfortable eye-

glasses, and this accident, coupled with her other anxieties and responsibilities, caused her to shed tears, an occurrence so unprecedented that Francesca and I kissed and comforted her and tucked her up on the sofa. Then we sent for the doctor, gave our opera tickets to the head waiter and chambermaid, and settled down to a cheerful home evening, our first in Ireland.

"If Himself were here, we should not be in this plight," I sighed.

"I don't know how you can say that," responded Salemina, with considerable spirit. "You know perfectly well that if your husband had found a mother and seven children helpless and deserted on that dock, he would have brought them all to this hotel, and then tried to find the father and grandfather."

"And it's not Salemina's fault," argued Francesca. "She could n't help the girl being born in Salem ; not that I believe that she ever heard of the place before she saw it printed on Salemina's trunk. I told you it was too big and red, dear, but you would n't listen ! I am the strongest American of the party, but I confess that U. S. A. in letters five inches long is too much for my patriotism."

"It would not be if you ever had charge of the luggage," retorted Salemina.

"And whatever you do, Francesca," I added beseechingly, "don't impugn the veracity of our

Derelict. While we think of ourselves as minister-
ing angels I can endure anything, but if we are
the dupes of an adventuress, there is nothing
pretty about it. By the way, I have consulted
the English manageress of this hotel, who was
not particularly sympathetic. 'Perhaps you
should n't have assumed charge of her, madam,'
she said, ' but having done so, had n't you better
see if you can get her into a hospital? ' It is n't
a bad suggestion, and after a day or two we will
consider it, or I will get a trained nurse to take
full charge of her. I would be at any reasonable
expense rather than have our pleasure interfered
with any further."

It still seems odd to make a proposition of
this kind. In former times, Francesca was the
Crœsus of the party, Salemina came second, and
I last, with a most precarious income. Now I am
the wealthy one, Francesca is reduced to the second place, and Salemina to the third, but it
makes no difference whatever, either in our relations, our arrangements, or, for that matter, in
our expenditures.

IV

" A fair maiden wander'd
    All wearied and lone,
Sighing, ' I 'm a poor stranger,
    And far from my own.'
We invited her in,
We offered her share
Of our humble cottage
And our humble fare ;
We bade her take comfort,
No longer to moan,
And made the poor stranger
Be one of our own."

Old Irish Song.

THE next morning dawned as lovely as if it had slipped out of Paradise, and as for freshness, and emerald sheen, the world from our windows was like a lettuce leaf just washed in dew. The windows of my bedroom looked out pleasantly on St. Stephen's Green, commonly called Stephen's Green, or, by citizens of the baser sort, Stephens's Green. It is a good English mile in circumference, and many are the changes in it from the time it was first laid out, in 1670, to the present day, when it was made into a public park by Lord Ardilaun.

When the celebrated Mrs. Delany, then Mrs. Pendarves, first saw it, the centre was a swamp, where in winter a quantity of snipe congregated, and Harris in his " History of Dublin " alludes to the presence of snipe and swamp as an agreeable and uncommon circumstance not to be met with perhaps in any other great city in the world.

A double row of spreading lime trees bordered its four sides, one of which, known as Beaux' Walk, was a favorite lounge for fashionable idlers. Here stood Bishop Clayton's residence, a large building with a front like Devonshire House in Piccadilly, so writes Mrs. Delany. It was splendidly furnished, and the bishop lived in a style which proves that Irish prelates of the day were not all given to self-abnegation and mortification of the flesh.

A long line of vehicles, outside cars and cabs, some of them battered and shaky, others sufficiently well looking, was gathering on two sides of the green, for Dublin, you know, is " the cardrivingest city in the world." Francesca and I had our first experience yesterday in the intervals of nursing, driving to Dublin Castle, Trinity College, the Four Courts, and Grafton Street (the Regent Street of Dublin). It is easy to tell the stranger, stiff, decorous, terrified, clutching the rail with one or both hands, but we took for our model a pretty Irish girl, who looked like nothing so much as a bird on a swaying bough. It

is no longer called the "jaunting," but the outside car, and there is another charming word lost
to the world. There was formerly an inside car
too, but it is almost unknown in Dublin, though
still found in some of the smaller towns. An outside car has its wheels practically inside the body
of the vehicle, but an inside car carries its
wheels outside. This definition was given us by
an Irish driver, but lucid definition is not perhaps
an Irishman's strong point. It is clearer to say
that the passenger sits outside of the wheels on
the one, inside on the other. There are seats for
two persons over each of the two wheels, and a
dickey for the driver in front, should he need to
use it. Ordinarily he sits on one side, driving,
while you perch on the other, and thus you jog
along, each seeing your own side of the road, and
discussing the topics of the day across the "well,"
as the covered-in centre of the car is called.
There are those who do not agree with its champions, who call it "Cupid's own conveyance;"
they find the seat too small for two, yet feel it a
bit unsociable when the companion occupies the
opposite side. To me a modern Dublin car with
rubber tires and a good Irish horse is the jolliest
vehicle in the universe; there is a liveliness,
an irresponsible gayety, in the spring and sway
of it; an ease in the half-lounging position against
the cushions, a unique charm in "traveling edge-
ways" with your feet planted on the step. You

must not be afraid of a car if you want to enjoy
it. Hold the rail if you must, at first, though it's
just as bad form as clinging to your horse's mane
while riding in the Row. Your driver will take
all the chances that a crowded thoroughfare gives
him; he would scorn to leave more than an inch
between your feet and a Guinness' beer dray; he
will shake your flounces and furbelows in the
very windows of the passing trams, but he is beloved by the gods, and nothing ever happens to
him.

The morning was enchanting, as I said, and,
above all, the Derelict was better.

"It's a grand night's slape I had wid her intirely," said the housemaid; "an' sure it's not
to-day she'll be dyin' on you at all, at all; she's
had the white drink in the bowl twyst, and a
grand cup o' tay on the top o' that."

Salemina fortified herself with breakfast before
she went in to an interview, which we all felt to
be important and decisive. The time seemed
endless to us, and endless were our suppositions.

"Perhaps she has had morning prayers and
fainted again."

"Perhaps she has turned out to be Salemina's
long-lost cousin."

"Perhaps she is upbraiding Salemina for kidnapping her when she was insensible."

"Perhaps she is relating her life history; if it
is a sad one, Salemina is adopting her legally at
this moment."

"Perhaps she is one of Mr. Beresford's wards, and has come over to complain of somebody's ill treatment."

Here Salemina entered, looking flushed and embarrassed. We thought it a bad sign that she could not meet our eyes without confusion, but I made room for her on the sofa, and Francesca drew her chair closer.

"She is from Salem," began the poor dear; "she has never been out of Massachusetts in her life."

"Unfortunate girl!" exclaimed Francesca, adding prudently, as she saw Salemina's rising color, "though of course if one has to reside in a single state, Massachusetts offers more compensations than any other."

"She knows every nook and corner in the place," continued Salemina; "she has even seen the house where I was born, and her name is Benella Dusenberry."

"Impossible!" cried Francesca. "Dusenberry is unlikely enough, but who ever heard of such a name as Benella! It sounds like a flavoring extract."

"She came over to see the world, she says."

"Oh! then she has money?"

"No — or at least, yes; or at least she had enough when she left America to last for two or three months, or until she could earn something."

"Of course she left her little all in a chamois-skin bag under her pillow on the steamer," suggested Francesca.

"That is precisely what she did," Salemina replied, with a pale smile. "However, she was so ill in the steerage that she had to pay twenty-five or thirty dollars extra to go into the second cabin, and this naturally reduced the amount of her savings, though it makes no difference since she left them all behind her, save a few dollars in her purse. She says she is usually perfectly well, but that she was very tired when she started, that it was her first sea voyage, and the passage was unusually rough."

"Where is she going?"

"I don't know; I mean, she does n't know. Her maternal grandmother was born in Trim, near Tara, in Meath, but she does not think she has any relations over here. She is entirely alone in the world, and that gives her a certain sentiment in regard to Ireland, which she heard a great deal about when she was a child. The maternal grandmother must have gone to Salem at a very early age, as Benella herself savors only of New England soil."

"Has she any trade, or is she trained to do anything whatsoever?" asked Francesca.

"No, she hoped to take some position of 'trust.' She does not care at all what it is, so long as the occupation is 'interestin' work,' she says. That is rather vague, of course, but she speaks and appears like a nice conscientious person."

"Tell us the rest; conceal nothing," I said sternly.

" She — she thinks that we have saved her life, and she feels that she belongs to us," faltered Salemina.

" Belongs to us ! " we cried in a duet. " Was there ever such a base reward given to virtue ; ever such an unwelcome expression of gratitude ! Belong to us, indeed ! We can't have her ; we won't have her. Were you perfectly frank with her ? "

" I tried to be, but she almost insisted ; she has set her heart upon being our maid."

" Does she know how to be a maid ? "

" No, but she is extremely teachable, she says."

" I have my doubts," remarked Francesca ; " a liking for personal service is not a distinguishing characteristic of New Englanders ; they are not the stuff of which maids are made. If she were French or German or Senegambian, in fact anything but a Saleminian, we might use her ; we have always said we needed some one."

Salemina brightened. " I thought myself it might be rather nice, that is, I thought it might be a way out of the difficulty. Penelope had thought at one time of bringing a maid, and it would save us a great deal of trouble. The doctor thinks she could travel a short distance in a few days; perhaps it is a Providence in disguise."

"The disguise is perfect," murmured Francesca.

"You see," Salemina continued, "when the poor thing tottered along the wharf the stewardess laid her on the pile of wool sacks," —

"Like a dying Chancellor," again interpolated the irrepressible.

"And ran off to help another passenger. When she opened her eyes, she saw straight in front of her, in huge letters, ' Salem, Mass., U. S. A.' It loomed before her despairing vision, I suppose, like a great ark of refuge, and seemed to her in her half-dazed condition not only a reminder, but almost a message from home. She had then no thought of ever seeing the owner; she says she felt only that she should like to die quietly on anything marked 'Salem, Mass.' Go in to see her presently, Penelope, and make up your own mind about her. See if you can persuade her to — to — well, to give us up. Try to get her out of the notion of being our maid. She is so firm; I never saw so feeble a person who could be so firm; and what in the world shall we do with her if she keeps on insisting, in her nervous state?"

"My idea would be," I suggested, "to engage her provisionally, if we must, not because we want her, but because her heart is weak. I shall

tell her that we do not feel like leaving her behind, and yet we ourselves cannot be detained in
Dublin indefinitely ; that we will try the arrangement for a month, and that she can consider
herself free to leave us at any time on a week's
notice."

"I approve of that," agreed Francesca, "because it makes it easier to dismiss her in case she
turns out to be a Massachusetts Borgia. You
remember, however, that we bore with the vapors
and vagaries, the sighs and moans, of Jane Grieve
in Pettybaw, all those weeks, and not one of us
had the courage to throw off her yoke. Never
shall I forget her at your wedding, Penelope ; the
teardrop glistened in her eye as usual ; I think
it is glued there ! Ronald was sympathetic, because he fancied she was weeping for the loss of
you, but on inquiry it transpired that she was
thinking of a marriage in that 'won'erfu' fine family in Glasgy,' with whose charms she had made
us all too familiar. She asked to be remembered
when I began my own housekeeping, and I told
her truthfully that she was not a person who
could be forgotten ; I repressed my feeling that
she is too tearful for a Highland village where it
rains most of the year, also my conviction that
Ronald's parish would chasten me sufficiently
without her aid."

I did as Salemina wished, and had a confer-
ence with Miss Dusenberry. I hope I was quite

clear in my stipulations as to the perfect freedom of the four contracting parties. I know I intended to be, and I was embarrassed to see Francesca and Salemina exchange glances next day when Benella said she would show us what a good sailor she could be, on the return voyage to America, adding that she thought a person would be much less liable to seasickness when traveling in the first cabin.

V

THE WEARING OF THE GREEN

"Sir Knight, I feel not the least alarm,
No son of Erin will offer me harm —
For tho' they love woman and golden store,
Sir Knight, they love honor and virtue more!"
Thomas Moore.

" THIS is an anniversary," said Salemina, coming into the sitting-room at breakfast time with a book under her arm. "Having given up all hope of any one's waking in this hotel, which, before nine in the morning, is precisely like the Sleeping Beauty's castle, I dressed and determined to look up Brian Boru."

" From all that I can recall of him he was not a person to meet before breakfast," yawned Francesca; "still I shall be glad of a little fresh light, for my mind is in a most chaotic state, induced by the intellectual preparation that you have made me undergo during the past month. I dreamed last night that I was conducting a mothers' meeting in Ronald's new parish, and the subject for discussion was the Small Livings Scheme, the object of which is to augment the stipends of the ministers of the Church of Scotland to a minimum of £200 per annum. I tried to keep the members to the point, but was distracted by the sudden appearance, in all corners of the church, of people who had n't been 'asked to the party.' There was Brian Boru, Tony Lumpkin, Finn McCool, Felicia Hemans, Ossian, Mrs. Delany, Sitric of the Silken Beard, St. Columba, Mickey Free, Strongbow, Maria Edgeworth, and the Venerable Bede. Imagine leading a mothers' meeting with those people in the pews, — it was impossible! St. Columbkille and the Venerable Bede seemed to know about parochial charges and livings and stipends and glebes, and Maria Edgeworth was rather helpful; but Brian and Sitric glared at each other and brandished their hymn books threateningly, while Ossian refused to sit in the same pew with Mickey Free, who behaved in an odious manner, and interrupted each of the speakers in turn. Incidentally a group of persons huddled together in a far corner rose out of the dim light, and flapping huge wings, flew over my head and out of the window above the altar. This I took to be the Flight of the Earls, and the terror of it awoke me. Whatever my parish duties may be in the future, at least they cannot be any more dreadful and disorderly than the dream."

"I don't know which is more to blame, the seed that I sowed, or the soil on which it fell," said Salemina, laughing heartily at Francesca's whimsical nightmares; "but as I said, this is an

anniversary. The famous battle of Clontarf was
fought here in Dublin on this very day eight hundred years ago, and Brian Boru routed the Danes
in what was the last struggle between Christian-
ity and heathenism. The greatest slaughter took
place on the streets along which we drove yesterday from Ballybough Bridge to the Four Courts.
Brian Boru was king of Munster, you remember,"
(Salemina always says this for courtesy's sake),
"or at least you have read of that time in Ireland's history when a fair lady dressed in fine silk
and gold and jewels could walk unmolested the
length of the land, because of the love the people
bore King Brian and the respect they cherished
for his wise laws. Well, Mailmora, the king of
Leinster, had quarreled with him, and joined
forces with the Danish leaders against him.
Broder and Amlaff, two vikings from the Isle of
Man, brought with them a 'fleet of two thousand
Danmarkians and a thousand men covered with
mail from head to foot,' to meet the Irish, who
always fought in tunics. Joyce says that Broder
wore a coat of mail that no steel would bite, that
he was both tall and strong, and that his black locks
were so long that he tucked them under his belt,
— there's a portrait for your gallery, Penelope.
Brian's army was encamped on the Green of Aha-
Clee, which is now Phœnix Park, and when he
set fire to the Danish districts, the fierce Norse-
men within the city could see a blazing, smoking

pathway that reached from Dublin to Howth. The quarrel must have been all the more virulent in that Mailmora was Brian's brother-in-law, and Brian's daughter was the wife of Sitric of the Silken Beard, Danish king of Dublin."

" I refuse to remember their relationships or alliances," said Francesca. " They were always intermarrying with their foes in order to gain strength, but it generally seems to have made things worse rather than better ; still I don't mind hearing what became of Brian after his victory ; let us quite finish with him before the eggs come up. I suppose it will be eggs ? "

" Broder the Viking rushed upon him in his tent where he was praying, cleft his head from his body, and he is buried in Armagh Cathedral," said Salemina, closing the book. " Penelope, do ring again for breakfast, and just to keep us from realizing our hunger read ' Remember the Glories of Brian the Brave.' "

We had brought letters of introduction to a dean, a bishop, and a Rt. Hon. Lord Justice, so there were a few delightful invitations when the morning post came up ; not so many as there might have been, perhaps, had not the Irish capital been in a state of complete dementia over the presence of the greatest Queen in the world.[1]

---

[1] Penelope's experiences in Scotland, given in a former volume, ended, the meticulous proof-reader will remember, with her marriage in the year of the Queen's Jubilee. It is apparent in the

Privately, I think that those nations in the habit of having kings and queens at all should have four, like those in a pack of cards; then they could manage to give all their colonies and dependencies a frequent sight of royalty, and prevent much excitement and heart-burning.

It was worth something to be one of the lunatic populace when the little lady in black, with her parasol bordered in silver shamrocks, drove along the gayly decorated streets, for the Irish, it seems to me, desire nothing better than to be loyal, if any persons to whom they can be loyal are presented to them.

"Irish disaffection is, after all, but skin-deep," said our friend the dean; "it is a cutaneous malady, produced by external irritants. Below the surface there is a deep spring of personal loyalty, which needs only a touch like that of the prophet's wand to enable it to gush forth in healing floods. Her Majesty might drive through these crowded streets in her donkey chaise unguarded, as secure as the lady in that poem of Moore's

opening chapters of this story that Penelope came to Ireland the following spring, which, though the matter is hardly important, was not that of the Queen's memorable visit.

The Irish experiences are probably the fruit of several expeditions, and Penelope has chosen to include this vivid impression of Her Majesty's welcome to Ireland, even though it might convict her of an anachronism. Perhaps as this is not an historical novel, but a "chronicle of small beer," the trifling inaccuracy may be pardoned. K. D. W.

which portrayed the safety of woman in Brian Boru's time. The old song has taken on a new meaning. It begins, you know, —

> 'Lady, dost thou not fear to stray
> So lone and lonely through this dark way?'

and the Queen might answer as did the heroine,

> 'Sir Knight, I feel not the least alarm,
> No son of Erin will offer me harm.'"

It was small use for the parliamentary mis-representatives to advise treating Victoria of the Good Deeds with the courtesy due to a foreign sovereign visiting the country. Under the miles of flags she drove, red, white, and blue, tossing themselves in the sweet spring air, and up from the warm hearts of the surging masses of people, men and women alike, Crimean soldiers and old crones in rags, gentry and peasants, went a greeting I never before heard given to any sovereign, for it was a sigh of infinite content that trembled on the lips and then broke into a deep sob, as a knot of Trinity College students in a spontaneous burst of song, flung out the last verse of " The New Wearing of the Green." [1]

"And so upon St. Patrick's Day, Victoria, she has said
Each Irish regiment shall wear the Green beside the Red ;
And she's coming to ould Ireland, who away so long has been,
And dear knows but into Dublin she'll ride wearing of the Green."

The first cheers were faint and broken, and the

[1] Alfred Perceval Graves.

emotion that quivered on every face and the tears
that gleamed in a thousand eyes made it the most
touching spectacle in the world. "Foreign Sovereign, indeed!" She was the Queen of Ireland,
and the nation of courtiers and hero worshipers
was at her feet. There was the history of five hundred years in that greeting, and to me it spoke
volumes.

Plenty of people there were in the crowd, too,
who were heartily "agin the government;" but
Daniel O'Connell is not the only Irishman who
could combine a detestation of the Imperial Parliament with a passionate loyalty to the sovereign.

There was a woman near us who "remembered the last time Her Noble Highness come,
thirty-nine years back, — glory be to God, thim
was the times!" — and who kept ejaculating,
"She's the best woman in the wurrld, bar none,
and the most varchous faymale!" As her husband made no reply, she was obliged in her excitement to thump him with her umbrella and
repeat, "The most varchous faymale, do you
hear?" At which he retorted, "Have conduct,
woman; sure I've nothin' agin it."

"Look at the size of her now," she went on,
"sittin' in that grand carriage, no bigger than
me own Kitty, and always in the black, the darlin'. Look at her, a widdy woman, raring that
large and heavy family of children; and how

well she's married off her daughters (more luck
to her!), though to be sure they must have been
well fortuned! They do be sayin' she's come
over because she's plazed with seein' estated
gintlemen lave iverything and go out and be shot
by thim bloody Boers, bad scran to thim! Sure
if I had the sons, sorra a wan but I'd lave go!
Who's the iligant sojers in the silver stays,
Thady? Is it the Life Guards you're callin'
thim?"

There were two soldiers' wives standing on the
pavement near us, and one of them showed a half-
sovereign to the other, saying, "'T is the last day's
airnin' iver I seen by him, Mrs. Muldoon, ma'am!
Ah, there's thim says for this war, an' there's
thim says agin this war, but Heaven lave Himself
where he is, I says, for of all the ragin' Turco-
maniacs iver a misfortunate woman was curst
with, Pat Brady, my full private, he bates 'em
all!"

Here the band played Come back to Erin, and
the scene was indescribable. Nothing could
have induced me to witness it had I realized
what it was to be, for I wept at Holyrood when I
heard the plaintive strains of Bonnie Charlie's
now Awa floating up to the Gallery of Kings from
the palace courtyard, and I did not wish Francesca to see me shedding national, political, and
historical tears so soon again. Francesca herself
is so ardent a republican that she weeps only for

presidents and cabinet officers. For my part, although I am thoroughly loyal, I cannot become sufficiently attached to a president in four years to shed tears when I see him driving at the head of a procession.

VI

DUBLIN, THEN AND NOW

> " I found in Innisfail the fair,
>   In Ireland, while in exile there,
>   Women of worth, both grave and gay men,
>   Many clerics, and many laymen."
>
> *James Clarence Mangan.*

MRS. DELANY, writing from Dublin in 1731, says: " As for the generality of people that I meet with here, they are much the same as in England — a mixture of good and bad. All that I have met with behave themselves very decently according to their rank ; now and then an oddity breaks out, but never so extraordinary but that I can match it in England. There is a heartiness among them that is more like Cornwall than any I have known, and great sociableness." This picturesque figure in the life of her day gives charming pictures in her memoirs of the Irish society of the time, descriptions which are confirmed by contemporary writers. She was the wife of Dr. Delany, Dean of Down, the companion of duchesses and queens, and the friend of Swift. Hannah More, in a poem called Sensibility, published in 1778, gives this quaint and stilted picture of her : —

" Delany shines, in worth serenely bright,
Wisdom's strong ray, and virtue's milder light.
And she who blessed the friend and graced the page
Of Swift, still lends her lustre to our age.
Long, long protract thy light, O star benign,
Whose setting beams with added brightness shine ! "

The Irish ladies of Delany's day, who scarcely ever appeared on foot in the streets, were famous for their grace in dancing, it seems, as the men were for their skill in swimming. The hospitality of the upper classes was profuse, and by no means lacking in brilliancy or in grace. The humorous and satirical poetry found in the fugitive literature of the period shows conclusively that there were plenty of bright spirits and keen wits at the banquets, routs, and balls. The curse of absenteeism was little felt in Dublin, where the Parliament secured the presence of most of the aristocracy and of much of the talent of the country, and during the residence of the viceroy there was the influence of the court to contribute to the sparkling character of Dublin society.

How they managed to sparkle when discussing some of the heavy dinner menus of the time I cannot think. Here is one of the Dean of Down's bills of fare : —

> Turkeys endove
> Boyled leg of mutton
> Greens, etc.
> Soup
> Plum Pudding
> Roast loin of veal

Venison pasty
Partridge
Sweetbreads
Collared Pig
Creamed apple tart
Crabs
Fricassée of eggs
Pigeons
No dessert to be had.

Although there is no mention of beverages we may be sure that this array of viands was not eaten dry, but was washed down with a plentiful variety of wines and liquors.

The hosts, either in Dublin or London, who numbered among their dinner guests such Irishmen as Sheridan or Lysaght, Mangan or Lever, Curran or Lover, Father Prout or Dean Swift, had as great a feast of wit and repartee as one will be apt soon to hear again ; although it must have been Lever or Lover who furnished the cream of Irish humor, and Father Prout and Swift the curds.

If you are fortunate enough to be bidden to the right houses in Ireland to-day, you will have as much good talk as you are likely to hear in any other city in this degenerate age, which has mostly forgotten how to converse in learning to chat ; and any one who goes to the Spring Show at Ball's Bridge, or to the Punchestown or Leopardstown races, or to the Dublin horse show, will have to confess that the Irishwomen can dispute the palm with any nation.

" Light on their feet now they passed me and sped,
   Give you me word, give you me word,
Every girl wid a turn o' the head
   Just like a bird, just like a bird;
And the lashes so thick round their beautiful eyes
Shinin' to tell you it 's fair time o' day wid them,
Back in me heart wid a kind of surprise,
I think how the Irish girls has the way wid them!"

Their charm is made up of beautiful eyes and
lashes, lustre of hair, poise of head, shapeliness
of form, vivacity and coquetry; and there is a
matchless grace in the way they wear the "whatever," be it the chiffons of the fashionable dame,
or the shawl of the country colleen, who can draw
the two corners of that faded article of apparel
shyly over her lips and look out from under it
with a pair of luminous gray eyes in a manner
that is fairly "disthractin'."

Yesterday was a red-letter day, for I dined in
the evening at Dublin Castle, and Francesca was
bidden to the concert in the Throne Room afterwards. It was a brilliant scene when the assembled guests awaited their host and hostess, the
shaded lights bringing out the satins and velvets,
pearls and diamonds, uniforms, orders, and medals. Suddenly the hum of voices ceased as one
of the aides-de-camp who preceded the vice-regal
party announced "Their Excellencies." We made
a sort of passage as these dignitaries advanced
to shake hands with a few of those they knew
best. The Lord Lieutenant then gave his arm

to the lady of highest rank (alas, it was not I !) ;
Her Excellency chose her proper squire, and
we passed through the beautifully decorated
rooms to St. Patrick's Hall in a nicely graded
procession, magnificence at the head, humility at
the tail.   A string band was discoursing sweet
music the while, and I fitted to its measures certain well-known lines descriptive of the entrance
of the beasts into the ark.

> " The animals went in two by two,
>   The elephant and the kangaroo."

As my escort was a certain brilliant lord justice,
and as the wittiest dean in Leinster was my other
neighbor, I almost forgot to eat, in my pleasure
and excitement.   I told the dean that we had
chosen Scottish ancestors before going to our
first great dinner in Edinburgh, feeling that we
should be more in sympathy with the festivities
and more acceptable to our hostess, but that I
had forgotten to provide myself for this occasion,
my first function in Dublin ; whereupon the good
dean promptly remembered that there was a Penelope O'Connor, daughter of the King of Connaught.   I could not quite give up Tam o' the
Cowgate (Thomas Hamilton) or Jenny Geddes
of fauld-stule fame, also a Hamilton, but I added
the King of Connaught to the list of my chosen
forbears with much delight, in spite of the polite
protests of the Rev. Father O'Hogan, who sat opposite, and who remarked that

" Man for his glory
    To ancestry flies,
But woman's bright story
    Is told in her eyes.
While the monarch but traces
Through mortal his line,
Beauty born of the Graces
    Ranks next to divine."

I asked the Reverend Father if he were descended from Galloping O'Hogan, who helped Patrick Sarsfield to spike the guns of the Williamites at Limerick.

"By me sowl, ma'am, it's not discinded at all I am ; I am one o' the common sort, jist," he answered, broadening his brogue to make me smile. A delightful man he was, exactly such an one as might have sprung full grown from a Lever novel ; one who could talk equally well with his flock about pigs or penances, purgatory or potatoes, and quote Tom Moore and Lover when occasion demanded.

Story after story fell from his genial lips, and at last he said apologetically, "One more, and I have done," when a pretty woman, sitting near him, interpolated slyly, "We might say to you, your reverence, what the old woman said to the eloquent priest who finished his sermon with ' One word, and I have done.' "

"An' what is that, ma'am?" asked Father O'Hogan.

"Och ! me darlin' pracher, may ye niver be done ! "

We all agreed that we should like to recon-
struct the scene for a moment and look at a
drawing-room of two hundred years ago, when
Her Excellency after the minuets at eleven
o'clock went to her basset table, while her pages
attended behind her chair, and when on ball
nights the ladies scrambled for sweetmeats on
the dancing-floor.   As to their probable toi-
lettes one could not give purer pleasure than by
quoting Mrs. Delany's description of one of
them : —

"The Duchess's dress was of white satin embroidered, the bottom of the petticoat brown hills
covered with all sorts of weeds, and every breadth
had an *old stump of a tree*, that ran up almost to
the top of the petticoat, broken and ragged, and
worked with brown chenille, round which twined
nasturtiums, ivy, honeysuckles, periwinkles, and
all sorts of running flowers, which spread and
covered the petticoat. . . . The robings and facings were little green banks covered with all
sorts of weeds, and the sleeves and the rest of
the gown loose twining branches of the same sort
as those on the petticoat.   Many of the leaves
were finished with gold, and part of the stumps
of the trees looked like the gilding of the sun.   I
never saw a piece of work so prettily fancied."

She adds a few other details for the instruction
of her sister Anne : —

"Heads are variously adorned; pompons with

some accompaniment of feathers, ribbons, or flowers; lappets in all sorts of curli-murlis; long hoods are worn close under the chin; the earrings go round the neck (!), and tie with bows and ends behind. Night-gowns are worn without hoops."

PART SECOND
MUNSTER

VII

A TOUR AND A DÉTOUR

" ' An' there,' sez I to meself, 'we 're goin' wherever we go,
But where we 'll be whin we git there it 's never a know I 'll
know.' "

Jane Barlow.

We had planned to go direct from Dublin to
Valencia Island, where there is not, I am told,
"one dhry step 'twixt your fut an' the States;"
but we thought it too tiring a journey for Benella,
and arranged for a little visit to Cork first. We
nearly missed the train owing to the late arrival
of Salemina at the Kingsbridge station. She had
been buying malted milk, Mellin's Food, an alco-
hol lamp, a tin cup, and getting all the doctor's
prescriptions renewed.

We intended, too, to go second or third class
now and then, in order to study the humors of
the natives, but of course we went "first" on this
occasion on account of Benella. I told her that
we could not follow British usage and call her
by her surname. Dusenberry was too long and
too — well, too extraordinary for daily use abroad.

"P'r'aps it is," she assented meekly; "and
still, Mis' Beresford, when a man's name is Du-

senberry, you can't hardly blame him for wanting
his child to be called by it, can you?"

This was incontrovertible, and I asked her
middle name. It was Frances, and that was too
like Francesca.

"You don't like the sound o' Benella?" she
inquired. "I 've always set great store by my
name, it is so unlikely. My father's name was
Benjamin and my mother's Ella, and mine is
made from both of 'em; but you can call me any
kind of a name you please, after what you 've
done for me," and she closed her eyes patiently.

> "Call me Daphne, call me Chloris,
> Call me Lalage or Doris,
> Only, only call me thine,"

which is exactly what we are not ready to do, I
thought, in a poetic parenthesis.

Benella looks frail and yet hardy. She has an
unusual and perhaps unnecessary amount of imagination for her station, some native common
sense, but limited experience; she is somewhat
vague and inconsistent in her theories of life, but
I am sure there is vitality, and energy too, in her
composition, although it has been temporarily
drowned in the Atlantic Ocean. If she were a
clock, I should think that some experimenter had
taken out her original works, and substituted
others to see how they would run. The clock
has a New England case and strikes with a New
England tone, but the works do not match it al-

together. Of course I know that one does not ordinarily engage a lady's maid because of these piquant peculiarities; but in our case the circumstances were extraordinary. I have explained them fully to Himself in my letters, and Francesca too has written pages of illuminating detail to Ronald Macdonald.

The similarity in the minds of men must sometimes come across them with a shock, unless indeed it appeals to their sense of humor. Himself in America, and the Rev. Mr. Macdonald in the north of Scotland, both answered, in course of time, that a lady's maid should be engaged because she is a lady's maid and for no other reason.

Was ever anything duller than this, more conventional, more commonplace or didactic, less imaginative? Himself added, "You are a romantic idiot, and I love you more than tongue can tell." Francesca did not say what Ronald added; probably a part of this same sentence (owing to the aforesaid similarity of men's minds), reserving the rest for the frank intimacy of the connubial state.

Everything looked beautiful in the uncertain glory of the April day. The thistledown clouds opened now and then to shake out a delicate, brilliant little shower, then ceased in a trice, and the sun smiled through the light veil of rain, turning every falling drop to a jewel. It was as if the fairies were busy at aerial watering pots, without any more serious purpose than to amuse themselves and make the earth beautiful; and we realized that Irish rain is as warm as an Irish welcome, and soft as an Irish smile.

Everything was bursting into new life, everything but the primroses, and their glory was departing. The yellow carpet seemed as bright as ever on the sunny hedgerow banks and on the fringe of the woods, but when we plucked some at a wayside station we saw that they were just past their golden prime. There was a gray-green hint of verdure in the sallows that stood against a dark background of firs and the branches of the fruit trees were tipped with pink, rosy hued promises of May just threatening to break through their silvery April sheaths. Raindrops were still glistening on the fronds of the tender young ferns and on the great clumps of pale, delicately scented bog violets that we found in a marshy spot and brought in to Salemina, who was not in her usual spirits; who indeed seemed distinctly anxious.

She was enchanted with the changeful charm of the landscape, and found Mrs. Delany's Memoirs a book after her own heart, but ever and anon her eyes rested on Benella's pale face. Nothing could have been more doggedly conscientious and assiduous than our attentions to the Derelict. She had beef juice at Kildare, malted

milk at Ballybrophy, tea at Dundrum ; nevertheless, as we approached Limerick Junction we
were obliged to hold a consultation. Salemina
wished to alight from the train at the next station, take a three or four hours' rest, then jog on
to any comfortable place for the night, and to
Cork in the morning.

" I shall feel much more comfortable," she said,
" if you go on and amuse yourselves as you like,
leaving Benella to me for a day, or even for two
or three days. I can't help feeling that the chief
fault, or at least the chief responsibility, is mine.
If I had n't been born in Salem, or had n't had
the word painted on my trunk in such red letters,
she would n't have fainted on it, and I need n't
have saved her life. It is too late to turn back
now ; it is saved, or partly saved, and I must per-
severe in saving it, at least until I find that it 's
not worth saving."

" Poor darling," said Francesca sympathiz-
ingly. " I 'll look in Murray and find a nice interesting place. You can put Benella to bed in
the Southern Hotel at Limerick Junction, and
perhaps you can then drive within sight of the
Round Tower of Cashel. Then you can take
up the afternoon train and go to — let me see
— how would you like Buttevant ? (Boutez en
avant, you know, the ' Push forward ' motto of
the Barrymores.) It 's delightful, Penelope," she
continued ; "we 'd better get off, too. It is a

garrison town, and there is a military hotel.
Then in the vicinity is Kilcolman, where Spenser
wrote the Faerie Queene : so there is the beginning of your literary pilgrimage the very first day,
without any plotting or planning. The little river
Aubeg, which flows by Kilcolman Castle, Spenser
called the Mulla, and referred to it as ' Mulla
mine, whose waves I whilom taught to weep.'
That, by the way, is no more than our Jane Grieve
could have done for the rivers of Scotland. What
do you say? and won't you be a 'prood woman
the day' when you sign the hotel register ' Miss
Peabody and maid, Salem, Mass., U. S. A.' "

I thought most favorably of Buttevant, but on
prudently inquiring the guard's opinion, he said
it was not a comfortable place for an invalid lady,
and that Mallow was much more the thing. At
Limerick Junction, then, we all alighted, and in
the ten minutes' wait saw Benella escorted up the
hotel stairway by a sympathetic head waiter.

Detached from Salemina's fostering care and
prudent espionage, separated, above all, from the
depressing Miss Dusenberry, we planned every
conceivable folly in the way of guidebook expeditions. The exhilarating sense of being married,
and therefore properly equipped to undertake any
sort of excursion with perfect propriety, gave
added zest to the affair in my eyes. Sleeping at
Cork in an Imperial Hotel was far too usual a
proceeding, — we scorned it. As the very apex

of boldness and reckless defiance of common
sense, we let our heavy luggage go on to the
capital of Munster, and, taking our handbags, entered a railway carriage standing on a side track,
and were speedily on our way, — we knew not
whither, and cared less. We discovered all too
soon that we were going to Waterford, the Star
of the Suir, —

> " The gentle Shure, that making way
> By sweet Clonmell, adorns rich Waterford ; "

and we were charmed at first sight with its quaint
bridge spanning the silvery river. It was only
five o'clock, and we walked about the fine old
ninth-century town, called by the Cavaliers the
Urbs Intacta, because it was the one place in
Ireland which successfully resisted the all-conquering Cromwell. Francesca sent a telegram at
once to

MISS PEABODY AND MAID, Great Southern Ho-
    tel, Limerick Junction.
    Came to Waterford instead Cork. Strong-
bow landed here 1771, defeating Danes and Irish.
Youghal to-morrow, pronounced Yawl. Address
Green Park, Miss Murphy's. How's Derelict ?
                    FRANELOPE.

It was absurd, of course, but an absurdity that
can be achieved at the cost of eighteen pence is
well worth the money.

Nobody but a Baedeker or a Murray could write an account of our doings the next two days. Feeling that we might at any hour be recalled to Benella's bedside, we took a childlike pleasure in crowding as much as possible into the time. This zeal was responsible for our leaving the Urbs Intacta, and pushing on to pass the night in something smaller and more idyllic.

I dissuaded Francesca from seeking a lodging in Ballybricken by informing her that it was the heart of the bacon industry, and the home of the best known body of pig-buyers in Ireland ; but her mind was fixed upon Kills and Ballies. On asking our jarvey the meaning of Bally as a prefix, he answered reflectively : " I don't think there's annything onderhanded in the manin', melady ; I think it means *bally* jist."

The name of the place where we did go shall never be divulged, lest a curious public follow in our footsteps ; and if perchance it have not our youth, vigor, and appetite for adventure, it might die there in the principal hotel, unwept, unhonored, and unsung. The house is said to be three hundred and seventy-five years old, but we are convinced that this is a wicked understatement of its antiquity. It must have been built since the Deluge, else it would at least have had one general spring cleaning in the course of its existence. Cromwell had been there, too, and in the confusion of his departure they must have forgotten to sweep under the beds. We entered our rooms at ten in the evening, having dismissed our car, knowing well that there was no other place to stop the night. We gave the jarvey twice his fare to avoid altercation, "but divil a penny less would he take," although it was he who had recommended the place as a cosy hotel. "It looks like a small little house, melady, but 't is large inside, and it has a power o' beds in it." We each generously insisted on taking the dirtiest bedroom (they had both been last occupied by the Cromwellian soldiers, we agreed), but relinquished the idea, because the more we compared them the more impossible it was to decide which was the dirtiest. There were no locks on the doors. "And sure what matther for that, Miss? Nobody has a right (*i. e.* business), to be comin' in here but meself" said the aged woman who showed us to our rooms.

VIII

"But he lay like a warrior taking his rest
With his martial cloak around him."
Charles Wolfe.

At midnight I heard a faint tap at my door, and Francesca walked in, her eyes wide and bright, her cheeks flushed, her long dark braid of hair hanging over her black traveling cloak. I laughed as I saw her, she looked so like Sir Patrick Spens in the ballad play at Pettybaw, — a memorable occasion when Ronald Macdonald caught her acting that tragic rôle in his ministerial gown, the very day that Himself came from Paris to marry me in Pettybaw, dear little Pettybaw!

"I came in to find out if your bed is as bad as mine, but I see you have not slept in it," she whispered.

"I was just coming in to see if yours could be any worse," I replied. "Do you mean to say that you have tried it, courageous girl? I blew out my candle, and then, after an interval in which to forget, sat down on the outside as a preliminary; but the moon rose just then, and I could get no further."

I had not unpacked my bag. I had simply slipped on my mackintosh, selected a wooden chair, and, putting a Cromwellian towel over it, seated myself shudderingly on it and put my feet on the rounds, quoting Moore meantime —

> " And the best of all ways
> To lengthen our days,
> Is to steal a few hours from the night, my dear ! "

Francesca followed my example, and we passed the night in reading Celtic romances to each other. We could see the faint outline of sweet Slievenamann from our windows, — the mountain of the fair women of Feimheann, celebrated as the hunting ground of the Finnian chiefs.

> " One day Finn and Oscar
> Followed the chase in Sliabh-na-mban-Feimheann,
> With three thousand Finnian chiefs
> Ere the sun looked out from his circle."

In the Finnian legend, the great Finn McCool, when much puzzled in the choice of a wife, seated himself on its summit. At last he decided to make himself a prize in a competition of all the fair women in Ireland. They should start at the foot of the mountain, and the one who first reached the summit should be the great Finn's bride. It was Grainne Oge, the Gallic Helen, and daughter of Cormac, the king of Ireland, who won the chieftain, " being fleetest of foot and longest of wind."

We almost forgot our discomforts in this en-

thralling story, and slept on each other's nice
clean shoulders a little, just before the dawn.
And such a dawn ! Such infinite softness of air,
such dew-drenched verdure ! It is a backward
spring, they say, but to me the woods are even
lovelier than in their summer wealth of foliage,
when one can hardly distinguish the beauty of
the single tree from that of its neighbors, since
the colors are blended in one universal green.
Now we see the feathery tassels of the beech
bursting out of their brown husks, the russet
hues of the young oak leaves, and the countless emerald gleams that " break from the ruby-
budded lime." The greenest trees are the larch,
the horse-chestnut, and the sycamore, three natu-
ralized citizens who apparently still keep to their
native fashions, and put out their foliage as they
used to do in their own homes. The young al-
ders and the hawthorn hedges are greening, but
it will be a fortnight before we can realize the
beauty of that snow-white bloom, with its bitter-
sweet fragrance. The cuckoo-flower came this
year before instead of after the bird, they tell
us, showing that even Nature, in these days of
anarchy and misrule, is capable of taking liber-
ties with her own laws. There is a fragrance of
freshly turned earth in the air, and the rooks are
streaming out from the elms by the little church
and resting for a bit in a group of plume-like
yews. The last few days of warmth and sunshine

have inspired the birds, and as Francesca and I sit at our windows breathing in the sweetness and freshness of the morning, there is a concert of thrushes and blackbirds in the shrubberies. The little birds furnish the chorus or the undertone of song, the hedge-sparrows, redbreasts, and chaffinches, but the meistersingers "call the tune" and lead the feathered orchestra with clear and certain notes. It is a golden time for the minstrels, for nest-building is finished, and the feeding of the younglings a good time yet in the future. We can see one little brown lady hovering warm eggs under her breast, her bright eyes peeping through a screen of leaves as she glances up at her singing lord, pouring out his thanks for the morning sun. There is only a hint of breeze, it might almost be the whisper of uncurling fern fronds, but soft as it is, it stirs the branches here and there, and I know that it is rocking hundreds of tiny cradles in the forest.

When I was always painting, in those other days before I met Himself, one might think my eyes would have been even keener to see beauty than now, when my brushes are more seldom used ; but it is not so. There is something, deep hidden in my consciousness, that makes all loveliness lovelier, that helps me to interpret it in a different and in a larger sense. I have a feeling that I have been lifted out of the individual and given my true place in the general scheme of the

universe, and, in some subtle way that I can
hardly explain, I am more nearly related to all
things good, beautiful, and true than I was when
I was wholly an artist, and therefore less a woman. The bursting of the leaf buds brings me a
tender thought of the one dear heart that gives
me all its spring ; and whenever I see the smile
of a child, a generous look, the flash of sympathy
in an eye, it makes me warm with swift remem-
brance of the one I love the best of all, just " as
a lamplight will set a linnet singing for the sun."

Love is doing the same thing for Francesca ;
for the smaller feelings merge themselves in the
larger ones, as little streams lose themselves in
oceans. Whenever we talk quietly together of
that strange, new, difficult life that she is going
so bravely and so joyously to meet, I know by
her expression that Ronald's noble face, a little
shy, a little proud, but altogether adoring, serves
her for courage and for inspiration, and she feels
that his hand is holding hers across the distance,
in a clasp that promises strength.

At five o'clock we longed to ring for hot water,
but did not dare. Even at six there was no sound
of life in the cosy inn which we have named
The Cromwell Arms (" Mrs. Duddy, Manageress ;
Comfort, Cleanliness, Courtesy ; Night Porter ;
Cycling Shed "). From seven to half past we
read pages and pages of delicious history and
legend, and decided to go from Cappoquin to

Youghal by steamer, if we could possibly reach
the place of departure in time. At half past
seven we pulled the bell energetically. Nothing
happened, and we pulled again and again, discovering at last that the connection between the bell
rope and the bell wire had long since disappeared,
though it had been more than once established
with bits of twine, fishing line, and shoe laces.
Francesca then went across the hall to examine
her methods of communication, and presently I
heard a welcome tinkle, and another, and another,
followed in due season by a cheerful voice, saying, "Don't desthroy it intirely, ma'am; I'll be
coming direckly." We ordered jugs of hot water,
and were told that it would be some time before
it could be had, as ladies were not in the habit of
calling for it before nine in the morning, and as
the damper of the kitchen range was out of order.
Did we wish it in a little canteen with whiskey
and a bit of lemon peel, or were we afther wantin'
it in a jug? We replied promptly that it was not
the hour for toddy, but the hour for baths, with
us, and the decrepit and very sleepy night porter
departed to wake the cook and build the fire; advising me first, in a friendly way, to take the
hearth brush that was "kapin' the windy up and
rap on the wall if I needed annything more."
At eight o'clock we heard the porter's shuffling
step in the hall, followed by a howl and a polite
objurgation. A strange dog had passed the night

under Francesca's bed, and the porter was giving him what he called "a good hand and fut downstairs." He had put down the hot water for this operation, and on taking up the burden again we heard him exclaim : "Arrah ! look at that now ! May the divil fly away with the excommunicated ould jug !" It was past saving, the jug, and leaked so freely that one had to be exceedingly nimble to put to use any of the smoky water in it. "Thim fools o' turf do nothing but smoke on me," apologized the venerable servitor, who then asked "would we be pleased to order breakquist." We were wise in our generation, and asked for nothing but bacon, eggs, and tea ; and after a smoky bath and a change of raiment we were seated at our repast in the coffee room, feeling wonderfully fresh and cheerful. By looking directly at each other most of the time, and making experimental journeys from plate to mouth, thus barring out any intimate knowledge of the table-cloth and the waiter's linen, we managed to make a breakfast. Francesca is enough to give any one a good appetite. Ronald Macdonald will be a lucky fellow, I think, to begin his day by sitting opposite her, for her eyes shine like those of a child, and one's gaze lingers fondly on the cool freshness of her cheek. Breakfast over and the bill settled, we speedily shook off as much of the dust of Mrs. Duddy's hotel as could be shaken off, and departed on the most decrepit side car

that ever rolled on two wheels, being wished a
safe journey by a slatternly maid who stood in
the doorway, by the wide Mrs. Duddy herself,
who realized in her capacious person the picturesque Irish phrase "the full-of-the-door of a
woman," and by our friend the head waiter, who
leaned against Mrs. Duddy's ancestral pillars in
such a way that the morning sun shone full upon
his costume and revealed its weaknesses to our
reluctant gaze.

The driver said it was eleven miles to Cappoquin, the guide-book fourteen, but this difference
of opinion, we find, is only the difference between
Irish and English miles, for which our driver had
an unspeakable contempt, as of a vastly inferior
quality. He had, on the other hand, a great respect for Mrs. Duddy and her comfortable, cleanly,
and courteous establishment (as per advertise-
ment), and the warmest admiration for the village
in which she had appropriately located herself, a
village which he alluded to as "wan of the natest
towns in the ring of Ireland, for if ye made a slip
in the street of it, be the help of God ye were
always sure to fall into a public house!"

"We had better not tell the full particulars of
this journey to Salemina," said Francesca prudently, as we rumbled along; "though, oddly
enough, if you remember, whenever any one
speaks disparagingly of Ireland, she always takes
up cudgels in its behalf."

"Francesca, now that you are within three or four months of being married, can you manage to keep a secret?"

"Yes," she whispered eagerly, squeezing my hand and inclining her shoulder cosily to mine. "Yes, oh yes, and how it would raise my spirits after a sleepless night!"

"When Salemina was eighteen she had a romance, and the hero of it was the son of an Irish gentleman, an M. P., who was traveling in America, or living there for a few years, — I can't remember which. He was nothing more than a lad, less than twenty-one years old, but he was very much in love with Salemina. How far her feelings were involved I never knew, but she felt that she could not promise to marry him. Her mother was an invalid, and her father a delightful, scholarly, autocratic, selfish old gentleman, who ruled his household with a rod of iron. Salemina coddled and nursed them both during all her young life; indeed, little as she realized it, she never had any separate existence or individuality until they both died, when she was thirty-one or two years old."

"And what became of the young Irishman? Was he faithful to his first love, or did he marry?"

"He married, many years afterward, and that was the time I first heard the story. His marriage took place in Dublin, on the very day, I believe, that Salemina's father was buried ; for Fate has the most relentless way of arranging these coincidences. I don't remember his name, and I don't know where he lives or what has become of him. I imagine the romance has been dead and buried in rose leaves for years ; Salemina never has spoken of it to me, but it would account for her sentimental championship of Ireland."

IX

THE LIGHT OF OTHER DAYS

" Oft in the stilly night,
    Ere slumber's chain has bound me,
Fond memory brings the light
    Of other days around me."

Thomas Moore.

If you want to fall head over ears in love with Ireland at the very first sight of her charms, take, as we did, the steamer from Cappoquin to Youghal, and float down the vale of the Black-water, —

" Swift Awniduff, which of the Englishman
    Is cal' de Black-water."

The shores of this Irish Rhine are so lovely that the sail on a sunny day is one of unequaled charm. Behind us the mountains ranged themselves in a mysterious melancholy background; ahead the river wended its way southward in and out, in and out, through rocky cliffs and well wooded shores.

The first tributary stream that we met was the little Finisk, on the higher banks of which is Affane House. The lands of Affane are said to have been given by one of the FitzGeralds to Sir

Walter Raleigh for a breakfast, a very high price
to pay for bacon and eggs, and it was here that he
planted the first cherry-tree in Ireland, bringing it
from the Canary Islands to the Isle of Weeping.

Looking back just below here, we saw the tower
and cloisters of Mount Melleray, the Trappist
monastery. Very beautiful and very lonely
looked "the little town of God," in the shadows
of the gloomy hills. We wished we had known
the day before how near we were to it, for we
could have claimed a night's lodging at the ladies' guest-house, where all creeds, classes, and
nationalities are received with a *céad-mile-fáilte*,[1]
and where any offering for food or shelter is given
only at the visitor's pleasure. The Celtic pro-
verb, "Melodious is the closed mouth," might be
written over the cloisters; for it is a village of
silence, and only the monks who teach in the
schools or who attend visitors are absolved from
the vow.

Next came Dromana Castle, where the extraordinary old Countess of Desmond was born, —
the wonderful old lady whose supposed one hundred and forty years so astonished posterity.
She must have married Thomas, twelfth Earl of
Desmond, after 1505, as his first wife is known to
have been alive in that year. Raleigh saw her in
1589, and she died in 1604: so it would seem
that she must have been at least one hundred and

[1] Hundred thousand welcomes.

ten or one hundred and twelve when she met her
untimely death, — a death brought about entirely
by her own youthful impetuosity and her fondness
for athletic sports. Robert Sydney, second Earl of
Leicester, makes the following reference to her
in his Table-Book, written when he was ambassador at Paris, about 1640 : —

"The old Countess of Desmond was a marryed
woman in Edward IV. time in England, and lived
till towards the end of Queen Elizabeth, so she
must needes be neare one hundred and forty
yeares old. She had a new sett of teeth not long
afore her death, and might have lived much
longer had she not mett with a kinde of violent
death ; for she would needes climbe a nut-tree to
gather nuts ; so falling down she hurt her thigh,
which brought a fever, and that fever brought
death. This, my cousin Walter Fitzwilliam told
me."

It is true that the aforesaid cousin Walter may
have been a better raconteur than historian ; still,
local tradition vigorously opposes any lessening of
the number of the countess's years, pinning its
faith rather on one Hayman, who says that she
presented herself at the English court at the age
of one hundred and forty years, to petition for her
jointure, which she lost by the attainder of the
last earl ; and it also prefers to have her fall from
the historic cherry-tree that Sir Walter planted,
rather than from a casual nut-tree.

Down the lovely river we went, lazily lying
back in the sun, almost the only passengers on
the little craft, as it was still far too early for tour-
ists; down past Villierstown, Cooneen Ferry,
Strancally Castle, with its "Murdering Hole"
made famous by the Lords of Desmond, through
the Broads of Clashmore; then past Temple Michael, an old castle of the Geraldines, which Cromwell battered down for "dire insolence," until we
steamed slowly into the harbor of Youghal, —
and, to use our driver's expression, there is no
more "onderhanded manin'" in Youghal than the
town of the Yew Wood, which is much prettier
to the eye and sweeter to the ear.

Here we found a letter from Salemina, and expended another eighteen pence in telegraphing to
her : —

PEABODY, Coolkilla House, near Mardyke Walk,
    Cork.
We are under Yew Tree at Myrtle Grove
where Raleigh and Spenser smoked read manu-
script Faerie Queene and planted first potato.
Delighted Benella better. Join you to-morrow.
Don't encourage archæologist.
                                PENESCA.

We had a charming hour at Myrtle Grove
House, an unpretentious gabled dwelling, for a
time the residence of the ill-fated soldier captain,

Sir Walter Raleigh. You remember, perhaps, that he was mayor of Youghal in 1588. After the suppression of the Geraldine rebellion, the vast estates of the Earl of Desmond and those of one hundred and forty of the leading gentlemen of Munster, his adherents, were confiscated, and proclamation was made all through England inviting gentlemen to " undertake " the plantation of this rich territory. Estates were offered at two or three pence an acre, and no rent was to be paid for the first five years. Many of these great " undertakers," as they were called, were English noblemen who never saw Ireland ; but among them were Raleigh and Spenser, who received forty-two thousand and twelve thousand acres respectively, and in consideration of certain patronage " undertook " to carry the business of the Crown through Parliament.

Francesca was greatly pleased with this information, culled mostly from Joyce's Child's History of Ireland. The volume had been bought in Dublin by Salemina and presented to us as a piece of genial humor, but it became our daily companion.

I made a rhyme for her, which she sent Miss Peabody, to show her that we were growing in wisdom, notwithstanding our separation from her.

> " You have thought of Sir Walter as soldier and knight,
> Edmund Spenser, you 've heard, was well able to write ;

> But Raleigh the planter, and Spenser verse-maker,
> Each, oddly enough, was by trade ' Undertaker.' "

It was in 1589 that the Shepherd of the Ocean, as Spenser calls him, sailed to England to superintend the publishing of the Faerie Queene : so from what I know of authors' habits, it is probable that Spenser did read him the poem under the Yew Tree in Myrtle Grove garden. It seems long ago, does it not, when the Faerie Queene was a manuscript, tobacco just discovered, the potato a novelty, and the first Irish cherry-tree just a wee thing newly transplanted from the Canary Islands? Were our own cherry-trees already in America when Columbus discovered us, or did the Pilgrim Fathers bring over " slips " or " grafts," knowing that they would be needed for George Washington later on, so that he might furnish an untruthful world with a sublime sentiment? We re-read Salemina's letter under the Yew Tree : —

COOLKILLA HOUSE, CORK.

MY DEAREST GIRLS, — It seems years instead of days since we parted, and I miss the two madcaps more than I can say. In your absence my life is always so quiet, discreet, dignified, — and, yes, I confess it, so monotonous ! I go to none but the best hotels, meet none but the best people, and my timidity and conservatism forever keep me in conventional paths. Dazzled and terrified as I still am when you precipitate adventures upon me, I always find afterwards that I have enjoyed them in spite of my fears. Life without you is like a stenographic report of a dull sermon ; with you it is by turns a dramatic story, a poem, and a romance. Sometimes it is a penny-dreadful, as when you deliberately leave your luggage on an express train going south, enter another standing upon a side track, and embark for an unknown destination. I watched you from an upper window of the Junction hotel, but could not leave Benella to argue with you. When your respected husband and lover have charge of you, you will not be allowed such pranks, I warrant you !

Benella has improved wonderfully in the last twenty-four hours, and I am trying to give her some training for her future duties. We can never forget our native land so long as we have her with us, for she is a perfect specimen of the Puritan spinster, though too young in years, perhaps, for determined celibacy. Do you know, we none of us mentioned wages in our conversations with her ? Fortunately she seems more alive to the advantages of foreign travel than to the filling of her empty coffers. (By the way, I have written to the purser of the ship that she crossed in, to see if I can recover the sixty or seventy dollars she left behind her.) Her principal idea in life seems to be that of finding some kind of work that will be " interestin' " whether it is lucrative or not.

I don't think she will be able to dress hair, or anything of that sort, — save in the way of plain sewing, she is very unskillful with her hands ; and she will be of no use as courier, she is so provincial and inexperienced. She has no head for business whatever, and cannot help Francesca with the accounts. She recites to herself again and again, " Four farthings make one penny, twelve pence make one shilling, twenty shillings make one pound ;" but when I give her a handful of money and ask her for six shillings and sixpence, five and three, one pound two, or two pound ten, she cannot manage the operation. She is docile, well mannered, grateful, and really likable, but her present philosophy of life is a thing of shreds and patches. She calls it "the science," as if there were but one ; and she became a convert to its teachings this past winter, while living in the house of a woman lecturer in Salem, a lecturer, not a "curist," she explains. She attended to the door, ushered in the members of classes, kept the lecture room in order, and so forth, imbibing by the way various doctrines, or parts of doctrines, which she is not the sort of person to assimilate, but with which she is experimenting : holding, meantime, a grim intuition of their foolishness, or so it seems to me. " The science " made it easier for her to seek her ancestors in a foreign country with only a hundred dollars in her purse ; for the Salem priestess proclaims the glad tidings that all the wealth of the world is ours, if we will but assert our heirship. Benella believed this more or less until a week's seasickness undermined all her new convictions of every sort. When she woke in the little bed-room at O'Carolan's, she says, her heart was quite at rest, for she knew that we were the kind of people one could rely on ! I mustered courage to say, "I hope so, and I hope also that we shall be able to rely upon you, Benella ! "

This idea evidently had not occurred to her, but she accepted it, and I could see that she turned it over in her mind. You can imagine that this vague philosophy of a Salem woman scientist su-perimposed on a foundation of orthodoxy makes a curious combination, and one which will only be temporary.

We shall expect you to-morrow evening, and we shall be quite ready to go on to the Lakes of Killarney or wherever you wish. By the way, I met an old acquaintance the morning I arrived here. I went to see Queen's College ; and as I was walking under the archway which has carved upon it, "Where Finbarr taught let Munster learn," I saw two gentlemen. They looked like professors, and I asked if I might see the college. They said certainly, and offered to take my card in to some one who would do the honors properly. I passed it to one of them : we looked at each other, and recognition was mutual. He (Dr.

La Touche) is giving a course of lectures here
on Irish Antiquities. It has been a great privilege to see this city and its environs with so
learned a man ; I wish you could have shared it.
Yesterday he made up a party and we went to
Passage, which you may remember in Father
Prout's verses : —

> " The town of Passage is both large and spacious,
>   And situated upon the say ;
>   'T is nate and dacent, and quite adjacent
>   To come from Cork on a summer's day.
>   There you may slip in and take a dippin'
>   Fornent the shippin' that at anchor ride ;
>   Or in a wherry cross o'er the ferry
>   To Carrigaloe, on the other side."

Dr. La Touche calls Father Prout an Irish potato
seasoned with Attic salt. Is not that a good
characterization ?

Good-by for the moment, as I must see about
Benella's luncheon.

Yours affectionately, S. P.

X

THE BELLES OF SHANDON

"The spreading Lee that, like an Island fayre,
Encloseth Corke with his divided floode."
Edmund Spenser.

WE had seen all that Youghal could offer to the tourist; we were yearning for Salemina; we wanted to hear Benella talk about "the science;" we were eager to inspect the archæologist, to see if he "would do" for Salemina instead of the canon, or even the minor canon, of the English Church, for whom we had always privately destined her. Accordingly we decided to go by an earlier train, and give our family a pleasant surprise. It was five o'clock in the afternoon when our car trundled across St. Patrick's Bridge, past Father Mathew's statue, and within view of the church and bells of Shandon, that sound so grand on the pleasant waters of the river Lee. Away to the west is the two-armed river. Along its banks rise hills, green and well wooded, with beautiful gardens and verdant pastures reaching to the very brink of the shining stream.

It was Saturday afternoon, and I never drove

through a livelier, quainter, more easy-going town.
The streets were full of people selling various
things and plying various trades, and among
them we saw many a girl pretty enough to recall
Thackeray's admiration of the Corkagian beauties
of his day. There was one in particular, driving
a donkey in a straw-colored governess cart, to
whose graceful charm we succumbed on the instant. There was an exquisite deluderin' wildness
about her, a vivacity, a length of eyelash with a
gleam of Irish gray eye, "the grayest of all things
blue, the bluest of all things gray," that might
well have inspired the English poet to write of
her as he did of his own Irish wife; for Spenser,
when he was not writing the Faerie Queene or
smoking Raleigh's fragrant weed, wooed and
wedded a fair colleen of County Cork.

> "Tell me, ye merchant daughters, did ye see
> So fayre a creature in your town before?
> Her goodlie eyes, like sapphyres shining bright;
> Her forehead, ivory white;
> Her lips like cherries, charming men to byte."

Now we turned into the old Mardyke walk, a
rus in urbe, an avenue a mile long lined with
noble elm-trees; forsaken now as a fashionable
promenade for the Marina, but still beautiful and
still beloved, though frequented chiefly by nurse-
maids and children. Such babies and such children, of all classes and conditions, — so jolly,
smiling, dimpled, curly-headed; such joyous dis-
regard of rags and dirt; such kindness one to

the other in the little groups, where a child of ten would be giving an anxious eye to four or five brothers and sisters, and mothering a contented baby in arms as well.

Our driver, though very loquacious, was not quite intelligible. He pronounced the simple phrase " St. Patrick Street " in a way to astonish the traveler ; it would seem impossible to crowd as many *h*'s into three words, and to wrap each in flannel, as he succeeded in doing. He seemed pleased with our admiration of the babies, and said that Irish children did be very fat and strong and hearty ; that they were the very best soldiers the Queen had, God kape her ! they could stand anny hardship and anny climate, for they were not brought up soft, like the English. He also said that, fine as all Irish children undoubtedly were, Cork produced the flower of them all, and the finest women and the finest men ; backing his opinion with a Homeric vaunt which Francesca took down on the spot : —

> " I 'd back one man from Corkshire
> To bate ten more from Yorkshire:
> Kerrymen
> Agin Derrymen,
> And Munster agin creation.
> Wirrasthrue ! 't is a pity we are n't a nation ! "

Here he slackened his pace as we passed a small bosthoon driving a donkey, to call out facetiously, " Be good to your little brother, *achree !* "

"We must be very near Coolkilla House by this time," said Francesca. "That is n't Salemina sitting on the bench under the trees, is it? There is a gentleman with her, and she never wears a wide hat, but it looks like her red umbrella. No, of course it is n't, for whoever it is belongs to that maid with the two children. Penelope, it is borne in upon me that we should n't have come here unannounced, three hours ahead of the time arranged. Perhaps, whenever we had chosen to come, it would have been too soon. Would n't it be exciting to have to keep out of Salemina's way, as she has always done for us? I could n't endure it; it would make me homesick for Ronald. Go slowly, driver, please."

Nevertheless, as we drew nearer we saw that it was Salemina; or at least it was seven eighths of her, and one eighth of a new person with whom we were not acquainted. She rose to meet us with an exclamation of astonishment, and after a hasty and affectionate greeting presented Dr. La Touche. He said a few courteous words, and to our relief made no allusions to round towers, duns, raths, or other antiquities, and bade us adieu, saying that he should have the honor of waiting upon us that evening with our permission.

A person in a neat black dress and little black bonnet with white lawn strings now brought up the two children to say good-by to Salemina. It was the Derelict, Benella Dusenberry, clothed in maid's apparel and looking, notwithstanding that disguise, like a New England schoolma'am. She was delighted to see us, scanned every detail of Francesca's traveling costume with the frankest admiration, and would have allowed us to carry our wraps and umbrellas upstairs if she had not been reminded by Salemina. We had a cosy cup of tea together, and told our various adventures, but Salemina was not especially communicative about hers. Oddly enough, she had met the La Touche children at the hotel in Mallow. They were traveling with a very raw Irish nurse, who had no control over them whatever. They shrieked and kicked when taken to their rooms at night, until Salemina was obliged to speak to them, in order that Benella's rest should not be disturbed.

" I felt so sorry for them," she said, — "the dear little girl put to bed with tangled hair and unwashed face, the boy in a rumpled, untidy nightgown, the bedclothes in confusion. I didn't know who they were nor where they came from, but while the nurse was getting her supper I made them comfortable, and Broona went to sleep with my strange hand in hers. Perhaps it was only the warm Irish heart, the easy friendliness of the Irish temperament, but I felt as if the poor little things must be neglected indeed, or they would not have clung to a woman whom

they had never seen before." (This is a mistake; anybody who has the opportunity always
clings to Salemina.) "The next morning they
were up at daylight, romping in the hall, stamp-
ing, thumping, clattering, with a tin cart on
wheels rattling behind them. I know it was not
my affair, and I was guilty of unpardonable rude-
ness, but I called the nurse into my room and
spoke to her severely. No, you need n't smile;
I was severe. 'Will you kindly do your duty and
keep the children quiet as they pass through the
halls?' I said. 'It is never too soon to teach
them to obey the rules of a public place, and to
be considerate of older people.' She seemed
awestruck. But when she found her tongue she
stammered, 'Sure, ma'am, I 've tould thim three
times this day already that when their father
comes he 'll bate thim with a blackthorn stick!'

"Naturally I was horrified. This, I thought,
would explain everything: no mother, and an
irritable, cruel father.

"'Will he really do such a thing?' I asked,
feeling as if I must know the truth.

"'Sure he will not, ma'am!' she answered
cheerfully. 'He would n't lift a feather to thim,
not if they murdthered the whole counthryside,
ma'am.'

"Well, they traveled third class to Cork, and
we came first, so we did not meet, and I did not
ask their surnames; but it seems that they were

being brought to their father, whom I met many years ago in America."

As she did not volunteer any further information, we did not like to ask her where, how many years ago, or under what circumstances. " Teasing " of this sort does not appeal to the sophisticated at any time, but it seems unspeakably vulgar to touch on matters of sentiment with a woman of middle age. If she has memories, they are sure to be sad and sacred ones ; if she has not, that perhaps is still sadder. We agreed, however, when the evening was over, that Dr. La Touche was probably the love of her youth, — unless indeed he was simply an old friend, and the degree of Salemina's attachment had been exaggerated; something that is very likely to happen in the gossip of a New England town, where they always incline to underestimate the feeling of the man, and overrate that of the woman, in any love affair. " I guess she 'd take him if she could get him " is the spoken or unspoken attitude of the public in rural or provincial New England.

The professor is grave, but very genial when he fully recalls the fact that he is in company, and has not, like the Trappist monks, taken vows of silence. Francesca behaved beautifully, on the whole, and made no embarrassing speeches, although she was in her gayest humor. Salemina blushed a little when the young sinner dragged

into the conversation the remark that, undoubtedly, from the beginning of the sixth century to
the end of the eighth Ireland was the university of
Europe, just as Greece was in the late days of
the Roman Republic, and asked our guest when
Ireland ceased to be known as " *Insula sanctorum
et doctorum,*" the island of saints and scholars.

We had seen her go into Salemina's bedroom,
and knew perfectly well that she had consulted
the Peabody notebook, lying open on the desk ;
but the professor looked as surprised as if he had
heard a pretty paroquet quote Gibbon. I don't
like to see grave and reverend scholars stare at
pretty paroquets, but I won't belittle Salemina's
exquisite and peculiar charm by worrying over the
matter.

> " Wirra, wirra ! Ologone !
>   Can't ye lave a lad alone,
> Till he 's proved there 's no tradition left of any other girl —
>   Not even Trojan Helen,
>   In beauty all excellin' —
> Who 's been up to half the divilment of Fan Fitzgerl ? "

Of course Francesca's heart is fixed upon Ronald Macdonald, but that fact has not altered
the glance of her eyes. They no longer say,
" Would n't you like to fall in love with me, if you
dared ? " but they still have a gleam that means,
" Don't fall in love with me ; it is no use ! " And
of the two, one is about as dangerous as the
other, and each has something of " Fan Fitzgerl's
divilment."

> " Wid her brows of silky black
>   Arched above for the attack,
> Her eyes they dart such azure death on poor admiring man ;
>   Masther Cupid, point your arrows,
>   From this out, agin the sparrows,
> For you 're bested at Love's archery by young Miss Fan."

Of course Himself never fell a prey to Francesca's fascinations, but then he is not susceptible ; you could send him off for a ten-mile drive in the moonlight with Venus herself, and not be in the least anxious.

Dr. La Touche is gray for his years, tall and spare in frame, and there are many lines of anxiety or thought in his forehead ; but a wonderful smile occasionally smooths them all out, and gives his face a rare though transient radiance. He looks to me as if he had loved too many books and too few people ; as if he had tried vainly to fill his heart and life with antiquities, which of all things, perhaps, are the most bloodless, the least warming and nourishing when taken in excess or as a steady diet. Himself (God bless him !) shall never have that patient look, if I can help it ; but how it will appeal to Salemina ! There are women who are born to be petted and served, and there are those who seem born to serve others. Salemina's first idea is always to make tangled things smooth (like little Broona's curly hair) ; to bring sweet and discreet order out of chaos ; to prune and graft and water and weed and tend things, until they blossom for very shame under her healing touch. Her mind is catholic, well ordered, and broad, — always full of other people's interests, never of her own ; and her heart always seems to me like some dim, sweet-scented guest-chamber in an old New England mansion, cool and clean and quiet, and fragrant of lavender. It has been a lovely, generous life, lived for the most part in the shadow of other people's wishes and plans and desires. I am an impatient person, I confess, and heaven seems so far away when certain things are in question : the righting of a child's wrong, or the demolition of a barrier between two hearts ; above all, for certain surgical operations, more or less spiritual, such as removing scales from eyes that refuse to see, and stops from ears too dull to hear. Nobody shall have our Salemina unless he is worthy, but how I should like to see her life enriched and crowned ! How I should enjoy having her dear little overworn second fiddle taken from her by main force, and a beautiful first violin, or even the baton for leading an orchestra, put into her unselfish hands !

And so good-by and " good luck to ye, Cork, and your pepper-box steeple," for we leave you to-morrow !

XI

"THE RALE THING"

"Her ancestors were kings before Moses was born,
Her mother descended from great Grana Uaile."
Charles Lever.

WE are in the province of Munster, the kingdom of Kerry, the town of Ballyfuchsia, and the house of Mrs. Mullarkey. Knockarney House is not her name for it; I made it myself. Killarney is church of the sloe-trees; and as kill is church, the "onderhanded manin'" of "arney" must be something about sloes; then, since knock means hill, Knockarney should be hill of the sloe-trees.

I have not lost the memory of Jenny Geddes and Tam o' the Cowgate, but Penelope O'Connor, daughter of the king of Connaught, is more frequently present in my dreams. I have by no means forgotten that there was a time when I was not Irish, but for the moment I am of the turf, turfy. Francesca is really as much in love with Ireland as I, only, since she has in her heart a certain tender string pulling her all the while to the land of the heather, she naturally avoids comparisons. Salemina, too, endeavors to appear neutral, lest she should betray an inexplicable interest in Dr. La Touche's country. Benella and I alone are really free to speak the brogue, and carry our wild harps slung behind us, like Moore's minstrel boy. Nothing but the ignorance of her national dishes keeps Benella from entire allegiance to this island; but she thinks a people who have grown up without a knowledge of doughnuts, baked beans, and blueberry pie must be lacking in moral foundations. There is nothing extraordinary in all this; for the Irish, like the Celtic tribes everywhere, have always had a sort of fascinating power over people of other races settling among them, so that they become completely fused with the native population, and grow to be more Irish than the Irish themselves.

We stayed for a few days in the best hotel; it really was quite good, and not a bit Irish. There was a Swiss manager, an English housekeeper, a French head waiter, and a German office clerk. Even Salemina, who loves comforts, saw that we should not be getting what is known as the real thing, under these circumstances, and we came here to this — what shall I call Knockarney House? It was built originally for a fishing lodge by a sporting gentleman, who brought parties of friends to stop for a week. On his death it passed somehow into Mrs. Mullarkey's

fair hands, and in a fatal moment she determined
to open it occasionally to " paying guests," who
might wish a quiet home far from the madding
crowd of the summer tourist. This was exactly
what we did want, and here we encamped, on the
half-hearted advice of some Irish friends in the
town, who knew nothing else more comfortable to
recommend.

" With us, small, quiet, or out-of-the-way places
are never clean ; or if they are, then they are not
Irish," they said. " You had better see Ireland
from the tourist's point of view for a few years
yet, until we have learned the art of living ; but
if you are determined to know the humors of the
people, cast all thought of comfort behind you."

So we did, and we afterward thought that this
would be a good motto for Mrs. Mullarkey to
carve over the door of Knockarney House. (My
name for it is adopted more or less by the family,
though Francesca persists in dating her letters to
Ronald from "The Rale Thing," which it undoubtedly is.) We take almost all the rooms in
the house, but there are a few other guests. Mrs.
Waterford, an old lady of ninety-three, from
Mullinavat, is here primarily for her health, and
secondarily to dispose of threepenny shares in
an antique necklace, which is to be raffled for the
benefit of a Roman Catholic chapel. Then we
have a fishing gentleman and his bride from
Glasgow, and occasional bicyclers who come in

for a dinner, a tea, or a lodging. These three comforts of a home are sometimes quite indistinguishable with us : the tea is frequently made up of fragments of dinner, and the beds are always sprinkled with crumbs. Their source is a mystery, unless they fall from the clothing of the chambermaids, who frequently drop hairpins and brooches and buttons between the sheets, and strew whisk brooms and scissors under the blankets.

We have two general servants, who are supposed to do all the work of the house, and who are as amiable and obliging and incapable as they well can be. Oonah generally waits upon the table, and Molly cooks ; at least she cooks now and then when she is not engaged with Peter in the vegetable garden or the stable. But whatever happens, Mrs. Mullarkey, as a descendant of one of the Irish kings, is to be looked upon only as an inspiring ideal, inciting one to high and ever higher flights of happy incapacity. Benella ostensibly oversees the care of our rooms, but she is comparatively helpless in such a kingdom of misrule. Why demand clean linen when there is none ; why seek for a towel at midday when it is never ironed until evening ; how sweep when a broom is all inadequate to the task ? Salemina's usual remark, on entering a humble hostelry anywhere, is : " If the hall is as dirty as this, what must the kitchen be ! Order me two hard-boiled eggs, please ! "

" Use your 'science,' Benella," I say to that discouraged New England maiden, who has never looked at her philosophy from its practical or humorous side. "If the universe is pure mind and there is no matter, then this dirt is not a real thing, after all. It seems, of course, as if it were thicker under the beds and bureaus than elsewhere, but I suppose our evil thoughts focus themselves there rather than in the centre of the room. Similarly, if the broom handle is broken, deny the dirt away, — denial is much less laborious than sweeping; bring 'the science' down to these simple details of everyday life, and you will make converts by dozens, only pray don't remove, either by suggestion or any cruder method, the large key that lies near the table leg, for it is a landmark; and there is another, a crochet needle, by the washstand, devoted to the same purpose. I wish to show them to the Mullarkey when we leave."

Under our educational régime, the " metaphysical " veneer, badly applied in the first place, and wholly unsuited to the foundation material, is slowly disappearing, and our Benella is gradually returning to her normal self. Perhaps nothing has been more useful to her development than the confusion of Knockarney House.

Our windows are supported on decrepit tennis rackets and worn-out hearth brushes ; the blinds refuse to go up or down ; the chairs have weak

backs or legs; the door knobs are disassociated
from their handles. As for our food, we have
bacon and eggs, with coffee made, I should think,
of brown beans and licorice, for breakfast; a bit
of sloppy chicken, or fish and potato, with custard pudding or stewed rhubarb, for dinner; and
a cold supper of — oh! anything that occurs to
Molly at the last moment. Nothing ever occurs
either to Molly or Oonah at any previous moment, and in that they are merely conforming
to the universal habit. Last week, when we
were starting for Valencia Island, the Ballyfuchsia station master was absent at a funeral;
meantime the engine had " gone cold on the engineer," and the train could not leave till twelve
minutes after the usual time. We thought we
must have consulted a wrong time-table, and
asked confirmation of a man who seemed to have
some connection with the railway. Goaded by
his ignorance, I exclaimed, "Is it possible you
don't know the time the trains are going?"

"Begorra, how should I?" he answered.
"Faix, the thrains don't always be knowin'
thimselves!"

The starting of the daily " Mail Express " from
Ballyfuchsia is a time of great excitement and
confusion, which on some occasions increases to
positive panic. The station master, armed with
a large dinner bell, stands on the platform, wearing an expression of anxiety ludicrously unsuited

to the situation. The supreme moment had really arrived some time before, but he is waiting for Farmer Brodigan with his daughter Kathleen, and the Widdy Sullivan, and a few other local worthies who are a "thrifle late on him." Finally they come down the hill, and he paces up and down the station ringing the bell and uttering the warning cry, "*This thrain never shtops! This thrain never shtops! This thrain never shtops!*" — giving one the idea that eternity, instead of Killarney, must be the final destination of the passengers. The clock in the Ballyfuchsia telegraph and post office ceases to go for twenty-four hours at a time, and nobody heeds it, while the postman always has a few moments' leisure to lay down his knapsack of letters and pitch quoits with the Royal Irish Constabulary. However, punctuality is perhaps an individual virtue more than an exclusively national one. I am not sure that we Americans would not be more agreeable if we spent a month in Ireland every year, and perhaps Ireland would profit from a month in America.

At the Brodigans' (Mr. Brodigan is a large farmer, and our nearest neighbor) all the clocks are from ten to twenty minutes fast or slow; and what a peaceful place it is! The family does n't care when it has its dinner, and, *mirabile dictu*, the cook does n't care either!

"If you have no exact time to depend upon,

how do you catch trains?" I asked Mr. Brodigan.

"Sure that's not an everyday matter, and why
be foostherin' over it? But we do, four times
out o' five, ma'am!"

"How do you like it that fifth time when you
miss it?"

"Sure it's no more throuble to you to miss it
the wan time than to hurry five times! A clock
is an overrated piece of furniture, to my mind,
Mrs. Beresford, ma'am. A man can ate whin
he's hungry, go to bed whin he's sleepy, and get
up whin he's slept long enough; for faith and
it's thim clocks he has inside of himself that
don't need anny winding!"

"What if you had a business appointment with
a man in the town, and missed the train?" I per-
severed.

"Trains is like misfortunes; they never come
singly, ma'am. Wherever there's a station the
trains do be dhroppin' in now and again, and
what's the differ which of thim you take?"

"The man who is waiting for you at the other
end of the line may not agree with you," I suggested.

"Sure, a man can always amuse himself in a
town, ma'am. If it's your own business you're
coming on, he knows you'll find him; and if it's
his business, then begorra let him find you!"
Which quite reminded me of what the Irish elf

says to the English elf in Moira O'Neill's fairy
story : "A waste of time ? Why, you 've come to
a country where there 's no such thing as a waste
of time. We have no value for time here.
There is lashings of it, more than anybody knows
what to do with."

I suppose there is somewhere a golden mean
between this complete oblivion of time and our
feverish American hurry. There is a " tedious
haste " in all peoples who make wheels and pis-
tons and engines, and live within sound of their
everlasting buzz and whir and revolution ; and
there is ever a disposition to pause, rest, and
consider on the part of that man whose daily
tasks are done in serene collaboration with dew
and rain and sun. One cannot hurry Mother
Nature very much, after all, and one who has much
to do with her falls into a peaceful habit of mind.
The mottoes of the two nations are as well
rendered in the vernacular as by any formal or
stilted phrases. In Ireland the spoken or unspoken slogan is, "Take it aisy ; " in America,
" Keep up with the procession ; " and between
them lie all the thousand differences of race, climate, temperament, religion, and government.

I don't suppose there is a nation on the earth
better developed on what might be called the
train-catching side than we of the Big Country,
and it is well for us that there is born every now
and again among us a dreamer who is (blessedly)

oblivious of time-tables and market reports ; who has been thinking of the rustling of the corn, not of its price. It is he, if we do not hurry him out of his dream, who will sound the ideal note in our hurly-burly and bustle of affairs. He may never discover a town site, but he will create new worlds for us to live in, and in the course of a century the coming Matthew Arnold will not be minded to call us an unimaginative and uninteresting people.

XII

LIFE AT KNOCKARNEY HOUSE

> " See where Mononia's heroes lie, proud Owen More's descend-
>   ants, —
>   'T is they that won the glorious name and had the grand attend-
>   ants ! "

> *James Clarence Mangan.*

IT was a charming thing for us when Dr. La
Touche gave us introductions to the Colquhouns
of Ardnagreena ; and when they, in turn, took
us to tea with Lord and Lady Killbally at Balkilly Castle. I don't know what there is about
us : we try to live a sequestered life, but there
are certain kind forces in the universe that are
always bringing us in contact with the good, the
great, and the powerful. Francesca enjoys it,
but secretly fears to have her democracy undermined. Salemina wonders modestly at her good
fortune. I accept it as the graceful tribute of an
old civilization to a younger one ; the older men
grow the better they like girls of sixteen, and why
should n't the same thing be true of countries ?

As long ago as 1589, one of the English " undertakers " who obtained some of the confiscated

Desmond lands in Munster wrote of the "better
sorte" of Irish: "Although they did never see
you before, they will make you the best cheare
their country yieldeth for two or three days, and
take not anything therefor. . . . They have a
common saying which I am persuaded they
speake unfeinedly, which is, 'Defend me and
spend me.' Yet many doe utterly mislike this or
any good thing that the poor Irishman dothe."

This certificate of character from an "under-
taker" of the sixteenth century certainly speaks
volumes for Irish amiability and hospitality, since
it was given at a time when grievances were as
real as plenty ; when unutterable resentment must
have been rankling in many minds ; and when
those traditions were growing which have colored
the whole texture of Irish thought, until, with the
poor and unlettered, to be "agin the government" is an inherited instinct, to be obliterated
only by time.

We supplement Mrs. Mullarkey's helter-skelter
meals with frequent luncheons and dinners with
our new friends, who send us home on our jaunting car laden with flowers, fruit, even with jellies
and jams. Lady Killbally forces us to take three
cups of tea and a half dozen marmalade sandwiches whenever we go to the Castle ; for I apologized for our appetites, one day, by confessing
that we had lunched somewhat frugally, the meal
being sweetened, however, by Molly's explanation

that there was a fresh sole in the house, but she thought she would not inthrude on it before dinner!

We asked, on our arrival at Knockarney House, if we might breakfast at a regular hour, — say eight thirty. Mrs. Mullarkey agreed, with that suavity which is, after her untidiness, her distinguishing characteristic; but notwithstanding this arrangement we break our fast sometimes at nine forty, sometimes at nine twenty, sometimes at nine, but never earlier. In order to achieve this much, we are obliged to rise early and make a combined attack on the executive and culinary departments. One morning I opened the door leading from the hall into the back part of the establishment, but closed it hastily, having interrupted the toilets of three young children, whose existence I had never suspected, and of Mr. Mullarkey, whom I had thought dead for many years. Each child had donned one article of clothing, and was apparently searching for the mate to it, whatever it chanced to be. Mrs. Mullarkey was fully clothed, and was about to administer correction to one of the children, who, unhappily for him, was not. I retired to my apartment to report progress, but did not describe the scene minutely, nor mention the fact that I had seen Salemina's ivory-backed hairbrush put to excellent if somewhat unusual and unaccustomed service.

Each party in the house eats in solitary splen-

dor, like the MacDermott, Prince of Coolavin.
That royal personage of County Sligo did not, I
believe, allow his wife or his children (who must
have had the MacDermott blood in their veins,
even if somewhat diluted) to sit at table with
him.   This method introduces the last element of confusion into the household arrangements, and on two occasions we have had our
custard pudding or stewed fruit served in our
bedrooms a full hour after we have finished
dinner.   We have reasons for wishing to be first
to enter the dining-room, and we walk in with
eyes fixed on the ceiling, by far the cleanest part of
the place.   Having wended our way through an
underbrush of corks, with an empty bottle here
and there, and stumbled over the holes in the carpet, we arrive at our table in the window.   It is
as beautiful as heaven outside, and the tablecloth
is at least cleaner than it will be later, for Mrs.
Waterford of Mullinavat has an unsteady hand.

When Oonah brings in the toast rack now she
balances it carefully, remembering the morning
when she dropped it on the floor, but picked up
the slices and offered them to Salemina.   Never
shall I forget that dear martyr's expression, which
was as if she had made up her mind to renounce
Ireland and leave her to her fate.   I know she
often must wonder if Dr. La Touche's servants,
like Mrs. Mullarkey's, feel of the potatoes to see
whether they are warm or cold !

At ten thirty there is great confusion and laughter and excitement, for the sportsmen are setting out for the day and the car has been waiting at the door for an hour. Oonah is caroling up and down the long passage, laden with dishes, her cheerfulness not in the least impaired by having served seven or eight separate breakfasts. Molly has spilled a jug of milk, and is wiping it up with a child's undershirt. The Glasgy man is telling them that yesterday they forgot the corkscrew, the salt, the cup, and the jam from the luncheon basket, — facts so mirth-provoking that Molly wipes tears of pleasure from her eyes with the milky undershirt, and Oonah sets the hotwater jug and the coffee-pot on the stairs to have her laugh out comfortably. When once the car departs, comparative quiet reigns in and about the house until the passing bicyclers appear for luncheon or tea, when Oonah picks up the napkins that we have rolled into wads and flung under the dining table, and spreads them on tea trays, as appetizing details for the weary traveler. There would naturally be more time for housework if so large a portion of the day were not spent in pleasant interchange of thought and speech. I can well understand Mrs. Colquhoun's objections to the housing of the Dublin poor in tenements, — even in those of a better kind than the present horrible examples; for wherever they are huddled together in any numbers they will

devote most of their time to conversation. To
them, talking is more attractive than eating; it
even adds a new joy to drinking; and if I may
judge from the groups I have seen gossiping over
a turf fire till midnight, it is preferable to sleeping. But do not suppose they will bubble over
with joke and repartee, with racy anecdote, to
every casual newcomer. The tourist who looks
upon the Irishman as the merry-andrew of the
English-speaking world, and who expects every
jarvey he meets to be as whimsical as Mickey
Free, will be disappointed. I have strong suspi-
cions that ragged, jovial Mickey Free himself,
delicious as he is, was created by Lever to satisfy
the Anglo-Saxon idea of the low-comedy Irishman. You will live in the Emerald Isle for many
a month, and not meet the clown or the villain so
familiar to you in modern Irish plays. Drama-
tists have made a stage Irishman to suit themselves, and the public and the gallery are disappointed if anything more reasonable is substituted
for him. You will find, too, that you do not easily gain Paddy's confidence. Misled by his careless, reckless impetuosity of demeanor, you
might expect to be the confidant of his joys and
sorrows, his hopes and expectations, his faiths
and beliefs, his aspirations, fears, longings, at the
first interview. Not at all; you will sooner be
admitted to a glimpse of the traveling Scotsman's
or the Englishman's inner life, family history,

personal ambition. Glacial enough at first and far less voluble, he melts soon enough, if he likes you. Meantime, your impulsive Irish friend gives himself as freely at the first interview as at the twentieth ; and you know him as well at the end of a week as you are likely to at the end of a year. He is a product of the past, be he gentleman or peasant. A few hundred years of necessary reserve concerning articles of political and religious belief have bred caution and prudence in stronger natures, cunning and hypocrisy in weaker ones.

Our days are very varied. We have been several times into the town and spent an hour in the Petty Sessions Court with Mr. Colquhoun, who sits on the bench. Each time we have come home laden with stories "as good as any in the books," so says Francesca. Have we not with our own eyes seen the settlement of an assault and battery case between two of the most notorious brawlers in that alley of the town which we have dubbed "The Pass of the Plumes."[1] Each barrister in the case had a handful of hair which he introduced on behalf of his client, both ladies apparently having pulled with equal energy. These most unattractive exhibits were shown to

[1] The original Pass of the Plumes is near Maryborough, and was so called from the number of English helmet plumes that were strewn about after O'Moore's fight with five hundred of the Earl of Essex's men.

the women themselves, each recognizing her own
hair, but denying the validity of the other exhibit
firmly and vehemently.   Prisoner number one
kneeled at the rail and insisted on exposing the
place in her head from which the hair had been
plucked ; upon which prisoner number two
promptly tore off her hat, scattered hairpins to
the four winds, and exposed her own wounds to
the judicial eye.   Both prisoners "had a dhrop
taken" just before the affair, that soft impeach-
ment they could not deny.   One of them explained, however, that she had taken it to help
her over a hard job of work, and through a little
miscalculation of quantity it had "overaided her."
The other termagant was asked flatly by the
magistrate if she had ever seen the inside of a
jail before, but evaded the point with much grace
and ingenuity by telling his Honor that he could n't
expect to meet a woman annywhere who had not
suffered a misforchin somewhere betwixt the
cradle and the grave.

Even the all too common drunk-and-disorderly
cases had a flavor of their own, for one man,
being dismissed with a small fine uhder condition
that he would sign the pledge, assented will-
ingly ; but on being asked for how long he would
take it replied, "I mostly take it for life, your
worship."

We also heard the testimony of a girl who had
run away from her employer before the comple-

tion of her six months' contract, her plea being that the fairies pulled her great toe at night so that she could not sleep, whereupon she finally became so lame that she was unable to work. She left her employer's house one evening, therefore, and went home, and curiously enough the fairies "shtopped pulling the toe on her as soon as iver she got there!"

Not the least enlivening of the prisoners was a decently educated person who had been arrested for disturbing the peace. The constable asserted that he was intoxicated, but the gentleman himself insisted that he was merely a poet in a more than usually inspired state.

"I am in the poetical advertising line, your worship. It is true I was surrounded by a crowd, but I was merely practicing my trade. I don't mind telling your worship that this holiday time makes things a little lively, and the tradesmen drink my health a trifle oftener than usual; poetry is dry work, your worship, and a poet needs a good deal of liquid refreshment. I do not disturb the peace, your worship, at least not more than any other poet. I go to a grocer's, and standing outside I make up some rhymes about his nice sweet sugar or his ale. If I want to please a butcher, — well, I 'll give you a specimen : —

> 'Here 's to the butcher who sells good meat —
> In this world it 's hard to beat;

> It's the very best that's to be had,
> And makes the human heart feel glad.
> There's no necessity to purloin,
> So step in and buy a good sirloin.'

I can go on in this style, like Tennyson's brook, forever, your worship." His worship was afraid that he might make the offer good, and the poet was released, after promising to imbibe less frequently when he felt the divine afflatus about to descend upon him.

These disagreements between light-hearted and bibulous persons who haunt the courts week after week have nothing especially pathetic about them, but there are many that make one's heart ache; many that seem absolutely beyond any solution, and beyond reach of any justice.

XIII

" O ! THE SOUND OF THE KERRY DANCING "

> " The light-hearted daughters of Erin,
>   Like the wild mountain deer they can bound ;
>   Their feet never touch the green island,
>   But music is struck from the ground.
>   And oft in the glens and green meadows,
>   The ould jig they dance with such grace,
>   That even the daisies they tread on,
>   Look up with delight in their face."
>
> *James M'Kowen.*

ONE of our favorite diversions is an occasional glimpse of a " crossroads dance " on a pleasant Sunday afternoon, when all the young people of the district are gathered together. Their religious duties are over with their confessions and their masses, and the priests encourage these decorous Sabbath gayeties. A place is generally chosen where two or four roads meet, and the dancers come from the scattered farmhouses in every direction. In Ballyfuchsia, they dance on a flat piece of road under some fir-trees and larches, with stretches of mountain covered with yellow gorse or purple heather and the quiet lakes lying in the distance. A message comes down to us at Ardnagreena — where we commonly spend our

Sunday afternoons — that they expect a good
dance, and the blind boy is coming to fiddle ; and
"so if you will be coming up, it's welcome you'll
be." We join them about five o'clock, — passing,
on our way, groups of "boys" of all ages from sixteen upwards, walking in twos and threes, and parties of three or four girls by themselves ; for it
would not be etiquette for the boys and girls to
walk together, such strictness is observed in these
matters about here.

When we reach the rendezvous we find quite a
crowd of young men and maidens assembled ;
the girls all at one side of the road, neatly
dressed in dark skirts and light blouses, with the
national woolen shawl over their heads. Two
wide stone walls, or dikes, with turf on top, make
capital seats, and the boys are at the opposite
side, as custom demands. When a young man
wants a partner, he steps across the road and
asks a colleen, who lays aside her shawl, generally giving it to a younger sister to keep until the
dance is over, when the girls go back to their own
side of the road and put on their shawls again.
Upon our arrival we find the " sets " are already
in progress ; a " set " being a dance like a very
intricate and very long quadrille. We are greeted
with many friendly words, and the young boat-
men and farmers' sons ask the ladies, "Will you
be pleased to dance, miss ? " Some of them are
shy, and say they are not familiar with the steps ;

but their would-be partners remark encouragingly: "Sure, and what matter? I'll see you through." Soon all are dancing, and the state of the road is being discussed with as much interest as the floor of a ballroom. Eager directions are given to the more ignorant newcomers, such as, "Twirl your girl, captain!" or "Turn your back to your face!"—rather a difficult direction to carry out, but one which conveys its meaning. Salemina confided to her partner that she feared she was getting a bit old to dance. He looked at her gray hair carefully for a moment, and then said chivalrously: "I'd not say that that was old age, ma'am. I'd say it was eddication."

When the sets, which are very long and very decorous, are finished, sometimes a jig is danced for our benefit. The spectators make a ring, and the chosen dancers go into the middle, where their steps are watched by a most critical and discriminating audience with the most minute and intense interest. Our Molly is one of the best jig dancers among the girls here (would that she were half as clever at cooking!); but if you want to see an artist of the first rank, you must watch Kitty O'Rourke, from the neighboring village of Dooclone. The half door of the barn is carried into the ring by one or two of her admirers, whom she numbers by the score, and on this she dances her famous jig polthogue, sometimes

alone and sometimes with Art Rooney, the only
worthy partner for her in the kingdom of Kerry.
Art's mother, "Bid" Rooney, is a keen match-
maker, and we heard her the other day advising
her son, who was going to Dooclone to have a
"weeny court" with his colleen, to put a clane
shirt on him in the middle of the week, and dis-
thract Kitty intirely by showin' her he had three
of thim, annyway!

Kitty is a beauty, and does n't need to be
made "purty wid cows," — a feat that the old
Irishman proposed to do when he was consummat-
ing a match for his plain daughter. But the gifts
of the gods seldom come singly, and Kitty is well
fortuned as well as beautiful; fifty pounds, her
own bedstead and its fittings, a cow, a pig, and a
web of linen are supposed to be the dazzling total,
so that it is small wonder her deluderin' ways are
maddening half the boys in Ballyfuchsia and
Dooclone. She has the prettiest pair of feet in
the County Kerry, and when they are encased in
a smart pair of shoes, bought for her by Art's
rival, the big constable from Ballyfuchsia barracks, how they do twinkle and caper over that
half barn door, to be sure! Even Murty, the
blind fiddler, seems intoxicated by the plaudits of
the bystanders, and he certainly never plays so
well for anybody as for Kitty of the Meadow.
Blindness is still common in Ireland, owing to
the smoke in these wretched cabins, where some-

times a hole in the roof is the only chimney ; and although the scores of blind fiddlers no longer traverse the land, finding a welcome at all firesides, they are still to be found in every community. Blind Murty is a favorite guest at the Rooneys' cabin, which is never so full that there is not room for one more. There is a small wooden bed in the main room, a settle that opens out at night, with hens in the straw underneath, where a board keeps them safely within until they have finished laying. There are six children besides Art, and my ambition is to photograph, or, still better, to sketch the family circle together ; the hens cackling under the settle, the pig ("him as pays the rint") snoring in the doorway, as a proprietor should, while the children are picturesquely grouped about. I never succeed, because Mrs. Rooney sees us as we turn into the lane, and calls to the family to make itself ready, as quality's comin' in sight. The older children can scramble under the bed, slip shoes over their bare feet, and be out in front of the cabin without the loss of a single minute. "Mickey jew'l," the baby, who is only four, but "who can handle a stick as bould as a man," is generally clad in a ragged skirt, slit every few inches from waist to hem, so that it resembles a cotton fringe. The little coateen that tops this costume is sometimes, by way of diversion, transferred to the dog, who runs off with it ; but if we appear at this unlucky moment, there is a stylish yoke of pink ribbon and soiled lace which one of the girls pins over Mickey jew'l's naked shoulders.

Moya, who has this eye for picturesque propriety, is a great friend of mine, and has many questions about the Big Country when we take our walks. She longs to emigrate, but the time is not ripe yet. "The girls that come back has a lovely style to thim," she says wistfully, "but they're so polite they can't live in the cabins anny more and be contint." The "boys" are not always so improved, she thinks. "You'd niver find a boy in Ballyfuchsia that would say annything rude to a girl; but when they come back from Ameriky, it's too free they've grown intirely." It is a dull life for them, she says, when they have once been away; though to be sure Ballyfuchsia is a pleasanter place than Dooclone, where the priest does not approve of dancing, and, however secretly you may do it, the curate hears of it, and will speak your name in church.

It was Moya who told me of Kitty's fortune. "She's not the match that Farmer Brodigan's daughter Kathleen is, to be sure; for he's a rich man, and has given her an iligant eddication in Cork, so that she can look high for a husband. She won't be takin' up wid anny of our boys, wid her two hundred pounds and her twenty cows and her pianya. Och, it's a thriminjus player she is, ma'am. She's that quick and that strong that you'd say she would n't lave a string on it."

Some of the young men and girls never see each other before the marriage, Moya says. "But sure," she adds shyly, "I'd niver be contint with that, though some love matches does n't turn out anny better than the others."

"I hope it will be a love match with you, and that I shall dance at your wedding, Moya," I say to her smilingly.

"Faith, I'm thinkin' my husband's intinded mother died an old maid in Dublin," she answers merrily. "It's a small fortune I'll be havin', and few lovers; but you'll be soon dancing at Kathleen Brodigan's wedding, or Kitty O'Rourke's, maybe."

I do not pretend to understand these humble romances, with their foundations of cows and linen, which are after all no more sordid than bank stock and trousseaux from Paris. The sentiment of the Irish peasant lover seems to be frankly and truly expressed in the verses : —

"Oh! Moya's wise and beautiful, has wealth in plenteous store,
And fortune fine in calves and kine, and lovers half a score ;
Her faintest smile would saints beguile, or sinners captivate,
Oh! I think a dale of Moya, but I'll surely marry Kate.
. . . .
Now to let you know the raison why I cannot have my way,
Nor bid my heart decide the part the lover must obey —
The calves and kine of Kate are nine, while Moya owns but eight,
So with all my love for Moya I'm compelled to marry Kate!"

I gave Moya a lace neckerchief the other day, and she was rarely pleased, running into the cabin with it and showing it to her mother with great pride. After we had walked a bit down the boreen she excused herself for an instant, and, returning to my side, explained that she had gone back to ask her mother to mind the kerchief, and not let the " cow knock it " !

Lady Killbally tells us that some of the girls who work in the mills deny themselves proper food, and live on bread and tea for a month, to save the price of a gay ribbon. This is trying, no doubt, to a philanthropist, but is it not partly a starved sense of beauty asserting itself ? If it has none of the usual outlets, where can imagination express itself if not in some paltry thing like a ribbon?

XIV

MRS. MULLARKEY'S ILIGANT LOCKS

"Where spreads the beautiful water to gay or cloudy skies,
And the purple peaks of Killarney from ancient woods arise."
William Allingham.

MRS. MULLARKEY cannot spoil this paradise for us. When I wake in the morning, the fuchsia tree outside my window is such a glorious mass of color that it distracts my eyes from the unwashed glass. The air is still; the mountains in the far distance are clear purple; everything is fresh-washed and purified for the new day. Francesca and I leave the house sleeping, and make our way to the bogs. We love to sit under a blossoming sloe bush and see the silver pools glistening here and there in the turf cuttings, and watch the transparent vapor rising from the red-brown or the purple-shadowed bog fields. Dinnis Rooney, half awake, leisurely, silent, is moving among the stacks with his creel. How the missel thrushes sing in the woods, and the plaintive note of the curlew gives the last touch of mysterious tenderness to the scene. There is a moist, rich fragrance of meadowsweet and bog myrtle in the air; and how fresh and wild and verdant it is!

" For there's plenty to mind, sure, if on'y ye look to the grass at
   your feet,
For 't is thick wid the tussocks of heather, an' blossoms and herbs
   that smell sweet
If ye tread thim ; an' maybe the white o' the bog-cotton waves in
   the win',
Like the wool ye might shear off a night-moth, an' set an ould
   fairy to spin ;
Or wee frauns, each wan stuck 'twixt two leaves on a grand little
   stem of its own,
Lettin' on 't was a plum on a tree." [1] . . .

As for Lough Lein itself, who could speak its
loveliness, lying like a crystal mirror beneath the
black Reeks of the McGillicuddy, where, in the
mountain fastnesses, lie spellbound the sleeping
warriors who, with their bridles and broadswords
in hand, await but the word to give Erin her own !
When we glide along the surface of the lakes, on
some bright day after a heavy rain ; when we look
down through the clear water on tiny submerged
islets, with their grasses and drowned daisies
glancing up at us from the blue ; when we moor
the boat and climb the hillsides, we are dazzled
by the luxuriant beauty of it all. It hardly seems
real, — it is too green, too perfect, to be believed ;
and one thinks of some fairy drop scene, painted
by cunning-fingered elves and sprites, who might
have a wee folk's way of mixing roses and rain-
bows, dew-drenched greens and sun-warmed yel-
lows ; showing the picture to you first all bur-
nished, glittering and radiant, then "veiled in

[1] Jane Barlow.

mist and diamonded with showers." We climb, climb, up, up, into the heart of the leafy loveliness; peering down into dewy dingles, stopping now and again to watch one of the countless streams as it tinkles and gurgles down an emerald ravine to join the lakes. The way is strewn with lichens and mosses; rich green hollies and arbutus surround us on every side; the ivy hangs in sweet disorder from the rocks; and when we reach the innermost recess of the glen we can find moist green jungles of ferns and bracken, a very bending, curling forest of fronds : —

> "The fairy's tall palm tree, the heath bird's fresh nest,
>   And the couch the red deer deems the sweetest and best."

Carrantual rears its crested head high above the other mountains, and on its summit Shon the Outlaw, footsore, weary, slept; sighing, "For once, thank God, I am above all my enemies."

You must go to sweet Innisfallen, too, and you must not be prosaic or incredulous at the boatman's stories, or turn the "bodthered ear to them." These are no ordinary hillsides : not only do the wee folk troop through the frond forests nightly, but great heroic figures of romance have stalked majestically along these mountain summits. Every waterfall foaming and dashing from its rocky bed in the glen has a legend in the toss and swirl of the water.

Can't you see the O'Sullivan, famous for fleetness of foot and prowess in the chase, starting

forth in the cool o' the morn to hunt the red deer?
His dogs sniff the heather; a splendid stag bounds
across the path; swift as lightning the dogs follow the scent across moors and glens. Throughout the long day the chieftain chases the stag,
until at nightfall, weary and thirsty, he loses the
scent, and blows a blast on his horn to call the
dogs homeward.

And then he hears a voice: "O'Sullivan, turn
back!"

He looks over his shoulder to behold the great
Finn McCool, central figure in centuries of romance.

"Why do you dare chase my stag?" he asks.

"Because it is the finest man ever saw," answers the chieftain composedly.

"You are a valiant man," says the hero, pleased
with the reply; "and as you thirst from the long
chase, I will give you to drink." So he crunches
his giant heel into the rock, and forth burst the
waters, seething and roaring as they do to this
day; "and may the divil fly away wid me if I've
spoke an unthrue word, ma'am!"

Come to Lough Lein as did we, too early for
the crowd of sightseers; but when the "long
light shakes across the lakes," the blackest arts
of the tourist (and they are as black as they are
many) cannot break the spell. Sitting on one of
these hillsides, we heard a bugle call taken up
and repeated in delicate, ethereal echoes, — sweet

enough, indeed, to be worthy of the fairy buglers who are supposed to pass the sound along their lines from crag to crag, until it faints and dies in silence. And then came the Lament for Owen Roe O'Neill. We were thrilled to the very heart with the sorrowful strains; and when we issued from our leafy covert, and rounded the point of rocks from which the sound came, we found a fat man in uniform playing the bugle. "Blank's Tours" was embroidered on his cap, and I have no doubt that he is a good husband and father, even a good citizen, but he is a blight upon the landscape, and fancy cannot breathe in his presence. The typical tourist should be encouraged within bounds, both because he is of some benefit to Ireland, and because Ireland is of inestimable benefit to him ; but he should not be allowed to jeer and laugh at the legends (the gentle smile of sophisticated unbelief, with its twinkle of amusement, is unknown to and forever beyond him); and above all, he should never be allowed to carry or to play on a concertina, for this is the unpardonable sin.

We had an adventure yesterday. We were to dine at eight o'clock at Balkilly Castle, where Dr. La Touche is staying the week end with Lord and Lady Killbally. We had been spending an hour or two after tea in writing an Irish letter, and were a bit late in dressing. These letters, written in the vernacular, are a favorite diversion

of ours when visiting in foreign lands; and they
are very easily done when once you have caught
the idioms, for you can always supplement your
slender store of words and expressions with
choice selections from native authors.

What Francesca and I wore to the Castle dinner is, alas, no longer of any consequence to the
community at large. In the mysterious purposes
of that third volume which we seem to be living
in Ireland, Francesca's beauty and mine, her hats
and frocks as well as mine, are all reduced to the
background; but Salemina's toilet had cost us
some thought. When she first issued from the
discreet and decorous fastnesses of Salem society,
she had never donned any dinner dress that was
not as high at the throat and as long in the sleeves
as the Puritan mothers ever wore to meeting. In
England she lapsed sufficiently from the rigid
Salem standard to adopt a timid compromise; in
Scotland we coaxed her into still further modern-
ities, until now she is completely enfranchised.
We achieved this at considerable trouble, but do
not grudge the time spent in persuasion when we
see her *en grande toilette*. In day dress she has
always been inclined ever so little to a primness
and severity that suggest old-maidishness. In
her low gown of pale gray, with all her silver hair
waved softly, she is unexpectedly lovely,—her face
softened, transformed, and magically "brought
out" by the whiteness of her shoulders and slen-

der throat. Not an ornament, not a jewel, will she
wear; and she is right to keep the nunlike sim-
plicity of style which suits her so well, and which
holds its own even in the vicinity of Francesca's
proud and glowing young beauty.

On this particular evening, Francesca, who
wished her to look her best, had prudently hidden her eyeglasses, for which we are now trying
to substitute a silver-handled lorgnette. Two
years ago we deliberately smashed her spectacles,
which she had adopted at five and twenty.

"But they are more convenient than eyeglasses," she urged obtusely.

"That argument is beneath you, dear," we
replied. "If your hair were not prematurely
gray, we might permit the spectacles, hideous as
they are, but a combination of the two is impossible; the world shall not convict you of failing
sight when you are guilty only of petty astigma-
tism!"

The gray satin had been chosen for this dinner,
and Salemina was dressed, with the exception of
the pretty pearl-embroidered waist that has to be
laced at the last moment, and had slipped on a
dressing jacket to come down from her room in
the second story, to be advised in some trifling
detail. She looked unusually well, I thought:
her eyes were bright and her cheeks flushed, as
she rustled in, holding her satin skirts daintily
away from the dusty carpets.

Now, from the morning of our arrival we have had trouble with the Mullarkey door-knobs, which come off continually, and lie on the floors at one side of the door or the other. Benella followed Salemina from her room, and, being in haste, closed the door with unwonted energy. She heard the well-known rattle and clang, but little suspected that, as one knob dropped outside in the hall, the other fell inside, carrying the rod of connection with it. It was not long before we heard a cry of despair from above and we responded to it promptly.

"It's fell in on the inside, knob and all, as I always knew it would some day; and now we can't get back into the room!" said Benella.

"Oh, nonsense! We can open it with something or other," I answered encouragingly, as I drew on my gloves; "only you must hasten, for the car is at the door."

The curling iron was too large, the shoe hook too short, a lead pencil too smooth, a crochet needle too slender: we tried them all, and the door resisted all their insinuations. "Must you necessarily get in before we go?" I asked Salemina thoughtlessly.

She gave me a glance that almost froze my blood, as she replied, "The waist of my dress is in the room."

Francesca and I spent a moment in irrepressible mirth, and then summoned Mrs. Mullarkey.

Whether the Irish kings could be relied upon in an emergency I do not know, but their descendants cannot. Mrs. Mullarkey had gone to the convent to see the Mother Superior about something; Mr. Mullarkey was at the Dooclone market; Peter was not to be found; but Oonah and Molly came, and also the old lady from Mullinavat, with a package of raffle tickets in her hand.

We left this small army under Benella's charge, and went down to my room for a hasty consultation.

"Could you wear any evening bodice of Francesca's?" I asked.

"Of course not. Francesca's waist measure is three inches smaller than mine."

"Could you manage my black lace dress?"

"Penelope, you know it would only reach to my ankles! No, you must go without me, and go at once. We are too new acquaintances to keep Lady Killbally's dinner waiting. Why did I come to this place like a pauper, with only one evening gown, when I should have known that if there is a castle anywhere within forty miles you always spend half your time in it!"

This slur was totally unjustified, but I pardoned it, because Salemina's temper is ordinarily perfect, and the circumstances were somewhat tragic. "If you had brought a dozen costumes, they would all be in your room at this moment," I replied; "but we must think of something. It is impossible for you to remain behind ; we were invited more on your account than on our own, for you are Dr. La Touche's friend, and the dinner is especially in his honor. Molly, have you a ladder?"

"Sorra a wan, ma'am."

"Could we borrow one?"

"We could not, Mrs. Beresford, ma'am."

"Then see if you can break down the door ; try hard, and if you succeed I will buy you a nice new one! Part of Miss Peabody's dress is inside the room, and we shall be late to the Castle dinner."

The entire corps, with Mrs. Waterford of Mullinavat on top, cast itself on the door, which withstood the shock to perfection. Then in a moment we heard : "Weary's on it, it will not come down for us, ma'am. It's the iligant locks we do be havin' in the house ; they're mortial shtrong, ma'am!"

"Strong indeed!" exclaimed the incensed Benella, in a burst of New England wrath. "There's nothing strong about the place but the impidence of the people in it! If you had told Peter to get a carpenter or a locksmith, as I've been asking you to these two weeks, it would have been all right ; but you never do anything till a month after it's too late. I've no patience with such a set of doshies, dawdling around and leaving everything to go to rack and ruin!"

" Sure it was yourself that ruinated the thing,"
responded Molly, with spirit, for the unaccustomed word " doshy " had kindled her quick
Irish temper. " It's aisy handlin' the knob is
used to, and faith it would 'a' stuck there for you
a twelvemonth ! "

" They will be quarreling soon," said Salemina
nervously. " Do not wait another instant ; you
are late enough now, and I insist on your going.
Make any excuse you see fit : say I am ill, say I
am dead, if you like, but don't tell the real excuse, — it is too shiftless and wretched and embarrassing. Don't cry, Benella. Molly, Oonah,
go downstairs to your work. Mrs. Waterford, I
think perhaps you have forgotten that we have
already purchased raffle tickets, and we'll not
take any more for fear that we may draw the
necklace. Good-by, dears ; tell Lady Killbally I
shall see her to-morrow."

XV

PENELOPE WEAVES A WEB

> Why the shovel and tongs
> To each other belongs,
> And the kettle sings songs
> Full of family glee,
> While alone with your cup,
> Like a hermit you sup,
> Och hone, Widow Machree."
>
> *Samuel Lover.*

FRANCESCA and I were gloomy enough, as we drove along facing each other in Ballyfuchsia's one "inside" car, — a strange and fearsome vehicle, partaking of the nature of a broken-down omnibus, a hearse, and an overgrown black beetle. It holds four, or at a squeeze six, the seats being placed from stem to stern lengthwise, and the balance being so delicate that the passengers, when going uphill, are shaken into a heap at the door, which is represented by a ragged leather flap. I have often seen it strew the hard highroad with passengers, as it jolts up the steep incline that leads to Ardnagreena, and the "fares" who succeed in staying in always sit in one another's laps a good part of the way, — a method pleasing only to relatives or intimate friends. Francesca and I agreed to tell the real reason of Salemina's absence. "It is Ireland's fault, and I will not have America blamed for it," she insisted; "but it is so embarrassing to be going to the dinner ourselves, and leaving behind the most important personage. Think of Dr. La Touche's disappointment, think of Salemina's; and they'll never understand why she could n't have come in a dressing jacket. I shall advise her to discharge Benella after this episode, for no one can tell the effect it may have upon all our future lives, even those of the doctor's two poor motherless children."

It is a four-mile drive to Balkilly Castle, and when we arrived there we were so shaken that we had to retire to a dressing-room for repairs. Then came the dreaded moment when we entered the great hall and advanced to meet Lady Killbally, who looked over our heads to greet the missing Salemina. Francesca's beauty, my supposed genius, both fell flat; it was Salemina whose presence was especially desired. The company was assembled, save for one guest still more tardy than ourselves, and we had a moment or two to tell our story as sympathetically as possible. It had an uncommonly good reception, and, coupled with the Irish letter I read at dessert, carried the dinner along on a basis of such laughter and good-fellowship that finally there was no place for regret save in the hearts of those who knew and loved Salemina, — poor Salemina, spending her dull, lonely evening in our rooms, and later on in her own uneventful bed, if indeed she had been lucky enough to gain access to that bed. I had hoped Lady Killbally would put one of us beside Dr. La Touche, so that we might at least keep Salemina's memory green by tactful conversation ; but it was too large a company to rearrange, and he had to sit by an empty chair, which perhaps was just as salutary, after all. The dinner was very smart, and the company interesting and clever, but my thoughts were elsewhere. As there were fewer squires than dames at the feast, Lady Killbally kindly took me on her left, with a view to better acquaintance, and I was heartily glad of a possible chance to hear something of Dr. La Touche's earlier life. In our previous interviews, Salemina's presence had always precluded the possibility of leading the conversation in the wished-for direction.

When I first saw Gerald La Touche I felt that he required explanation. Usually speaking, a human being ought to be able, in an evening's conversation, to explain himself, without any adventitious aid. If he is a man, alive, vigorous, well poised, conscious of his own individuality, he shows you, without any effort, as much of his past as you need to form your impression, and as much of his future as you have intuition to read. As opposed to the vigorous personality, there is the colorless, flavorless, insubstantial sort, forgotten as soon as learned, and forever confused with that of the previous or the next comer. When I was a beginner in portrait painting, I remember that, after I had succeeded in making my background stay back where it belonged, my figure sometimes had a way of clinging to it in a kind of smudgy weakness, as if it were afraid to come out like a man and stand the inspection of my eye. How often have I squandered paint upon the ungrateful object without adding a cubit to its stature! It refused to look like flesh and blood, but resembled rather some half-made creature flung on the passive canvas in a liquid state, with its edges running over into the background. There are a good many of these people in literature, too, — heroes who, like home-made paper dolls, do not stand up well; or if they manage to perform that feat, one unexpectedly discovers, when they are placed in a strong light, that they have no vital organs whatever, and can be seen through without the slightest difficulty. Dr. La Touche does not belong to either of these two classes: he is not warm, magnetic, powerful, impressive; neither is he by any means destitute of vital organs; but his personality is blurred in some way. He seems a bit remote, absent-minded, and a trifle, just a trifle, over-resigned. Privately, I think a man can afford to be resigned only to one thing, and that is the will of God; against all other

odds I prefer to see him fight till the last armed
foe expires. Dr. La Touche is devotedly attached to his children, but quite helpless in their
hands ; so that he never looks at them with pleasure or comfort or pride, but always with an anxiety as to what they may do next. I understand
him better now that I know the circumstances of
which he has been the product. (Of course one
is always a product of circumstances, unless one
can manage to be superior to them.) His wife,
the daughter of an American consul in Ireland,
was a charming but somewhat feather-brained
person, rather given to whims and caprices ; very
pretty, very young, very much spoiled, very attractive, very undisciplined. All went well enough
with them until her father was recalled to America, because of some change in political adminis-
tration. The young Mrs. La Touche seemed to
have no resources apart from her family, and
even her baby "Jackeen" failed to absorb her as
might have been expected.

"We thought her a most trying woman at this
time," said Lady Killbally. "She seemed to
have no thought of her husband's interests, and
none of the responsibilities that she had assumed in marrying him ; her only idea of life
appeared to be amusement and variety and gayety. Gerald was a student, and always very
grave and serious ; the kind of man who invari-
ably marries a butterfly, if he can find one to

make him miserable. He was exceedingly patient; but after the birth of little Broona, Adeline became so homesick and depressed and discontented that, although the journey was almost an impossibility at the time, Gerald took her back to her people, and left her with them, while he returned to his duties at Trinity College. Their life, I suppose, had been very unhappy for a year or two before this, and when he came home to Dublin without his children, he looked a sad and broken man. He was absolutely faithful to his ideals, I am glad to say, and never wavered in his allegiance to his wife, however disappointed he may have been in her; going over regularly to spend his long vacations in America, although she never seemed to wish to see him. At last she fell into a state of hopeless melancholia; and it was rather a relief to us all to feel that we had judged her too severely, and that her unreasonableness and her extraordinary caprices had been born of mental disorder more than of moral obliquity. Gerald gave up everything to nurse her and rouse her from her apathy; but she faded away without ever once coming back to a more normal self, and that was the end of it all. Gerald's father had died meanwhile, and he had fallen heir to the property and the estates. They were very much encumbered, but he is gradually getting affairs into a less chaotic state; and while his fortune would seem a small one to you

extravagant Americans, he is what we Irish pau-
pers would call well to do."

Lady Killbally was suspiciously willing to give
me all this information, — so much so that I
ventured to ask about the children.

"They are captivating, neglected little things,"
she said. "Madam La Touche, an aged aunt,
has the ostensible charge of them, and she is a
most easy-going person. The servants are of
the 'old family' sort, the reckless, improvident,
untidy, devoted, quarrelsome creatures that always stand by the ruined Irish gentry in all their
misfortunes, and generally make their life a burden to them at the same time. Gerald is a saint,
and therefore never complains."

"It never seems to me that saints are altogether
adapted to positions like these," I sighed; "sinners
would do ever so much better. I should like to
see Dr. La Touche take off his halo, lay it carefully on the bureau, and wield a battle-axe. The
world will never acknowledge his merit; it will
even forget him presently, and his life will have
been given up to the evolution of the passive
virtues. Do you suppose he will ever marry
again? Do you suppose he will recognize the
tender passion if it ever does bud in his breast,
or will he think it a weed, instead of a flower,
and let it wither for want of attention?"

"I think his friends will have to enhance his
self-respect, or he will forever be too modest to

declare himself," said Lady Killbally. "Perhaps you can help us : he is probably going to America this winter to lecture at some of your universities, and he may stay there for a year or two, so he says. At any rate, if the right woman ever appears on the scene, I hope she will have the instinct to admire and love and reverence him as we do," and here she smiled directly into my eyes, and slipping her pretty hand under the tablecloth squeezed mine in a manner that spoke volumes.

It is not easy to explain one's desire to marry off all the unmarried persons in one's vicinity. When I look steadfastly at any group of people, large or small, they usually segregate themselves into twos under my prophetic eye. If they are nice and attractive, I am pleased to see them mated ; if they are horrid and disagreeable, I like to think of them as improving under the discipline of matrimony. It is joy to see beauty meet a kindling eye, but I am more delighted still to watch a man fall under the glamour of a plain, dull girl, and it is ecstasy for me to see a perfectly unattractive, stupid woman snapped up at last, when I have given up hopes of settling her in life. Sometimes there are men so uninspiring that I cannot converse with them a single moment without yawning ; but though failures in all other relations, one can conceive of their being tolerably useful as husbands and fathers ; not for one's self, you understand, but for one's neighbors.

Dr. La Touche's life now, to any understanding eye, is as incomplete as the unfinished window in Aladdin's tower. He is too wrinkled, too studious, too quiet, too patient for his years. His children need a mother, his old family servants need discipline, his baronial halls need sweeping and cleaning (I have n't seen them, but I know they do!), and his aged aunt needs advice and guidance. On the other hand, there are those (I speak guardedly) who have walked in shady sequestered paths all their lives, looking at hundreds of happy lovers on the sunny highroad, but never joining them; those who adore erudition, who love children, who have a genius for unselfish devotion, who are sweet and refined and clever, and who look perfectly lovely when they put on gray satin and leave off eyeglasses. They say they are over forty, and although this probably is exaggeration, they may be thirty-nine and three quarters; and if so, the time is limited in which to find for them a worthy mate, since half of the masculine population is looking for itself, and always in the wrong quarter, needing no assistance to discover rosy-cheeked idiots of nineteen, whose obvious charms draw thousands to a dull and uneventful fate.

These thoughts were running idly through my mind while the Honorable Michael McGillicuddy was discoursing to me of Mr. Gladstone's misunderstanding of Irish questions, — a misunderstanding, he said, so colossal, so temperamental, and so all-embracing, that it amounted to genius. I was so anxious to return to Salemina that I wished I had ordered the car at ten thirty instead of eleven ; but I made up my mind, as we ladies went to the drawing-room for coffee, that I would seize the first favorable opportunity to explore the secret chambers of Dr. La Touche's being. I love to rummage in out-of-the-way corners of people's brains and hearts if they will let me. I like to follow a courteous host through the public corridors of his house and come upon a little chamber closed to the casual visitor. If I have known him long enough I put my hand on the latch and smile inquiringly. He looks confused and conscious, but unlocks the door. Then I peep in, and often I see something that pleases and charms and touches me so much that it shows in my eyes when I lift them to his to say " Thank you." Sometimes, after that, my host gives me the key and says gravely, " Pray come in whenever you like."

When Dr. La Touche offers me this hospitality I shall find out whether he knows anything of that lavender-scented guest room in Salemina's heart. First, has he ever seen it ? Second, has he ever stopped in it for any length of time ? Third, was he sufficiently enamored of it to occupy it on a long lease?

XVI

SALEMINA HAS HER CHANCE

"And what use is one's life widout chances?
Ye 've always a chance wid the tide."
Jane Barlow.

I WAS walking with Lady Fincoss, and Francesca with Miss Clondalkin, a very learned personage who has deciphered more undecipherable inscriptions than any lady in Ireland, when our eyes fell upon an unexpected tableau.

Seated on a divan in the centre of the drawing-room, in a most distinguished attitude, in unexceptionable attire, and with the rose-colored lights making all her soft grays opalescent, was Miss Salemina Peabody. Our exclamations of astonishment were so audible that they must have reached the dining-room, for Lord Killbally did not keep the gentlemen long at their wine.

Salemina cannot tell a story quite as it ought to be told to produce an effect. She is too reserved, too concise, too rigidly conscientious. She does not like to be the centre of interest, even in a modest *contretemps* like being locked out of a room which contains part of her dress;

but from her brief explanation to Lady Killbally, her more complete and confidential account on the way home, and Benella's graphic story when we arrived there, we were able to get all the details.

When the inside car passed out of view with us, it appears that Benella wept tears of rage, at the sight of which Oonah and Molly trembled. In that moment of despair and remorse her mind worked as it must always have done before the Salem priestess befogged it with hazy philosophies, understood neither by teacher nor by pupil. Peter had come back, but could suggest nothing. Benella forgot her " science," which prohibits rage and recrimination, and called him a great, hulking, lazy vagabone, and told him she 'd like to have him in Salem for five minutes, just to show him a man with a head on his shoulders.

" You call this a Christian country," she said, " and you have n't got a screw-driver, nor a brad awl, nor a monkey wrench, nor a rat-tail file, nor no kind of a useful tool to bless yourselves with; and my Miss Peabody, that 's worth ten dozen of you put together, has got to stay home from the Castle and eat warmed-up scraps served in courses, with twenty minutes' wait between 'em. Now you do as I say : take the dining table and set it out under the window, and the carving table on top o' that, and see how fur up it 'll reach. I guess you can't stump a Salem woman by telling her there ain't no ladder."

The two tables were finally in position; but there still remained nine feet of distance to that key of the situation, Salemina's window, and Mrs. Waterford's dressing table went on top of this pile. "Now, Peter," were the next orders, "if you've got sprawl enough, and want to rest yourself by doin' something useful for once in your life, you just hold down the dining table; and you and Oonah, Molly, keep the next two tables stiddy, while I climb up."

The intrepid Benella could barely reach the sill, even from this ingeniously dizzy elevation, and Mrs. Waterford and Salemina were called on to "stiddy" the tables, while Molly was bidden to help by giving an heroic "boost" when the word of command came. The device was completely successful, and in a trice the conqueror disappeared, to reappear at the window holding the precious pearl-embroidered bodice wrapped in a towel. "I would n't stop to fool with the door-knob till I dropped you this," she said. "Oonah, you go and wash your hands clean, and help Miss Peabody into it, — and mind you start the lacing right at the top; and you, Peter, run down to Rooney's and get the donkey and the cart, and bring 'em back with you, — and don't you let the grass grow under your feet neither!"

There was literally no other mode of conveyance within miles, and time was precious. Salemina wrapped herself in Francesca's long black cloak, and climbed into the cart. Dinnis hauls turf in it, takes a sack of potatoes or a pig to market in it, and the stubborn little ass, blind of one eye, has never in his wholly elective course of existence taken up the subject of speed.

It was eight o'clock when Benella mounted the seat beside Salemina, and gave the donkey a preliminary touch of the stick.

"Be aisy wid him," cautioned Peter. "He's a very arch donkey for a lady to be dhrivin', and mebbe he'd lay down and not get up for you."

"Arrah! shut yer mouth, Pether. Give him a couple of belts añondher the hind leg, melady, and that'll put the fear o' God in him!" said Dinnis.

"I'd rather not go at all," urged Salemina timidly; "it's too late, and too extraordinary."

"I'm not going to have it on my conscience to make you lose this dinner party, — not if I have to carry you on my back the whole way," said Benella doggedly; "and this donkey won't lay down with me more'n once, — I can tell him that right at the start."

"Sure, melady, he'll go to Galway for you, when oncet he's started wid himself; and it's only a couple o' fingers to the Castle, annyways."

The four-mile drive, especially through the village of Ballyfuchsia, was an eventful one, but by

dint of prodding, poking, and belting, Benella
had accomplished half the distance in three
quarters of an hour, when the donkey suddenly
lay down " on her," according to Peter's predic-
tion. This was luckily at the town cross, where
a group of idlers rendered hearty assistance.
Willing as they were to succor a lady in dis-
thress, they did not know of any car which could
be secured in time to be of service, but one of
them offered to walk and run by the side of the
donkey, so as to kape him on his legs. It was
in this wise that Miss Peabody approached Balkilly Castle ; and when a gilded gentleman-in-
waiting lifted her from Rooney's "plain cart,"
she was just on the verge of hysterics. Fortunately his Magnificence was English, and be-
trayed no surprise at the arrival in this humble
fashion of a dinner guest, but simply summoned
the Irish housekeeper, who revived her with wine,
and called on all the saints to witness that she'd
never heard of such a shameful thing, and such
a disgrace to Ballyfuchsia. The idea of not
keeping a ladder in a house where the door-knobs
were apt to come off struck her as being the
worst feature of the accident, though this unexpected and truly Milesian view of the matter had
never occurred to us.

"Well, I got Miss Peabody to the dinner
party," said Benella triumphantly, when she was

laboriously unlacing my frock, later on, "or at least I got her there before it broke up. I had to walk every step o' the way home, and the donkey laid down four times, but I was so nerved up I didn't care a mite. I was bound Miss Peabody shouldn't lose her chance, after all she's done for me!"

"Her chance?" I asked, somewhat puzzled, for dinners, even castle dinners, are not rare in Salemina's experience.

"Yes, her chance," repeated Benella mysteriously; "you'd know well enough what I mean, if you'd ben born and brought up in Salem, Massachusetts!"

Copy of a letter read by Penelope O'Connor, descendant of the king of Connaught, at the dinner of Lord and Lady Killbally at Balkilly Castle. It needed no apology then, but in sending it to our American friends, we were obliged to explain that though the Irish peasants interlard their conversation with saints, angels, and devils, and use the name of the Virgin Mary, and even the Almighty, with, to our ears, undue familiarity and frequency, there is no profane or irreverent intent. They are instinctively religious, and it is only because they feel on terms of such friendly intimacy with the powers above that they speak of them so often.

At the Widdy Mullarkey's,
KNOCKARNEY HOUSE, BALLYFUCHSIA,
County Kerry.

Och! musha bedad, man alive, but it's a fine
counthry over here, and it bangs all the jewel
of a view we do be havin' from the windys, begorra! Knockarney House is in a wild remoted
place at the back of beyant, and faix we're as
much alone as Robinson Crusoe on a dissolute
island; but when we do be wishful to go to the
town, sure there's ivery convaniency. There's
ayther a bit of a jauntin' car wid a skewbald
pony for drivin', or we can borry the loan of Dinnis Rooney's blind ass wid the plain cart, or we can
just take a fut in a hand and leg it over the bog.
Sure it's no great thing to go do, but only a taste
of divarsion like, though it's three good Irish
miles an' powerful hot weather, with niver a
dhrop of wet these manny days. It's a great old
spring we're havin' intirely; it has raison to be
proud of itself, begob!

Paddy, the gossoon that drives the car (it's a
gossoon we call him, but faix he stands five fut
nine in his stockin's, when he wears anny), —
Paddy, as I'm afther tellin' you, lives in a cabin
down below the knockaun, a thrifle back of the
road. There's a nate stack of turf fornint it,
and a pitaty pot sets beside the doore, wid the
hins and chuckens rachin' over into it like aigles
tryin' to swally the smell.

Across the way there does be a bit of sthrame that's fairly shtiff wid troutses in the saison, and a growth of rooshes under the edge lookin' that smooth and greeny it must be a pleasure intirely to the grand young pig and the goat that spinds their time by the side of it when out of doores, which is seldom. Paddy himself is raggetty like, and a sight to behould wid the daylight shinin' through the ould coat on him; but he's a dacint spalpeen, and sure we'd be lost widout him. His mother's a widdy woman with nine moi-dtherin' childer, not countin' the pig an' the goat, which has aquil advantages. It's nine she has livin', she says, and four slapin' in the beds o' glory; and faix I hope thim that's in glory is quieter than the wans that's here, for the divil is busy wid thim the whole of the day. Here's wan o' thim now makin' me as onaisy as an ould hin on a hot griddle, slappin' big sods of turf over the dike, and ruinatin' the timpers of our poulthry. We've a right to be lambastin' thim this blessed minute, the crathurs; as sure as eggs is mate, if they was mine they'd sup sorrow wid a spoon of grief, before they wint to bed this night!

Misthress Colquhoun, that lives at Ardnagreena on the road to the town, is an iligant lady intirely, an' she's uncommon frindly, may the peace of heaven be her sowl's rist! She's rale charitable-like an' liberal with the whativer, an' as for Himself, sure he's the darlin' fine man! He taches the dead-and-gone languages in the grand sates of larnin', and has more eddication and comperhinson than the whole of County Kerry rowled together.

Then there's Lord and Lady Killbally; faix there's no iliganter family on this counthryside, and they has the beautiful quality stoppin' wid thim, begob! They have a pew o' their own in the church, an' their coachman wears top-boots wid yaller chimbleys to thim. They do be very open-handed wid the eatin' and the drinkin', and it bangs Banagher the figurandyin' we do have wid thim! So you see ould Ireland is not too disthressful a counthry to be divartin' ourselves in, an' we have our healths finely, glory be to God!

Well, we must be shankin' off wid ourselves now to the Colquhouns', where they're wettin' a dhrop o' tay for us this mortial instant.

It's no good for yous to write to us here, for we'll be quittin' out o' this before the letther has a chanst to come; though sure it can folly us as we're jiggin' along to the north.

Don't be thinkin' that you've shlipped hould of our ricollections, though the breadth of the ocean say's betune us. More power to your elbow! May your life be aisy, and may the heavens be your bed!

PENELOPE O'CONNOR BERESFORD.

PART THIRD

ULSTER

XVII

THE GLENS OF ANTRIM

"Silent, O Moyle,[1] be the roar of thy water;
  Break not, ye breezes, your chain of repose;
While murmuring mournfully, Lir's lovely daughter
  Tells to the night-star her tale of woes."

Thomas Moore.

SORLEY BOY HOTEL,
Glens of Antrim.

WE are here for a week, in the neighborhood of Cushendun, just to see a bit of the northeastern corner of Erin, where, at the end of the nineteenth century, as at the beginning of the seventeenth, the population is almost exclusively Catholic and Celtic. The Gaelic Sorley Boy is, in Irish state papers, Carolus Flavus, — yellow-haired Charles, — the most famous of the Macdonnell fighters; the one who, when recognized by Elizabeth as Lord of the Route, and given a patent for his estates, burned the document be-

---

1 The sea between Erin and Alban (Ireland and Scotland) was called in the olden time The Sea of Moyle, from the Moyle, or Mull, of Cantire.

fore his retainers, swearing that what had been won by the sword should never be held by the sheepskin. Cushendun was one of the places in our literary pilgrimage, because of its association with that charming Irish poetess and good glens-woman who calls herself " Moira O'Neill."

This country of the Glens, east of the river Bann, escaped "plantation," and that accounts for its Celtic character. When the great Ulster chieftains, the O'Donnells and the O'Neills of Donegal, went under, the third great house of Ulster, the " Macdonnells of the Isles," was more fortunate, and, thanks to its Scots blood, found favor with James I. It was a Macdonnell who was created first Earl of Antrim, and given a "grant of the Glens and the Route, from the Curran of Larne to the Cutts of Coleraine." Ballycastle is our nearest large town, and its great days were all under the Macdonnells, where, in the Franciscan abbey across the bay, it is said the ground "literally heaves with Clandonnell dust." Here are buried those of the clan who perished at the hands of Shane O'Neill, — Shane the Proud, who signed himself " Myself O'Neill," and who has been called "the shaker of Ulster;" here, too, are those who fell in the great fight at Slieve-an-Aura up in Glen Shesk, when the Mac-donnells finally routed the older lords, the Mc-Quillans. A clansman once went to the Countess of Antrim to ask the lease of a farm.

"Another Macdonnell?" asked the countess. "Why, you must all be Macdonnells in the Low Glens!"

"Ay," said the man. "Too many Macdonnells now, but not one too many on the day of Aura."

From the cliffs of Antrim we can see on any clear day the Sea of Moyle and the bonnie blue hills of Scotland, divided from Ulster at this point by only twenty miles of sea path. The Irish or Gaels or Scots of "Uladh" often crossed in their curraghs to this lovely coast of Alba, then inhabited by the Picts. Here, "when the tide drains out wid itself beyant the rocks," we sit for many an hour, perhaps on the very spot from which they pushed off their boats. The Mull of Cantire runs out sharply toward you; south of it are Ailsa Craig, and the soft Ayrshire coast; north of the Mull are blue, blue mountains in a semicircle, and just beyond them somewhere, Francesca knows, are the Argyleshire Highlands. And oh! the pearl and opal tints that the Irish atmosphere flings over the scene, shifting them ever at will, in misty sun or radiant shower; and how lovely are the too rare bits of woodland! The ground is sometimes white with wild garlic, sometimes blue with hyacinths; the primroses still linger in moist hidden places, and there are violets and marsh marigolds. Everything wears the color of Hope. If there are buds that will never bloom and birds that will never fly, the great mother-heart does not know it yet. "I wonder," said Salemina, "if that is why we think of autumn as sad, — because the story of the year is known and told?"

Long, long before the Clandonnell ruled these hills and glens and cliffs they were the home of Celtic legend. Over the waters of the wee river Margy, with its half-mile course, often sailed the four white swans, those enchanted children of Lir, king of the Isle of Man, who had been transformed into this guise by their cruel stepmother, with a stroke of her druidical fairy wand. After turning them into four beautiful white swans she pronounced their doom, which was to sail three hundred years on smooth Lough Derryvara, three hundred on the gloomy Sea of Moyle, and three hundred on the Sea of Erris, — sail, and sail, until the union of Largnen, the prince from the north, with Decca, the princess from the south; until the Taillkenn [1] should come to Erinn, bringing the light of a pure faith, and until they should hear the voice of a Christian bell. They were allowed to keep their own Gaelic speech, and to sing sweet, plaintive fairy music, which should excel all the music of the world, and which should lull to sleep all who listened to it. We could hear it, we three, for we loved the story; and love opens the ear as well as the heart to all sorts

[1] A name given by the druids to St. Patrick.

of sounds not heard by the dull and incredulous.
You may hear it, too, any fine soft day if you will
sit there looking out on Fair Head and Rathlin
Island, and read the old fairy tale. When you
put down the book you will see Finola, Lir's
lovely daughter, in any white-breasted bird; and
while she covers her brothers with her wings,
she will chant to you her old song in the Gaelic
tongue.

" Ah, happy is Lir's bright home to-day
   With mirth and music and poet's lay;
   But gloomy and cold his children's home,
   Forever tossed on the briny foam.

" Our wreathèd feathers are thin and light
   When the wind blows keen through the wintry night;
   Yet oft we were robed, long, long ago,
   In purple mantles and furs of snow.

" On Moyle's bleak current our food and wine
   Are sandy seaweed and bitter brine;
   Yet oft we feasted in days of old,
   And hazel-mead drank from cups of gold.

" Our beds are rocks in the dripping caves;
   Our lullaby song the roar of the waves;
   But soft rich couches once we pressed,
   And harpers lulled us each night to rest.

" Lonely we swim on the billowy main,
   Through frost and snow, through storm and rain;
   Alas! for the days when round us moved
   The chiefs and princes and friends we loved." [1]

1 Joyce's translation.

The Fate of the Children of Lir is the second of Erin's Three Sorrows of Story, and the third and greatest is the Fate of the Sons of Usnach, which has to do with a sloping rock on the north side of Fair Head, five miles from us. Here the three sons of Usnach landed when they returned from Alba to Erin with Deirdré, — Deirdré, who was "beautiful as Helen, and gifted like Cassandra with unavailing prophecy;" and by reason of her beauty many sorrows fell upon the Ultonians.

Naisi, son of Conor, king of Uladh, had fled with Deirdré, daughter of Phelim the king's story-teller, to a sea-girt islet on Lough Etive, where they lived happily by the chase. Naisi's two brothers went with them, and thus the three sons of Usnach were all in Alba. Then the story goes on to say that Fergus, one of Conor's nobles, goes to seek the exiles, and Naisi and Deirdré, while playing at the chess, hear from the shore "The cry of a man of Erin." It is against Deirdré's will that they finally leave Alba with Fergus, who says, "Birthright is first, for ill it goes with a man, although he be great and prosperous, if he does not see daily his native earth."

So they sailed away over the sea, and Deirdré sang this lay as the shores of Alba faded from her sight : —

"My love to thee, O Land in the East, and 't is

ill for me to leave thee, for delightful are thy
coves and havens, thy kind soft flowery fields,
thy pleasant green-sided hills ; and little was our
need of departing."

Then in her song she went over the glens of
their lordship, naming them all, and calling to
mind how here they hunted the stag, here they
fished, here they slept, with the swaying fern for
pillows, and here the cuckoo called to them. And
" Never," she sang, " would I quit Alba were it
not that Naisi sailed thence in his ship."

They landed first under Fair Head, and then
later at Rathlin Island, where their fate met them
at last, as Deirdré had prophesied. It is a sad
story, and we can easily weep at the thrilling moment when, there being no man among the Ultonians to do the king's bidding, a Norse captive takes
Naisi's magic sword and strikes off the heads of
the three sons of Usnach with one swift blow,
and Deirdré, falling prone upon the dead bodies,
chants a lament ; and when she has finished singing, she puts her pale cheek against Naisi's, and
dies ; and a great cairn is piled over them, and
an inscription in Ogam set upon it.

We were full of legendary lore, these days, for
we were fresh from a sight of Glen Ariff. Who
that has ever chanced to be there in a pelting
rain but will remember its innumerable little waterfalls, and the great falls of Ess-na-Crubh and
Ess-na-Craoibhe ! And who can ever forget the

atmosphere of romance that broods over these Irish glens !

We have had many advantages here as elsewhere; for kind Dr. La Touche, Lady Killbally, and Mrs. Colquhoun follow us with letters, and wherever there is an unusual personage in a district we are commended to his or her care. Sometimes it is one of the " grand quality," and often it is an Ossianic sort of person like Shaun O'Grady, who lives in a little whitewashed cabin, and who has, like Mr. Yeats' Gleeman, " the whole Middle Ages under his frieze coat." The longer and more intimately we know these peasants, the more we realize how much in imagination, or in the clouds, if you will, they live. The ragged man of leisure you meet on the road may be a philosopher, and is still more likely to be a poet; but unless you have something of each in yourself, you may mistake him for a mere beggar.

" The practical ones have all emigrated," a Dublin novelist told us, " and the dreamers are left. The heads of the older ones are filled with poetry and legends; they see nothing as it is, but always through some iridescent-tinted medium. Their waking moments, when not tormented by hunger, are spent in heaven, and they all live in a dream, whether it be of the next world or of a revolution. Effort is to them useless, submission to everybody and everything the only safe course ; in a word, fatalism expresses their attitude to life."

Much of this submission to the inevitable is a product of past poverty, misfortune, and famine, and the rest is undoubtedly a trace of the same spirit that we find in the lives and writings of the saints, and which is an integral part of the mystery and the tradition of Romanism. We who live in the bright (and sometimes staring) sunlight of common sense can hardly hope to penetrate the dim, mysterious world of the Catholic peasant, with his unworldliness and sense of failure.

Dr. Douglas Hyde, an Irish scholar and stanch Protestant says : " A pious race is the Gaelic race. The Irish Gael is pious by nature. There is not an Irishman in a hundred in whom is the making of an unbeliever. The spirit, and the things of the spirit, affect him more powerfully than the body, and the things of the body. . . . What is invisible for other people is visible for him. . . . He feels invisible powers before him, and by his side, and at his back, throughout the day and throughout the night. . . . His mind on the subject may be summed up in the two sayings : that of the early Church, ' Let ancient things prevail,' and that of St. Augustine, ' Credo quia impossibile.' Nature did not form him to be an unbeliever ; unbelief is alien to his mind and contrary to his feelings."

Here, only a few miles away, is the Slemish mountain where St. Patrick, then a captive of the rich cattle-owner Milcho, herded his sheep and swine. Here, when his flocks were sleeping, he poured out his prayers, a Christian voice in pagan darkness. It was the memory of that darkness, you remember, that brought him back, years after, to convert Milcho. Here, too, they say, lies the great bard Ossian ; for they love to think that Finn's son Oisin,[1] the hero poet, survived to the time of St. Patrick, three hundred years after the other "Fianna" had vanished from the earth, — the three centuries being passed in Tir-nan-og, the Land of Youth, where the great Oisin married the king's daughter, Niam of the Golden Hair. "Ossian after the Fianna" is a phrase which has become the synonym of all survivors' sorrow. Blinded by tears, broken by age, the hero bard when he returns to earth has no fellowship but with grief, and thus he sings : —

> "No hero now where heroes hurled, —
> Long this night the clouds delay —
> No man like me, in all the world,
>   Alone with grief, and gray.
>
> "Long this night the clouds delay —
> I raise their grave carn, stone on stone,
> For Finn and Fianna passed away —
>   I, Ossian left alone."

In more senses than one Irish folk-lore is Irish

[1] Pronounced Isheen' in Munster, Osh'in' in Ulster.

history. At least the traditions that have been handed down from one generation to another, contain not only the sometimes authentic record of events, but a revelation of the Milesian temperament, with its mirth and its melancholy, its exuberant fancy and its passion. So in these weird tales there is plenty of history, and plenty of poetry, to one who will listen to it; but the high and tragic story of Ireland has been cherished mainly in the sorrowful traditions of a defeated race, and the legends have not yet been wrought into undying verse. Erin's songs of battle could only recount weary successions of Flodden Fields, with never a Bannockburn and its nimbus of victory; for, as Ossian says of his countrymen, "They went forth to the war, but they always fell;" but somewhere in the green isle is an unborn poet who will put all this mystery, beauty, passion, romance, and sadness, these tragic memories, these beliefs, these visions of unfulfilled desire, into verse that will glow on the page and live forever. Somewhere is a mother who has kept all these things in her heart, and who will bear a son to write them. Meantime, who shall say that they have not been imbedded in the language, as flower petals might be in amber? — that language which, as an English scholar says, "has been blossoming there unseen, like a hidden garland of roses; and whenever the wind has blown from the west, English poetry has felt the vague perfume of it."

XVIII

LIMAVADY LOVE–LETTERS

" As beautiful Kitty one morning was tripping
  With a pitcher of milk from the fair of Coleraine,
  When she saw me she stumbled, the pitcher it tumbled,
  And all the sweet buttermilk watered the plain."

Anonymous.

WE wanted to cross to Rathlin Island, which
is " like an Irish stockinge, the toe of which point-
eth to the main lande."   That would bring Francesca six miles nearer to Scotland and her Scottish
lover ; and we wished to see the castle of Robert
the Bruce, where, according to the legend, he
learned his lesson from the " six times baffled
spider."   We delayed too long, however, and the
Sea of Moyle looked as bleak and stormy as it
did to the children of Lir.   We had no mind to
be swallowed up in Brecain's Caldron, where the
grandson of Niall and the Nine Hostages sank
with his fifty curraghs, so we took a day of golf
at the Ballycastle links.   Salemina, who is a neo-
phyte, found a forlorn lady driving and putting
about by herself, and they made a match just to
increase the interest of the game.   There was but
one boy in evidence, and the versatile Benella

offered to caddie for them, leaving the more experienced gossoon to Francesca and me. The Irish caddie does not, on the whole, perhaps manifest so keen an interest in the fine points of the game as his Scottish brother. He is somewhat languid in his search for a ball, and will occasionally, when serving amiable ladies, sit under a tree in the sun and speculate as to its whereabouts. As for staying by you while you "hole out" on your last green, he has no possible interest in that proceeding, and is off and away, giving his perfunctory and half-hearted polish to your clubs while you are passing through this thrilling crisis. Salemina, wishing to know what was considered a good score by local players on these links, asked our young friend "what they got round in, here," and was answered, "They tries to go round in as few as possible, ma'am, but they mostly takes more!" We all came together again at luncheon, and Salemina returned flushed with victory. She had made the nine hole course in one hundred and sixty, and had beaten her adversary five up and four to play.

The next morning, bright and early, we left for Coleraine, a great Presbyterian stronghold in what is called by the Roman Catholics the "black north." If we liked it, and saw anything of Kitty's descendants, or any nice pitchers to break, or any reason for breaking them, we in-

tended to stop ; if not, then to push on to the
walled town of Derry, —

> " Where Foyle his swelling waters
> Rolls northward to the main."

We thought it Francesca's duty, as she was to be
the wife of a Scottish minister of the Established
Church, to look up Presbyterianism in Ireland
whenever and wherever possible, with a view to
discoursing learnedly about it in her letters, —
though, as she confesses ingenuously, Ronald, in
his, never so much as mentions Presbyterianism.
As for ourselves, we determined to observe all
theological differences between Protestants and
Roman Catholics, but leave Presbyterianism to
gang its ain gait.   We had devoted hours — yes,
days — in Edinburgh to the understanding of the
subtle and technical barriers which separated the
Free Kirkers and the United Presbyterians ; and
the first thing they did, after we had completely
mastered the subject, was to unite.   It is all very
well for Salemina, who condenses her information
and stows it away neatly ; but we who have
small storage room and inferior methods of pack-
ing must be as economical as possible in amass-
ing facts.

If we had been touring properly, of course we
should have been going to the Giant's Causeway
and the swinging bridge at Carrick-a-rede ; but
propriety is the last thing we aim at, in our

itineraries. We were within worshiping distance
of two rather important shrines in our literary
pilgrimage ; for we had met a very knowledge-
able traveler at the Sorley Boy, and after a little
chat with him had planned a day of surprises for
the academic Miss Peabody. We proposed to
halt at Port Stewart, lunch at Coleraine, sleep at
Limavady ; and meantime Salemina was to read
all the books at her command, and guess, we
hoped vainly, the why and wherefore of these
stops.

On the appointed day, the lady in question
drove in state on a car with Benella, but Francesca and I hired a couple of very wheezy bicy-
cles for the journey. We had a thrilling start ;
for it chanced to be a Fair day in Ballycastle,
and we wheeled through a sea of squealing, bolt-
ing pigs, stupid sheep, and unruly cows, all pur-.
sued on every side by their drivers. To alight
from a bicycle in such a whirl of beasts always
seems certain death ; to remain seated diminishes,
I believe, the number of one's days of life to an
appreciable extent. Francesca chose the first
course, and, standing still in the middle of the
street, called upon everybody within hearing to
save her, and that right speedily. A crowd of
" jibbing " heifers encircled her on all sides,
while a fat porker, " who (his driver said) might
be a prize pig by his impidence," and a donkey
that was feelin' blue-mouldy for want of a batin',

tried to poke their noses into the group. Salemina's only weapon was her scarlet parasol, and, standing on the step of her side car, she brandished this with such terrible effect that the only bull in the cavalcade put up his head and roared. "Have conduct, woman dear!" cried his owner to Salemina. "Sure if you kape on moidherin' him wid that red ombrelly, you'll have him ugly on me immajently, and the divil a bit o' me can stop him." "Don't be cryin' that way, asthore," he went on, going to Francesca's side, and piloting her tenderly to the hedge. "Sure I'll nourish him wid the whip whin I get him to a more remoted place."

We had no more adventures, but Francesca was so unhinged by her unfortunate exit from Ballycastle that, after a few miles, she announced her intention of putting her machine and herself on the car; whereupon Benella proclaimed herself a competent cyclist, and climbed down blithely to mount the discarded wheel. Her ideas of propriety were by this time so developed that she rode ten or twelve feet behind me, where she looked quaint enough, in her black dress and little black bonnet with its white lawn strings.

"Sure it's a quare footman ye have, me lady," said a genial and friendly person who was siting by the roadside smoking his old dudeen. An Irishman, somehow, is always going to his work "jist," or coming from it, or thinking how it shall presently be done, or meditating on the next step in the process, or resting a bit before taking it up again, or reflecting whether the weather is on the whole favorable to its proper performance ; but however poor and needy he may be, it is somewhat difficult to catch him at the precise working moment. Mr. Alfred Austin says of the Irish peasants that idleness and poverty seem natural to them. "Life to the Scotsman or Englishman is a business to conduct, to extend, to render profitable. To the Irishman it is a dream, a little bit of passing consciousness on a rather hard pillow; the hard part of it being the occasional necessity for work, which spoils the tenderness and continuity of the dream."

Presently we passed the Castle, rode along a neat quay with a row of houses advertising lodgings to let; and here is Lever Cottage, where Harry Lorrequer was written ; for Lever was dispensary doctor in Port Stewart when his first book was appearing in the Dublin University Magazine.

We did not fancy Coleraine ; it looked like anything but Cuil-rathain, a ferny corner. Kitty's sweet buttermilk may have watered, but it had not fertilized the plain, though the town itself seemed painfully prosperous. Neither the Clothworkers' Inn nor the Corporation Arms looked a pleasant stopping place, and the humble inn we finally selected for a brief rest proved to be about as gay as a family vault, with a landlady who had all the characteristics of a poker except its occasional warmth, as the Liberator said of another stiff and formal person. Whether she was Scot or Saxon I know not; she was certainly not Celt, and certainly no Barney McCrea of her day would have kissed her if she had spilled ever so many pitchers of sweet buttermilk over the plain; so we took the railway, and departed with delight for Limavady, where Thackeray, fresh from his visit to Charles Lever, laid his poetical tribute at the stockingless feet of Miss Margaret of that town.

O'Cahan, whose chief seat was at Limavady, was the principal *urraght* of O'Neill, and when one of the great clan was "proclaimed" at Tullaghogue it was the magnificent privilege of the O'Cahan to toss a shoe over his head. We slept at O'Cahan's Hotel, and — well, one must sleep; and wherever we attend to that necessary function without due preparation, we generally make a mistake in the selection of the particular spot. Protestantism does not necessarily mean cleanliness, although it may have natural tendencies in that direction; and we find, to our surprise (a surprise rooted, probably, in bigotry), that Catholicism can be as clean as a penny whistle, now and again. There were no special privileges at O'Cahan's for maids, and Benella, therefore, had a delightful evening in the coffee room with a storm-bound commercial traveler. As for Francesca and me, there was plenty to occupy us in our regular letters to Ronald and Himself; and Salemina wrote several sheets of thin paper to somebody, — no one in America, either, for we saw her put on a penny stamp.

Our pleasant duties over, we looked into the cheerful glow of the turf sods while I read aloud Thackeray's Peg of Limavady. He spells the town with two *d*'s, by the way, to insure its being rhymed properly with Paddy and daddy.

" Riding from Coleraine
   (Famed for lovely Kitty),
Came a Cockney bound
   Unto Derry city ;
Weary was his soul,
   Shivering and sad he
Bumped along the road
   Leads to Limavaddy.
.   .   .   .   .

"Limavaddy inn 's
   But a humble baithouse,
Where you may procure
   Whisky and potatoes ;
Landlord at the door
   Gives a smiling welcome
To the shivering wights
   Who to his hotel come.
Landlady within
   Sits and knits a stocking,
With a wary foot
   Baby's cradle rocking.
.   .   .   .   .

"Presently a maid
   Enters with the liquor
(Half-a-pint of ale
   Frothing in a beaker).

Gads ! I did n't know
  What my beating heart meant :
Hebe's self I thought
  Enter'd the apartment.
As she came she smiled,
  And the smile bewitching,
On my word and honour,
  Lighted all the kitchen !

. . . . . .

" This I do declare,
  Happy is the laddy
Who the heart can share
  Of Peg of Limavaddy.
Married if she were,
  Blest would be the daddy
Of the children fair
  Of Peg of Limavaddy.
Beauty is not rare
  In the land of Paddy,
Fair beyond compare
  Is Peg of Limavaddy."

This cheered us a bit; but the wind sighed in
the trees, the rain dripped on the window panes,
and we felt for the first time a consciousness of
home-longing. Francesca sat on a low stool,
looking into the fire, Ronald's last letter in her
lap, and it was easy indeed to see that her heart
was in the Highlands. She had been giving us a
few extracts from the communication, an unusual
proceeding, as Ronald, in his ordinary correspond-
ence, is evidently not a quotable person. We
smiled over his account of a visit to his old parish
of Inchcaldy in Fifeshire. There is a certain
large orphanage in the vicinity, in which we had

all taken an interest, chiefly because our friends
the Macraes of Pettybaw House were among its
guardians.

It seems that Lady Rowardennan of the Castle
had promised the orphans, *en bloc*, that those who
passed through an entire year without once falling into falsehood should have a treat or festival
of their own choosing. On the eventful day of
decision, those orphans, male and female, who
had not for a twelvemonth deviated from the
truth by a hair's breadth, raised their little white
hands (emblematic of their pure hearts and lips),
and were solemnly counted. Then came the unhappy moment when a scattering of small grimy
paws was timidly put up, and their falsifying
owners confessed that they had fibbed more than
once during the year. These tearful fibbers were
also counted, and sent from the room, while the
non-fibbers chose their reward, which was to sail
around the Bass Rock and the Isle of May in a
steam tug.

On the festival day, the matron of the orphanage chanced on the happy thought that it might
have a moral effect on the said fibbers to see the
non-fibbers depart in a blaze of glory; so they
were taken to the beach to watch the tug start
on its voyage. The confessed criminals looked
wretched enough, Ronald wrote, when forsaken
by their virtuous playmates, who stepped jauntily
on board, holding their sailor hats on their heads

and carrying nice little luncheon baskets; so miserably unhappy, indeed, did they seem that certain sympathetic and ill-balanced persons sprang to their relief, providing them with sandwiches, sweeties, and pennies. It was a lovely day, and when the fibbers' tears were dried they played merrily on the sand, their games directed and shared by the aforesaid misguided persons.

Meantime a high wind had sprung up at sea, and the tug was tossed to and fro upon the foamy deep. So many and so varied were the ills of the righteous orphans that the matron could not attend to all of them properly, and they were laid on benches or on the deck, where they languidly declined luncheon, and wept for a sight of land. At five the tug steamed up to the home landing. A few of the voyagers were able to walk ashore, some were assisted, others were carried; and as the pale, haggard, truthful company gathered on the beach, they were met by a boisterous, happy crowd of Ananiases and Sapphiras, sunburned, warm, full of tea and cakes and high spirits, and with the moral law already so uncertain in their minds that at the sight of the suffering non-liars it tottered to its fall.

Ronald hopes that Lady Rowardennan and the matron may perhaps have gained some useful experience by the incident, though the orphans, truthful and untruthful, are hopelessly mixed in their views of right doing.

He is staying now at the great house of the neighborhood, while his new manse is being put in order. Roderick, the piper, he says, has a grand collection of pipe tunes given him by an officer of the Black Watch. Francesca, when she and Ronald visit the Castle on their wedding journey, is to have Johnnie Cope to wake her in the morning, Brose and Butter just before dinner is served, a reel, a strathspey, and a march while the meal is going on, and last of all The Highland Wedding. Ronald does not know whether there are any Lowland Scots or English words to this pipe tune, but it is always played in the Highlands after the actual marriage, and the words in Gaelic are, " Alas for me if the wife I have married is not a good one, for she will eat the food and not do the work ! "

" You don't think Ronald meant anything personal in quoting that ? " I asked Francesca teasingly ; but she shot me such a reproachful look that I had n't the heart to persist, her face was so full of self-distrust and love and longing.

What creatures of sense we are, after all ; and in certain moods, of what avail is it if the beloved object is alive, safe, loyal, so long as he is absent ? He may write letters like Horace Walpole or Chesterfield, — better still, like Alfred de Musset, or George Sand, or the Brownings ; but one clasp of the hand that moved the pen is worth an ocean of words ! You believe only in the etherealized, the spiritualized passion of love ; you know that it can exist through years of separation, can live and grow where a coarser feeling would die for lack of nourishment ; still though your spirit should be strong enough to meet its spirit mate somewhere in the realms of imagination, and the bodily presence ought not really to be necessary, your stubborn heart of flesh craves sight and sound and touch. That is the only pitiless part of death, it seems to me. We have had the friendship, the love, the sympathy, and these are things that can never die ; they have made us what we are, and they are by their very nature immortal ; yet we would come near to bartering all these spiritual possessions for the " touch of a vanished hand, and the sound of a voice that is still."

How could I ever think life easy enough to be ventured on alone ! It is so beautiful to feel one's self of infinite value to one other human creature ; to hear beside one's own step the tread of a chosen companion on the same road. And if the way be dusty or the hills difficult to climb, each can say to the other : " I love you, dear ; lean on me and walk in confidence. I can always be counted on, whatever happens."

XIX

"IN OULD DONEGAL"

"Here's a health to you, Father O'Flynn!
Slainté, and slainté, and slainté agin;
Pow'rfulest preacher and tenderest teacher,
And kindliest creature in ould Donegal."

Alfred Perceval Graves.

COOMNAGEEHA HOTEL,
In ould Donegal.

It is a far cry from the kingdom of Kerry to
"ould Donegal," where we have been traveling
for a week, chiefly in the hope of meeting Father
O'Flynn. We miss our careless, genial, ragged,
southern Paddy just a bit; for he was a picturesque, likable figure, on the whole, and easier to
know than this Ulster Irishman, the product of a
mixed descent.

We did not stop long in Belfast; for if there is
anything we detest, when on our journeys, it is
to mix too much with people of industry, thrift,
and business sagacity. Sturdy, prosperous, calcu-
lating, well-to-do Protestants are well enough in
their way, and undoubtedly they make a very good
backbone for Ireland; but we crave something
more romantic than the citizen virtues, or we

should have remained in our own country, where they are tolerably common, although we have not as yet anything approaching overproduction.

Belfast, it seems, is and has always been, a centre of Presbyterianism. The members of the Presbytery protested against the execution of Charles I., and received an irate reply from Milton, who said that "the blockish presbyters of Claudeboy" were "egregious liars and impostors," who meant to stir up rebellion "from their unchristian synagogue at Belfast in a barbarous nook of Ireland."

Dr. La Touche writes to Salemina that we need not try to understand all the religious and political complications which surround us. They are by no means as violent or as many as in Thackeray's day, when the great English author found nine shades of politico-religious differences in the Irish Liverpool. As the impartial observer must, in such a case, necessarily displease eight parties, and probably the whole nine, Thackeray advised a rigid abstinence from all intellectual curiosity. Dr. La Touche says, if we wish to know the north better, it will do us no harm to study the Plantation of Ulster, the United Irish movement, Orangeism, Irish Jacobitism, the effect of French and Swiss Republicanism in the evolution of public sentiment, and the close relation and affection that formerly existed between the north of Ireland and New England. (This last topic seems to appeal to Salemina particularly.) He also alludes to Tories and Rapparees, Rousseau and Thomas Paine and Owen Roe O'Neill, but I have entirely forgotten their connection with the subject. Francesca and I are thoroughly enjoying ourselves, as only those people can who never take notes, and never try, when Pandora's box is opened in their neighborhood, to seize the heterogeneous contents and put them back properly, with nice little labels on them.

Ireland is no longer a battlefield of English parties, neither is it wholly a laboratory for political experiment; but from having been both the one and the other, its features are a bit knocked out of shape and proportion, as it were. We have bought two hideous engravings of The Battle of the Boyne and The Secret of England's Greatness; and whenever we stay for a night in any inn where perchance these are not, we pin them on the wall, and are received into the landlady's heart at once. I don't know which is the finer study: the picture of his Majesty William III. crossing the Boyne, or the plump little Queen presenting a huge family Bible to an apparently uninterested black youth. In the latter work of art the eye is confused at first as the three principal features approach each other very nearly in size, and Francesca asked innocently, "Which *is* the secret of England's greatness, — the Bible, the Queen, or the black man?"

This is a thriving town, and we are at a smart hotel which had for two years an English manager. The scent of the roses hangs round it still, but it is gradually growing fainter under the stress of small patronage and other adverse circumstances. The table linen is a trifle ragged, though clean ; but the circle of red and green wineglasses by each plate, an array not borne out by the number of vintages on the wine list, the tiny ferns scattered everywhere in innumerable pots, and the dozens of minute glass vases, each holding a few blue hyacinths, give an air of urban elegance to the dining-room. The guests are requested in printed placards to be punctual at meals, especially at the seven-thirty *table d'hôte* dinner, and the management itself is punctual at this function about seven forty-five. This is much better than at the south, where we, and sixty other travelers, were once kept waiting fifteen minutes between the soup and the fish course. When we were finally served with half-cooked turbot, a pleasant-spoken waitress went about to each table, explaining to the irate guests that the cook was " not at her best." We caught a glimpse of her as she was being borne aloft, struggling and eloquent, and were able to understand the reason of her unachieved ideals.

There is nothing sacred about dinner to the average Irishman ; he is willing to take anything that comes, as a rule, and cooking is not regarded

as a fine art here. Perhaps occasional flashes
of starvation and seasons of famine have rendered the Irish palate easier to please ; at all
events, wherever the national god may be, its
pedestal is not in the stomach. Our breakfast,
day after day, week after week, has been bacon
and eggs. One morning we had tomatoes on bacon, and concluded that the cook had experienced
religion or fallen in love, since both these operations send a flush of blood to the brain and stimulate the mental processes. But no; we found
simply that the eggs had not been brought in time
for breakfast. There is no consciousness of mo-
notony, — far from it; the nobility and gentry
can at least eat what they choose, and they choose
bacon and eggs. There is no running of the family gamut, either, from plain boiled to omelet ;
poached or fried eggs on bacon, it is, week days
and Sundays. The luncheon, too, is rarely inspired : they eat cold joint of beef with pickled
beet root, or mutton and boiled potatoes, with
unfailing regularity, finishing off at most hotels
with semolina pudding, a concoction intended for,
and appealing solely to, the taste of the tooth-
less infant, who, having just graduated from rubber rings, has not a jaded palate.

How the long breakfast bill at an up-to-date
Belfast hostelry awed us, after weeks of bacon
and eggs ! The viands on the menu swam together before our dazed eyes.

Porridge
Fillets of Plaice
Whiting
Fried Sole
Savoury Omelet
Kidneys and Bacon
Cold Meats

I looked at this array like one in a dream, realizing that I had lost the power of selection, and remembering the scientific fact that unused faculties perish for want of exercise. The man who was serving us rattled his tray, shifted his weight wearily from one foot to the other and cleared his throat suggestively ; until at last I said hastily, " Bacon and eggs, please," and Salemina, the most critical person in the party, murmured, " The same."

It is odd to see how soon, if one has a strong sense of humanity, one feels at home in a foreign country. I, at least, am never impressed by the differences, but only by the similarities, between English - speaking peoples. We take part in the life about us here, living each experience as fully as we can, whether it be a " hiring fair " in Donegal or a pilgrimage to the Doon " Well of Healing." Not the least part of the pleasure is to watch its effect upon the Derelict. Where, or in what way, could three persons hope to gain as much return from a monthy expenditure of twenty dollars, added to her living and traveling expenses, as we have had in Miss Benella

Dusenberry? We sometimes ask ourselves what we found to do with our time before she came into the family, and yet she is as busy as possible herself.

Having twice singed Francesca's beautiful locks, she no longer attempts hair - dressing; while she never accomplishes the lacing of an evening dress without putting her knee in the centre of your back once, at least, during the operation. She can button shoes, and she can mend and patch and darn to perfection; she has a frenzy for small laundry operations, and, after washing the windows of her room, she adorns every pane of glass with a fine cambric handkerchief, and, stretching a line between the bedpost and the bureau knob, she hangs out her white neckties and her bonnet strings to dry. She has learned to pack reasonably well, too. But if she has another passion beside those of washing and mending, it is for making bags. She buys scraps of gingham and print, and makes cases of every possible size and for every possible purpose; so that all our personal property, roughly speaking, — hairbrushes, shoes, writing materials, pincushions, photographs, underclothing, gloves, medicines, — is bagged. The strings in the bags pull both ways, and nothing is commoner than to see Benella open and close seventeen or eighteen of them when she is searching for Francesca's rubbers or my gold thimble. But what other lady's maid or traveling companion ever had half the Derelict's unique charm and interest, half her conversational power, her unusual and original defects and virtues? Put her in a third-class carriage when we go " first," and she makes friends with all her fellow travelers, discussing Home Rule or Free Silver with the utmost prejudice and vehemence, and freeing her mind on any point, to the delight of the natives. Occasionally, when borne along by the joy of argument, she forgets to change at the point of junction, and has to be found and dragged out of the railway carriage; occasionally, too, she is left behind when taking a cheerful cup of tea at a way station, but this is comparatively seldom. Her stories of life below stairs in the various inns and hotels, her altercations with housemaid or boots or landlady in our behalf, all add a zest to the day's doings.

Benella's father was an itinerant preacher, her mother the daughter of a Vermont farmer; and although she was left an orphan at ten years, educating and supporting herself as best she could after that, she is as truly a combination of both parents as her name is a union of their two names.

" I 'm so 'fraid I shan't run across any of grandmother's folks over here, after all," she said yesterday, " though I ask every nice-appearin' person I meet anywheres if he or she 's any kin to

Mary Boyce of Trim ; and then, again, I 'm scared
to death for fear I shall find I 'm own cousin to
one of these here critters that ain't brushed their
hair nor washed their apurns for a month o' Sundays ! I declare, it keeps me real nerved up. . . .
I think it 's partly the climate that makes 'em so
slack," she philosophized, pinning a new bag on
her knee, and preparing to backstitch the seam.
" There 's nothin' like a Massachusetts winter for
puttin' the git-up-an'-git into you. Land ! you 've
got to move round smart, or you 'd freeze in your
tracks. These warm, moist places always makes
folks lazy ; and when they 're hot enough, if you
take notice, it makes heathen of 'em. It always
seems so queer to me that real hot weather and
the Christian religion don't seem to git along together. P'r'aps it 's just as well that the idol-wor-
shipers should git used to heat in this world, for
they 'll have it consid'able hot in the next one, I
guess ! And see here, Mrs. Beresford, will you
get me ten cents' — I mean sixpence worth o'
red gingham to make Miss Monroe a bag for
Mr. Macdonald's letters ? They go sprawlin' all
over her trunk ; and there 's so many of 'em, I
wish to the land she 'd send 'em to the bank
while she 's travelin' ! "

XX

WE EVICT A TENANT

"Soon as you lift the latch, little ones are meeting you,
Soon as you 're 'neath the thatch, kindly looks are greeting you ;
Scarcely have you time to be holding out the fist to them —
Down by the fireside you 're sitting in the midst of them."

Francis Fahy.

ROOTHYTHANTHRUM COTTAGE,
KNOCKCOOL, County Tyrone.

OF course, we have always intended sooner or later to forsake this life of hotels and lodgings, and become either Irish landlords or tenants, or both, with a view to the better understanding of one burning Irish question. We heard of a charming house in County Down, which could be secured by renting it the first of May for the season ; but as we could occupy it only for a month at most, we were obliged to forego the opportunity.

"We have been told from time immemorial that absenteeism has been one of the curses of Ireland," I remarked to Salemina ; "so, whatever the charms of the cottage in Rostrevor, do not let us take it, and in so doing become absentee landlords."

" It was you two who hired the 'wee theekit hoosie' in Pettybaw," said Francesca. "I am going to be in the vanguard of the next house-hunting expedition; in fact, I have almost made up my mind to take my third of Benella and be an independent householder for a time. If I am ever to learn the management of an establishment before beginning to experiment on Ronald's, now is the proper moment."

"Ronald must have looked the future in the face when he asked you to marry him," I replied, "although it is possible that he looked only at you, and therefore it is his duty to endure your maiden incapacities; but why should Salemina and I suffer you to experiment upon us, pray?"

It was Benella, after all, who inveigled us into making our first political misstep; for, after avoiding the sin of absenteeism, we fell into one almost as black, inasmuch as we evicted a tenant. It is part of Benella's heterogeneous and unusual duty to take a bicycle and scour the country in search of information for us : to find out where shops are, post office, lodgings, places for good sketches, ruins, pretty roads for walks and drives, and many other things, too numerous to mention. She came home from one of these expeditions flushed with triumph.

"I've got you a house!" she exclaimed proudly. "There's a lady in it now, but she'll move out to-morrow when we move in; and we are to pay seventeen dollars fifty — I mean three pound ten — a week for the house, with privilege of renewal, and she throws in the hired girl." (Benella is hopelessly provincial in the matter of language ; butler, chef, boots, footman, scullery maid, all come under the generic term of "help.")

"I knew our week at this hotel was out to-morrow," she continued, "and we 've about used up this place, anyway, and the new village that I 've b'en to is the prettiest place we 've seen yet ; it 's got an up-and-down hill to it, just like home, and the house I 've partly rented is opposite a Fair green, where there 's a market every week, and Wednesday 's the day; and we 'll save money, for I shan't cost you so much when we can housekeep."

"Would you mind explaining a little more in detail," asked Salemina quietly, " and telling me whether you have hired the house for yourself or for us ? "

" For us all," she replied genially, — "you don't suppose I 'd leave you ? I liked the looks of this cottage the first time I passed it, and I got acquainted with the hired girl by going in the side yard and asking for a drink. The next time I went I got acquainted with the lady, who 's got the most outlandish name that ever was wrote down, and here it is on a paper ; and to-day I asked her if she did n't want to rent her house for a week to three quiet ladies without children

and only one of them married and him away.
She said it wa'n't her own house, and I asked her
if she could n't sublet to desirable parties, — I
knew she was as poor as Job's turkey by her
looks ; and she said it would suit her well enough,
if she had any place to go. I asked her if she
would n't like to travel, and she said no. Then I
says, 'Would n't you like to go to visit some of
your folks ? ' And she said she s'posed she could
stop a week with her son's wife, just to oblige us.
So I engaged a car to drive you down this afternoon just to look at the place ; and if you like it
we can easy move over to-morrow. The sun 's so
hot I asked the stableman if he had n't got a top
buggy, or a surrey, or a carryall; but he never
heard tell of any of 'em ; he did n't even know a
shay. I forgot to tell you the lady is a Protestant,
and the hired girl's name is Bridget Thunder, and
she 's a Roman Catholic, but she seems extra
smart and neat. I was kind of in hopes she
would n't be, for I thought I should enjoy trainin'
her, and doin' that much for the country."

And so we drove over to this village of Knockcool (Knockcool, by the way, means "Hill of
Sleep"), as much to make amends for Benella's
eccentricities as with any idea of falling in with
her proposal. The house proved everything she
said, and in Mrs. Wogan Odevaine Benella had
found a person every whit as remarkable as herself. She is evidently an Irish gentlewoman of

very small means, very flexible in her views and convictions, very talkative and amusing, and very much impressed with Benella as a product of New England institutions. We all took a fancy to one another at first sight, and we heard with real pleasure that her son's wife lived only a few miles away. We insisted on paying the evicted lady the three pounds ten in advance for the first week. She seemed surprised, and we remembered that Irish tenants, though often capable of shedding blood for a good landlord, are generally averse to paying him rent. Mrs. Wogan Odevaine then drove away in high good humor, taking some personal belongings with her, and promising to drink tea with us some time during the week. She kissed Francesca good-by, told her she was the prettiest creature she had ever seen, and asked if she might have a peep at all her hats and frocks when she came to visit us.

Salemina says that Rhododendron Cottage (pronounced by Bridget Thunder "Roothythanthrum") being the property of one landlord and the residence of four tenants at the same time makes us in a sense participators in the old system of rundale tenure, long since abolished. The good will or tenant right was infinitely subdivided, and the tiniest holdings sometimes existed in thirty-two pieces. The result of this joint tenure was an extraordinary tangle, particularly when it went so far as the subdivision of "one cow's grass," or even of a horse, which, being owned jointly by three men, ultimately went lame, because none of them would pay for shoeing the fourth foot.

We have been here five days, and instead of reproving Benella, as we intended, for gross assumption of authority in the matter, we are more than ever her bond slaves. The place is altogether charming, and here it is for you.

Knockcool Street is Knockcool village itself, as with almost all Irish towns; but the line of little thatched cabins is brightened at the far end by the neat house of Mrs. Wogan Odevaine, set a trifle back in its own garden, by the pillared porch of a modest hotel, and by the barracks of the Royal Irish Constabulary. The sign of the Provincial Bank of Ireland almost faces our windows; and although it is used as a meal shop the rest of the week, they tell us that two thousand pounds in money is needed there on Fair days. Next to it is a little house, the upper part of which is used as a Methodist chapel; and old Nancy, the caretaker, is already a good friend of ours. It is a humble house of prayer, but Nancy takes much pride in it, and showed us the melodeon, "worked by a young lady from Rossantach," the Sunday-school rooms, and even the cupboard where she keeps the jugs for the love feast and the linen and wine for the sacrament, which is administered once in three years. Next comes the Hoeys' cabin, where we have always a cordial welcome, but where we never go all together, for fear of embarrassing the family, which is a large one, — three generations under one roof, and plenty of children in the last. Old Mrs. Hoey does not rightly know her age, she says; but her daughter Ellen was born the year of the Big Wind, and she herself was twenty-two when she was married, and you might allow a year between that and when Ellen was born, and make your own calculation.

She tells many stories of the Big Wind, which we learn was in 1839, making Ellen's age about sixty-one and her mother's eighty-four. The fury of the storm was such that it forced the water of the Lough far ashore, stranding the fish among the rocks, where they were found dead by hundreds. When next morning dawned there was confusion and ruin on every side : the cross had tumbled from the chapel, the tombstones were overturned in the graveyard, trees and branches blocked the roadways, cabins were stripped of their thatches, and cattle found dead in the fields ; so it is small wonder old Mrs. Hoey remembers the day of Ellen's birth, weak as she is on all other dates.

Ellen's husband, Miles M'Gillan, is the carpenter on an estate in the neighborhood. His shop opens out of the cabin, and I love to sit by the Hoey fireside, where the fan bellows, turned

by a crank, brings in an instant a fresh flame to
the sods of smouldering turf, and watch a wee
Colleen Bawn playing among her daddy's shav-
ings, tying them about her waist and fat wrists,
hanging them on her ears and in among her brown
curls. Mother Hoey says that I do not speak
like an American, — that I have not so many
"caperin's" in my language, whatever they may
be ; and so we have long delightful chats together
when I go in for a taste of Ellen's griddle bread,
cooked over the peat coals. Francesca, meantime, is calling on Mrs. O'Rourke, whose son has
taken more than fifty bicycle prizes ; and no
stranger can come to Knockcool without inspect-
ing the brave show of silver, medals, and china
that adorn the bedroom, and make the O'Rourkes
the proudest couple in ould Donegal. Phelim
O'Rourke smokes his dudeen on a bench by the
door, and invites the passer-by to enter and examine the trophies. His trousers are held up with
bits of rope arranged as suspenders ; indeed, his
toilet is so much a matter of strings that it must
be a work of time to tie on his clothing in the
morning, in case he takes it off at night, which is
open to doubt ; nevertheless it is he that's the
satisfied man, and the luck would be on him as
well as on e'er a man alive, were he not kilt wid
the cough intirely ! Mrs. Phelim's skirt shows a
triangle of red flannel behind, where the two ends
of the waistband fail to meet by about six inches,

but are held together by a piece of white ball fringe. Any informality in this part of her costume is, however, more than atoned for by the presence of a dingy bonnet of magenta velvet, which she always dons for visitors.

The O'Rourke family is the essence of hospitality, so their kitchen is generally full of children and visitors; and on the occasion when Salemina issued from the prize bedroom, the guests were so busy with conversation that, to use their own language, divil a wan of thim clapt eyes on the O'Rourke puppy, and they did not notice that the baste was floundering in a tub of soft, newly made butter standing on the floor. He was indeed desperately involved, being so completely wound up in the waxy mass that he could not climb over the tub's edge. He looked comical and miserable enough in his plight: the children and the visitors thought so, and so did Francesca and I; but Salemina went directly home, and kept her room for an hour. She is so sensitive! Och, thin, it's herself that's the marthyr intirely! We cannot see that the incident affects us so long as we avoid the O'Rourkes' butter; but she says, covering her eyes with her handkerchief and shuddering: "Suppose there are other tubs and other pup— Oh, I cannot bear the thought of it, dears! Please change the subject, and order me two hard-boiled eggs for dinner."

Leaving Knockcool behind us, we walk along the country road between high, thick hedges: here a clump of weather-beaten trees, there a stretch of bog with silver pools and piles of black turf, then a sudden view of hazy hills, a grove of beeches, a great house with a splendid gateway, and sometimes, riding through it, a figure new to our eyes, a Lady Master of the Hounds, handsome in her habit with red facings. We pass many an " evicted farm," the ruined house with the rushes growing all about it, and a lonely goat browsing near ; and on we walk, until we can see the roofs of Lisdara's solitary cabin row, huddled under the shadow of a gloomy hill topped by the ruin of an old fort. All is silent, and the blue haze of the peat smoke curls up from the thatch. Lisdara's young people have mostly gone to the Big Country ; and how many tears have dropped on the path we are treading, as Peggy and Mary, Cormac and Miles, with a wooden box in the donkey cart behind them, or perhaps with only a bundle hanging from a blackthorn stick, have come down the hill to seek their fortune. Perhaps Peggy is barefooted ; perhaps Mary has little luggage beyond a pot of shamrock or a mountain thrush in a wicker cage ; but what matter for that ? They are used to poverty and hardship and hunger, and although they are going quite penniless to a new country, sure it can be no worse than the old. This is the happy-go-

lucky Irish philosophy, and there is mixed with it
a deal of simple trust in God.

How many exiles and wanderers, both those
who have no fortune and those who have failed
to win it, dream of these cabin rows, these sweet-
scented boreens with their "banks of furze un-
profitably gay," these leaking thatches with the
purple loosestrife growing in their ragged seams,
and, looking backward across the distance of time
and space, give the humble spot a tender thought,
because after all it was in their dear native isle !

> " Pearly are the skies in the country of my fathers,
> Purple are thy mountains, home of my heart;
> Mother of my yearning, love of all my longings,
> Keep me in remembrance long leagues apart."

I have been thinking in this strain because of
an old dame in the first cabin in Lisdara row,
whose daughter is in America, and who can talk
of nothing else. She shows us the last letter,
with its postal order for sixteen shillings, that
Mida sent from New York, with little presents
for blind Timsy, "dark since he were three year
old," and for lame Dan, or the " Bocca," as he is
called in Lisdara. Mida was named for the virgin saint of Killeedy in Limerick.[1] "And it's
she that's good enough to bear a saint's name,
glory be to God ! " exclaims the old mother, returning Mida's photograph to a hole in the wall
where the pig cannot possibly molest it.

[1] Saint Midé, the Brigit of Munster.

At the far end of the row lives "Omadhaun Pat." He is a "little sthrange," you understand; not because he was born with too small a share of wit, but because he fell asleep one evening when he was lying on the grass up by the old fort, and — "well, he was niver the same thing since." There are places in Ireland, you must know, where if you lie down upon the green earth and sink into untimely slumber, you will "wake silly;" or, for that matter, although it is doubtless a risk, you may escape the fate of waking silly, and wake a poet! Carolan fell asleep upon a faery rath, and it was the faeries who filled his ears with music, so that he was haunted by the tunes ever afterward; and perhaps all poets, whether they are conscious of it or not, fall asleep on faery raths before they write sweet songs.

Little Omadhaun Pat is pale, hollow-eyed, and thin; but that, his mother says, is "because he is over-studyin' for his confirmation." The great day is many weeks away, but to me it seems likely that, when the examination comes, Pat will be where he will know more than the priests!

Next door lives old Biddy Tuke. She is too aged to work, and she sits in her doorway, always a pleasant figure in her short woolen petticoat, her little shawl, and her neat white cap. She has pitaties for food, with stirabout of Indian meal once a day (oatmeal is too dear), tea occasionally when there is sixpence left from the rent, and she has more than once tasted bacon in her eighty years of life ; more than once, she tells me proudly, for it 's she that 's had the good sons to help her a bit now and then, — four to carry her and one to walk after, which is the Irish notion of an ideal family.

"It 's no chuckens I do be havin' now, ma'am," she says, "but it 's a darlin' flock I had ten year ago, whin Dinnis was harvestin' in Scotland ! Sure it was two-and-twinty chuckens I had on the floore wid meself that year, ma'am."

"Oh, it 's a conthrary world, that 's a mortial fact !" as Phelim O'Rourke is wont to say when his cough is bad ; and for my life I can frame no better wish for ould Biddy Tuke and Omadhaun Pat, dark Timsy and the Bocca, than that they might wake, one of these summer mornings, in the harvest field of the seventh heaven. That place is reserved for the saints, and surely these unfortunates, acquainted with grief like Another, might without difficulty find entrance there.

I am not wise enough to say how much of all this squalor and wretchedness and hunger is the fault of the people themselves, how much of it belongs to circumstances and environment, how much is the result of past errors of government, how much is race, how much is religion. I only know that children should never be hungry, that there are ignorant human creatures to be taught

how to live: and if it is a hard task, the sooner
it is begun the better, both for teachers and
pupils. It is comparatively easy to form opinions and devise remedies, when one knows the
absolute truth of things; but it is so difficult to
find the truth here, or at least there are so many
and such different truths to weigh in the balance,
— the Protestant and the Roman Catholic truth,
the landlord's and the tenant's, the Nationalist's
and the Unionist's truth! I am sadly befogged,
and so, pushing the vexing questions all aside, I
take dark Timsy, Bocca Lynch, and Omadhaun
Pat up on the green hillside near the ruined fort,
to tell them stories, and teach them some of the
thousand things that happier, luckier children
know.

This is an island of anomalies; the Irish peasants will puzzle you, perplex you, disappoint you
with their inconsistencies, but keep from liking
them if you can! There are a few cleaner and
more comfortable homes in Lisdara and Knockcool than when we came, and Benella has been
invaluable, although her reforms, as might be
expected, are of an unusual character, and with
her the wheels of progress never move silently,
as they should, but always squeak. With the two
golden sovereigns given her to spend, she has
bought scissors, knives, hammers, boards, sewing
materials, knitting needles, and yarn, — everything to work with, and nothing to eat, drink, or

wear, though Heaven knows there is little enough of such things in Lisdara.

"The quicker you wear 'em out, the better you 'll suit me," she says to the awe-stricken Lisdarians. "I 'm a workin' woman myself, an' it 's my ladies' money I 've spent this time; but I 'll make out to keep you in brooms and scrubbin' brushes, if only you 'll use 'em! You must n't take offense at anything I say to you, for I 'm part Irish — my grandmother was Mary Boyce of Trim; and if she had n't come away and settled in Salem, Massachusetts, mebbe I would n't have known a scrubbin' brush by sight myself!"

XXI

LACHRYMÆ HIBERNICÆ

"What ails you, Sister Erin, that your face
  Is, like your mountains, still bedewed with tears?

   .   .   .   .   .   .

Forgive! forget! lest harsher lips should say,
Like your turf fire, your rancour smoulders long,
And let Oblivion strew Time's ashes o'er your wrong."
                          Alfred Austin.

AT tea time, and again after our simple dinner, — for Bridget Thunder's repertory is not
large, and Benella's is quite unsuited to the
Knockcool markets, — we wend our way to a
certain house that stands by itself on the road
to Lisdara. It is only a whitewashed cabin with
green window trimmings, but it is a larger and
more comfortable one than we commonly see,
and it is the perfection of neatness within and
without. The stone wall that incloses it is
whitewashed, too, and the iron picket railing at
the top is painted bright green; the stones on
the posts are green, also, and there is the prettiest possible garden, with nicely cut borders of
box. In fine, if ever there was a cheery place to
look at, Sarsfield Cottage is that one; and if

ever there was a cheerless gentleman, it is Mr.
Jordan, who dwells there. Mrs. Wogan Odevaine commended him to us as the man of all
others with whom to discuss Irish questions, if
we wanted, for once in a way, to hear a thoroughly disaffected, outraged, wrong-headed, and
rancorous view of things.

"He is an encyclopædia, and he is perfectly
delightful on any topic in the universe but the
wrongs of Ireland," said she ; "not entirely sane
and yet a good father, and a good neighbor, and
a good talker. Faith, he can abuse the English
government with any man alive ! He has a
smaller grudge against you Americans, perhaps,
than against most of the other nations, so possibly he may elect to discuss something more cheerful than our national grievances ; if he does, and
you want a livelier topic, just mention — let me
see — you might speak of Wentworth, who destroyed Ireland's woolen industry, though it is
true he laid the foundation of the linen trade, so
he would n't do, though Mr. Jordan is likely to
remember the former point, and forget the latter.
Well, just breathe the words 'Catholic Disqualification' or 'Ulster Confiscation,' and you will
have as pretty a burst of oratory as you'd care
to hear. You remember that exasperated Englishman who asked in the House why Irishmen
were always laying bare their grievances ? And
Major O'Gorman bawled across the floor, 'Because they want them redressed !' "

Salemina and I went to call on Mr. Jordan the very next day after our arrival at Knockcool. Over the sitting-room or library door at Sarsfield Cottage is a coat of arms with the motto of the Jordans, "Percussus surgus;" and as our friend is descended from Richard Jordan of Knock, who died on the scaffold at Claremorris in the memorable year 1798, I find that he is related to me, for one of the De Exeter Jordans married Penelope O'Connor, daughter of the king of Connaught. He took her to wife, too, when the espousal of anything Irish, names, language, apparel, customs, or daughters, was high treason, and meant instant confiscation of estates. I never thought of mentioning the relationship, for obviously a family cannot hold grievances for hundreds of years and bequeath a sense of humor at the same time.

The name Jordan is derived, it appears, from a noble ancestor who was banner-bearer in the Crusades and who distinguished himself in many battles, but particularly in one fought against the Infidels on the banks of the River Jordan in the Holy Land. In this conflict he was felled to the ground three times during the day, but owing to his gigantic strength, his great valor, and the number of the Saracens prostrated by his sword he succeeded in escaping death and keeping the banner of the Cross hoisted ; hence by way of eminence, he was called Jordan ; and the motto of this illustrious family ever since has been, "Though I fall I rise."

Mr. Jordan's wife has been long dead, but he has four sons, only one of them, Napper Tandy, living at home.   Theobald Wolfe Tone is practicing law in Dublin ; Hamilton Rowan is a physician in Cork; and Daniel O'Connell, commonly called "Lib" (a delicate reference to the Liberator), is still a lad at Trinity.   It is a great pity that Mr. Jordan could not have had a larger family, that he might have kept fresh in the national heart the names of a few more patriots ; for his library walls, "where Memory sits by the altar she has raised to Woe," are hung with engravings and prints of celebrated insurgents, rebels, agitators, demagogues, denunciators, conspirators, — pictures of anybody, in a word, who ever struck a blow, right or wrong, well or ill judged, for the green isle.   That gallant Jacobite, Patrick Sarsfield, Burke, Grattan, Flood, and Robert Emmet stand shoulder to shoulder with three Fenian gentlemen, named Allan, Larkin, and O'Brien, known in ultra-Nationalist circles as the "Manchester martyrs."   For some years after this trio was hanged in Salford jail, it appears that the infant mind was sadly mixed in its attempt to separate knowledge in the concrete from the more or less abstract information contained in the Catechism ; and many a bishop was shocked, when asking in the confirmation service,

" Who are the martyrs ? " to be told, " Allan, Larkin, and O'Brien, me lord ! "

Francesca says she longs to smuggle into Mr.
Jordan's library a picture of Tom Steele, one of
Daniel O'Connell's henchmen, to whom he gave
the title of Head Pacificator of Ireland. Many
amusing stories are told of this official, of his
gaudy uniform, his strut and swagger, and his
pompous language. At a political meeting on one
occasion, he attacked, it seems, one Peter Purcell,
a Dublin tradesman who had fallen out with the
Liberator on some minor question. " Say no
more on the subject, Tom," cried O'Connell, who
was in the chair, " I forgive Peter from the bottom of my heart."

" You may forgive him, liberator and saviour
of my country," rejoined Steele, in a characteristic burst of his amazingly fervent rhetoric. " Yes,
you, in the discharge of your ethereal functions
as the moral regenerator of Ireland, may forgive
him ; but, revered leader, I also have functions
of my own to perform ; and I tell you that, as
Head Pacificator of Ireland, I can never forgive
the diabolical villain that dared to dispute your
august will."

The doughty Steele, who appears to have been
but poorly fitted by nature for his office, was considered at the time to be half a madman, but as
Sir James O'Connell, Daniel's candid brother,
said, " And who the divil else would take such a

job?" At any rate, when we gaze at Mr. Jordan's gallery, imagining the scene that would ensue were the breath of life breathed into the patriots' quivering nostrils, we feel sure that the Head Pacificator would be kept busy.

Dear old white-haired Mr. Jordan, known in select circles as "Grievance Jordan," sitting in his library surrounded by his denunciators, conspirators, and martyrs, with incendiary documents piled mountains high on his desk, — what a pathetic anachronism he is after all!

The shillelagh is hung on the wall now, for the most part, and faction-fighting is at an end; but in the very last moments of it there were still "ructions" between the Fitzgeralds and the Moriartys, and the age-old reason of the quarrel was, according to the Fitzgeralds, the betrayal of the "Cause of Ireland." The particular instance occurred in the sixteenth century, but no Fitzgerald could ever afterward meet any Moriarty at a fair without crying, "Who dare tread on the tail of me coat?" and inviting him to join in the dishcussion with shticks. This practically is Mr. Jordan's position; and if an Irishman desires to live entirely in the past, he can be as unhappy as any man alive. He is writing a book, which Mrs. Wogan Odevaine insists is to be called The Groans of Ireland; but after a glance at a page of memoranda penciled in a collection of Swift's Irish tracts that he lent to me (the volume con-

taining that ghastly piece of irony, The Modest
Proposal for Preventing the Poor of Ireland from
being a Burden to their Parents and Country), I
have concluded that he is editing a Catalogue
of Irish Wrongs Alphabetically Arranged. This
idea pleased Mrs. Wogan Odevaine extremely ;
and when she drove over to tea, bringing several
cheerful young people to call upon us, she proposed, in the most light-hearted way in the world,
to play what she termed the Grievance Game, an
intellectual diversion which she had invented on
the instant. She proposed it, apparently, with
a view of showing us how small a knowledge of
Ireland's ancient wrongs is the property of the
modern Irish girl, and how slight a hold on her
memory and imagination have the unspeakably
bitter days of the long ago.

We were each given pencil and paper, and two
or three letters of the alphabet, and bidden to
arrange the wrongs of Ireland neatly under them,
as we supposed Mr. Jordan to be doing for the
instruction and the depression of posterity. The
result proved that Mrs. Odevaine was a true
prophet, for the youngest members of the coterie
came off badly enough, and read their brief list
of grievances with much chagrin at their lack of
knowledge ; the only piece of information they
possessed in common being the inherited idea
that England never had understood Ireland, never
would, never could, never should, never might
understand her.

Rosetta Odevaine succeeded in remembering, for A, F, and H, Absenteeism, Flight of the Earls, Famine, and Hunger; her elder sister, Eileen, fresh from college, was rather triumphant with O and P, giving us Oppression of the Irish Tenantry, Penal Laws, Protestant Supremacy, Poyning's Law, Potato Rot, and Plantations. Their friend, Rhona Burke, had V, W, X, Y, Z, and succeeded only in finding Wentworth and Woolen Trade Destroyed, until Miss Odevaine helped her with Wood's Halfpence, about which everybody else had to be enlightened ; and there was plenty of laughter when Francesca suggested, for V, Vipers Expelled by St. Patrick. Salemina carried off the first prize ; but we insisted that C and D were the easiest letters ; at any rate, her list showed great erudition, and would certainly have pleased Mr. Jordan. C. Church Cess, Catholic Disqualification, Crimes Act of 1887, Confiscations, Cromwell, Carrying Away of Lia Fail (Stone of Destiny) from Tara. D. Destruction of Trees on Confiscated Lands, Discoverers (of flaws in Irish titles), Debasing of the Coinage by James I.

Mrs. Odevaine came next with R and S. R. Recall of Lord Fitzwilliams by Pitt, Rundale Land Tenure, Rack-Rents, Ribbonism. S. Schism Act, Supremacy Act, Sixth Act of George I.

I followed with T and U, having unearthed Tithes and the Test Act for the first, and Undertakers, the Acts of Union and Uniformity, for the second; while Francesca, who had been given I, J, K, L, and M, disgraced herself by failing on all the letters but the last, under which she finally catalogued one particularly obnoxious wrong in Middlemen.

This ignorance of the past may have its bright side, after all, though, to speak truthfully, it did show a too scanty knowledge of national history. But if one must forget, it is as well to begin with the wrongs of far-off years, those "done to your ancient name or wreaked upon your race."

PART FOURTH
CONNAUGHT

PART FOURTH. CONNAUGHT.

XXII

THE WEEPING WEST

" Veiled in your mist, and diamonded with showers."
Alfred Austin.

SHAN VAN VOCHT HOTEL,
Heart of Connemara.

SHAN VAN VOCHT means in English the " Poor Little Old Woman," one of the many endearing names given to Ireland in the Gaelic. There is, too, a well-known rebel song called by this title, — one which was not only written in Irish and English, but which was translated into French for the soldiers at Brest who were to invade Ireland under Hoche.

We had come from Knockcool, Donegal, to Westport, in County Mayo, and the day was enlivened by two purely Irish touches, one at the beginning and one at the end. We alighted at a certain railway junction to await our train, and were interested in a large detachment of soldiers, — leaving for a long journey, we judged, by the number of railway carriages and the amount of

luggage and stores. In every crowded compart-
ment there were two or three men leaning out
over the locked doors; for the guard was making
ready to start. All were chatting gayly with
their sweethearts, wives, and daughters, save one
gloomy fellow sitting alone in a corner, searching
the crowd with sad eyes for a wished-for face or
a last greeting. The bell rang, the engine stirred;
suddenly a pretty, rosy girl flew breathlessly down
the platform, pushing her way through the groups
of on-lookers. The man's eyes lighted; he rose
to his feet, but the other fellows blocked the way;
the door was locked, and he had but one precious
moment. Still he was equal to the emergency,
for he raised his fist and with one blow shattered
the window, got his kiss, and the train rumbled
away, with his victorious smile set in a frame of
broken glass! I liked that man better than any
one I've seen since Himself deserted me for his
Duty! How I hope the pretty girl will be faithful, and how I hope that an ideal lover will not
be shot in South Africa!

And if he was truly Irish, so was the porter at
a little way station where we stopped in the dark,
after being delayed interminably at Claremorris
by some trifling accident. We were eight persons packed into a second-class carriage, and totally ignorant of our whereabouts; but the porter, opening the door hastily, shouted, "Is there
anny one there for here?" — a question so vague

and illogical that none of us said anything in reply, but simply gazed at one another, and then laughed as the train went on.

We are on a here-to-day-and-gone-to-morrow journey, determined to avoid the railways, and travel by private conveyance and the public "long cars," just for a glimpse of the Weeping West before we settle down quietly in County Meath for our last few weeks of Irish life.

Thus far it has been a pursuit of the picturesque under umbrellas ; in fact, we 're desthroyed wid the dint of the damp ! " Moist and agreeable, — that 's the Irish notion both for climate and company." If the barometer bore any relation to the weather, we could plan our drives with more discretion ; but it sometimes remains as steady as a rock during two days of sea mist, and Francesca, finding it wholly regardless of gentle tapping, lost her temper on one occasion and rapped it so severely as to crack the glass. That this peculiarity of Irish barometers has been noted before we are sure, because of this verse written by a native bard : —

> " When the glass is up to thirty,
> Be sure the weather will be dirty.
> When the glass is high, O very !
> There 'll be rain in Cork and Kerry.
> When the glass is low, O Lork !
> There 'll be rain in Kerry and Cork ! "

I might add : —

> And when the glass has climbed its best,
> The sky is weeping in the West.

The national rainbow is as deceitful as the barometer, and it is no uncommon thing for us to have half a dozen of them in a day, between heavy showers, like the smiles and tears of Irish character; though, to be sure, one does not need to be an Irish patriot to declare that a fine day in this country is worth three fine days anywhere else. The present weather is accounted for partially by the fact that, as Horace Walpole said, summer has set in with its usual severity, and the tourist is abroad in the land.

I am not sure but that we belong to the hated class for the moment, though at least we try to emulate tourist virtues, if there are any, and avoid tourist vices, which is next to impossible, as they are the fruit of the tour itself. It is the circular tour which, in its effect upon the great middle class, is the most virulent and contagious, and which breeds the most offensive habits of thought and speech. The circular tour is a magnificent idea, a praiseworthy business scheme; it has educated the minds of millions, and why it should have ruined their manners is a mystery, unless indeed they had none when they were at home. Some of our fellow travelers with whom we originally started disappear every day or two, to join us again. We lose them temporarily when we take a private conveyance or when they stop at a cheap hotel, but we come together again on coach or long car; and although they have torn off many coupons in the interval, their remaining stock seems to assure us of their society for days to come.

We have a Protestant clergyman who is traveling for his health, but beguiling his time by observations for a volume to be called The Relation between Priests and Pauperism. It seems, at first thought, as if the circular coupon system was ill fitted to furnish him with corroborative detail ; but inasmuch as every traveler finds in a country only, so to speak, what he brings to it, he will gather statistics enough. Those persons who start with a certain bias of mind in one direction seldom notice any facts that would throw out of joint those previously amassed ; they instinctively collect the ones that "match," all others having a tendency to disturb the harmony of the original scheme. The clergyman's traveling companion is a person who possesses not a single opinion, conviction, or trait in common with him ; so we conclude that they joined forces for economy's sake. This comrade we call "the man with the evergreen heart," for we can hardly tell by his appearance whether he is an old young man or a young old one. With his hat on he is juvenile ; when he removes it, he is so distinctly elderly that we do not know whether to regard him as damaged youth or well-preserved old age ; but he transfers his solicitous attentions to lady after lady, rebuffs not having the slightest effect upon his warm, susceptible, ardent nature. We suppose that he is single, but we know that he can be married at a moment's notice by anybody who is willing to accept the risks of the situation. Then we have a nice schoolmaster, so agreeable that Salemina, Francesca, and I draw lots every evening as to who shall sit beside him next day. He has just had seventy boys down with measles at the same time, giving prizes to those who could show the best rash! Salemina is no friend to the competitive system in education, but this appealed to her as being as wise as it was whimsical.

We have also in our company an indiscreet and inflammable Irishman from Wexford and a cutler from Birmingham, who lose no opportunity to have a conversational scrimmage. When the car stops to change or water the horses (and as for this last operation, our steeds might always manage it without loss of time by keeping their mouths open), we generally hear something like this; for although the two gentlemen have never met before, they fight as if they had known each other all their lives.

Mr. Shamrock. "Faith, then, if you don't like the hotels and the railroads, go to Paris or London; we've done widout you up to now, and we can kape on doing widout you! We'd have more money to spind in entertainin' you if the government had n't taken three million of pounds out of us to build fortifications in China."

Mr. Rose. "That's all bosh and nonsense; you wouldn't know how to manage a hotel if you had the money."

Mr. Shamrock. "If we can't make hotel-kapers, it's soldiers we can make; and be the same token you can't manage India or Canada widout our help! Faith England owes Ireland more than she can pay, and it's not her business to be thravelin' round criticisin' the throubles she's helped to projuce."

Mr. Rose. "William Ewart Gladstone did enough for your island to make up for all the harm that the other statesmen may or may not have done."

Mr. Shamrock, touched in his most vulnerable point, shrieks above the rattle of the wheels: "The wurrst statesman that iver put his name to paper was William Ewart Gladstone!"

Mr. Rose. "The best, I say!"

Mr. Shamrock. "I say the wurrst!"

Mr. Rose. "The best!!"

Mr. Shamrock. "The wurrst!!"

Mr. Rose (after a pause). "It's your absentee landlords that have done the mischief. I'd hang every one of them, if I had my way."

Mr. Shamrock. "Faith they'd be absint thin, sure enough!"

And at this everybody laughs, and the trouble is over for a brief space, much to the relief of Mrs. Shamrock, until her husband finds himself, after a little, sufficiently calm to repeat a Cockney anecdote, which is received by Mr. Rose in resentful silence ; it being merely a description of the common bat, an unfortunate animal that, according to Mr. Shamrock, " 'as no 'ole to 'ide in, no 'ands to 'old by, no 'orns to 'urt with, though Nature 'as given 'im 'ooks be'ind to 'itch 'imself up by."

The last two noteworthy personages in our party are a dapper Frenchman, who is in business at Manchester, and a portly Londoner, both of whom are seeing Ireland for the first time. The Frenchman does not grumble at the weather, for he says that in Manchester it rains twice a day all the year round, save during the winter, when it commonly rains all day.

Sir James Paget, in an address on Recreation, defined its chief element to be surprise. If that is true, the portly Londoner must be exhilarated beyond words. But with him the sensation does not stop with surprise : it speedily becomes amazement, and then horror ; for he is of the comparative type, and therefore sees things done and hears things said, on every hand, that are not said and done at all in the same way in London. He sees people — ay, and policemen — bicycling on footpaths and riding without lamps, and is horrified to learn that they are seldom, if ever, prosecuted. He is shocked at the cabins, and the rocks, and the beggar children, and the lack

of trees; at the lack of logic, also, and the lack
of shoes; at the prevalence of the brogue; above
all, at the presence of the pig in the parlor. He
is outraged at the weather, and he minds getting
wet the more because he hates Irish whiskey.
He keeps a little notebook, and he can hardly
wait for dinner to be over, he is so anxious to
send a communication (probably signed "Veritas") to the London Times.

The multiplicity of rocks and the absence of
trees are indeed the two most striking features of
the landscape; and yet Boate says, "In ancient
times, as long as the land was in full possession
of the Irish themselves, all Ireland was very full
of woods on every side, as evidently appeareth
by the writings of Giraldus Cambrensis." But
this was long ago, —

> "Ere the emerald gem of the western world
> Was set in the brow of a stranger."

In the long wars with the English these forests
were the favorite refuge of the natives, and it
was a common saying that the Irish could never
be tamed while the leaves were upon the trees.
Then passages were cut through the woods, and
the policy of felling them, as a military measure,
was begun and carried forward on a gigantic
scale in Elizabeth's reign.

At one of the cabins along the road they were
making great preparations, which we understood,
from having seen the same thing in Lisdara.

There are wee villages and solitary cabins so far
from chapel that the priests establish "stations"
for confession. A certain house is selected, and
all the old, infirm, and feeble ones come there to
confess and hear mass. The priest afterwards
eats breakfast with the family; and there is great
pride in this function, and great rivalry in the
humble arrangements. Mrs. Odevaine often
lends a linen cloth and flowers to one of her
neighbors, she tells us; to another a knife and
fork, or a silver teapot; and so on. This cabin
was at the foot of a long hill, and the driver gave
me permission to walk; so Francesca and I
slipped down, I with a parcel which chanced to
have in it some small purchases made at the last
hotel. We asked if we might help a bit, and give
a little teapot of Belleek ware and a linen doily
trimmed with Irish lace. Both the articles were
trumpery bits of souvenirs, but the old dame was
inclined to think that the angels and saints had
taken her in charge, and nothing could exceed
her gratitude. She offered us a potato from the
pot, a cup of tea or goat's milk, and a bunch of
wild flowers from a cracked cup; and this last
we accepted as we departed in a shower of blessings, the most interesting of them being, "May
the Blessed Virgin twine your brow with roses
when ye sit in the sates of glory!" and "The
Lord be good to ye and sind ye a duke for a
husband!" We felt more than repaid for our

impulsive interest, and as we disappeared from sight a last "Bannact dea leat!" (God's blessing be on your way!) was wafted to our ears.

I seem to have known all these people before, and indeed I have met them between the covers of a book; for Connemara has one prophet, and her name is Jane Barlow. In how many of these wild bog lands of Connaught have we seen a huddle of desolate cabins on a rocky hillside, turf stacks looming darkly at the doors, and empty black pots sitting on the thresholds, and fancied we have found Lisconnel! I should recognize Ody Rafferty, the Widow McGurk, Mad Bell, old Mrs. Kilfoyle, or Stacey Doyne, if I met them face to face, just as I should know other real human creatures of a higher type, — Beatrix Esmond, Becky Sharp, Meg Merrilies, or Di Vernon.

XXIII

BEAMS AND MOTES

" Mud cabins swarm in
  This place so charming,
  With sailor garments
  Hung out to dry ;
  And each abode is
  Snug and commodious,
  With pigs melodious
    In their straw-built sty."

Father Prout.

" ' DID the Irish elves ever explain themselves to you, Red Rose ? '

" ' No, I can't say that they did,' said the English Elf. ' You can't call it an explanation to say that a thing has always been that way, just; or that a thing would be a heap more bother any other way.' "

The west of Ireland is depressing, but it is very beautiful ; at least if your taste includes an appreciation of what is wild, magnificent, and sombre. Oppressed you must be, even if you are an artist, by its bleakness and its dreariness, its lonely lakes reflecting a dull gray sky, its desolate bog lands, its solitary chapels, its wretched cabins perched on hillsides that are very wildernesses of rocks. But for cloud effects, for wonderful shadows, for fantastic and unbelievable sunsets, when the mountains are violet, the lakes silver with red flashes, the islets gold and crimson and purple, and the whole cloudy west in a flame, it is unsurpassed; only your standard of beauty must not be a velvet lawn studded with copper beeches, or a primary-hued landscape bathed in American sunshine. Connemara is austere and gloomy under a dull sky, but it has the poetic charm that belongs to all mystery, and its bare cliffs and ridges are delicately penciled on a violet background, in a way peculiar to itself and enchantingly lovely.

The waste of all God's gifts; the incredible poverty; the miserable huts, often without window or chimney; the sad-eyed women, sometimes nothing but "skin, bones, and grief;" the wild, beautiful children, springing up like startled deer from behind piles of rocks or growths of underbrush; the stony little bits of earth which the peasants cling to with such passion, while good grass lands lie unused, yet seem forever out of reach, — all this makes one dream, and wonder, and speculate, and hope against hope that the worst is over and a better day dawning. We passed within sight of a hill village without a single road to connect it with the outer world. The only supply of turf was on the mountain top, and from thence it had to be brought, basket by basket, even in the snow. The only manure for such land is seaweed, and that must be carried from the shore to the tiny plats of sterile earth on the hillside. I remember it all, for I refused to buy a pair of stockings of a woman along the road. We had taken so many that my courage failed; but I saw her climbing the slopes patiently, wearily, a shawl over her white hair, — knitting, knitting, knitting, as she walked in the rain to her cabin somewhere behind the high hills. We never give to beggars in any case, but we buy whatever we can as we are able; and why did I draw the line at that particular pair of stockings, only to be haunted by that pathetic figure for the rest of my life? Beggars there are by the score, chiefly in the tourist districts; but it is only fair to add that there are hundreds of huts where it would be a dire insult to offer a penny for a glass of water, a sup of milk, or the shelter of a turf fire.

As we drive along the road, we see, if the umbrellas can be closed for a half hour, flocks of sheep grazing on the tops of the hills, where it is sunnier, where food is better and flies less numerous. Crystal streams and waterfalls are pouring down the hillsides to lose themselves in one of Connemara's many bays, and we have a glimpse of osmunda fern, golden green and beautiful. It was under a branch of this *Osmunda regalis* that the Irish princess lay hidden, they say, till she had evaded her pursuers. The blue turf smoke rises here and there, — now from a cabin with houseleek growing on the crumbling thatch, now from one whose roof is held on by ropes and stones, — and there is always a turf bog, stacks and stacks of the cut blocks, a woman in a gown of dark red flannel resting for a moment, with the empty creel beside her, and a man cutting in the distance. After climbing the long hill beyond the "station" we are rewarded by a glimpse of more fertile fields; the clumps of ragwort and purple loosestrife are reinforced with kingcups and lilies growing near the wayside, and the rare sight, first of a pot of geraniums in the window, and then of a garden all aglow with red fuchsias, torch plants, and huge dahlias, so cheers Veritas that he takes heart again. "This is something like home!" he exclaims breezily; whereupon Mr. Shamrock murmurs that if people find nothing to admire in a foreign country save what resembles their own, he wonders that they take the trouble to be traveling.

"It is a darlin' year for the pitaties," the driver says; and there are plenty of them planted here-abouts, even in stony spots not worth a *keenogue* for anything else, for "pitaties does n't require anny in*thrick*et farmin', you see, ma'am."

The clergyman remarks that only three things are required to make Ireland the most attractive country in the world, — " Protestantism, cleanliness, and gardens;" and Mr. Shamrock, who is of course a Roman Catholic, answers this tactful speech in a way that surprises the speaker and keeps him silent for hours.

The Birmingham cutler, who has a copy of Ismay's Children in his pocket, triumphantly reads aloud, at this moment, a remark put into the mouth of an Irish character: "The low Irish are quite destitute of all notion of beauty, — have not the remotest particle of artistic sentiment or taste; their cabins are exactly as they were six hundred years ago, for they never want to improve themselves."

Then Mr. Shamrock asserts that any show of prosperity on a tenant's part would only mean an advance of rent on the landlord's; and Mr. Rose retorts that while that might have been true in former times, it is utterly false to-day.

Mrs. Shamrock, who is a natural apologist, pleads that the Irish gentry have the most beautiful gardens in the world and the greatest natural taste in gardening, and there must be some reason why the lower classes are so different in this respect. May it not be due partly to lack of ground, lack of money to spend on seeds and fertilizers, lack of all refining, civilizing, and educating influences? Mr. Shamrock adds that the dwellers in cabins cannot successfully train creepers against the walls or flowers in the dooryard, because of the goat, pig, donkey, ducks, hens and chickens; and Veritas asks triumphantly, "Why don't you keep the pig in a sty then?"

The man with the evergreen heart (who has already been told this morning that I am happily married, Francesca engaged, Salemina a determined celibate, but Benella quite at liberty) peeps under Salemina's umbrella at this juncture, and says tenderly, "And what do you think about these vexed questions, dear madam?" Which gives her a chance to reply with some distinctness, "I shall not know what I think for several months to come; and at any rate, there are various things more needed on this coach than opinions."

At this the Frenchman murmurs, "Ah, she has right!" and the Birmingham cutler says, "'Ear! 'ear!"

On another day the parson began to tell the man with the evergreen heart some interesting things about America. He had never been there himself, but he had a cousin who had traveled extensively in that country, and had brought back much unusual information. "The Americans are an extraordinary people on the practical side," he remarked; "but having said that, you have said all, for they are sordid and absolutely devoid of ideality. Take an American at his roller-top desk, a telephone at one side and a typewriter at the other, talk to him of pork and dollars, and you have him at his very best. He always keeps on his Panama hat at business, and sits in a rocking-chair smoking a long cigar. The American wo-man wears a blue dress with a red lining, or a black dress with orange trimmings, showing a survival of African taste ; while another exhibits the American Indian type, — sallow, with high cheek bones. The manners of the servant classes are extraordinary. I believe they are called the 'help,' and they commonly sit in the drawing-room after the work is finished."

"You surprise me !" said Mrs. Shamrock.

"It is indeed amazing," he continued ; "and there are other extraordinary customs, among them the habit of mixing ices with all beverages. They plunge ices into mugs of ale, beer, porter, lemonade, or Apollinaris, and sip the mixture with a long ladle at the chemist's counter, where it is usually served."

"You surprise me !" exclaimed the cutler.

"You surprise me too !" I echoed in my in-most heart. Francesca would not have confined herself to that blameless mode of expression, you may be sure, and I was glad that she was on the back seat of the car. I did not know it at the time, but Veritas, who is a man of intelligence, had identified her as an American, and wishing to inform himself on all possible points, had asked her frankly why it was that the people of her nation gave him the impression of never being restful or quiet, but always so excessively and abnormally quick in motion and speech and thought.

"Casual impressions are not worth anything," she replied nonchalantly. "As a nation, you might sometimes give us the impression of being phlegmatic and slow-witted. Both ideas may have some basis of fact, yet not be absolutely true. We are not all abnormally quick in America. Look at our messenger boys, for example."

"We! Phlegmatic and slow-witted!" exclaimed Veritas. "You surprise me! And why do you not reward these government messengers for speed, and stimulate them in that way?"

"We do," Francesca answered; "that is the only way in which we ever get them to arrive anywhere, — by rewarding and stimulating them at both ends of the journey, and sometimes, in extreme cases, at a halfway station."

"This is most interesting," said Veritas, as he took out his damp notebook; "and perhaps you can tell me why your newspapers are so poorly edited, so cheap, so sensational?"

"I confess I can't explain it," she sighed, as if sorely puzzled. "Can it be that we have expended our strength on magazines, where you are so lamentably weak?"

At this moment the rain began, as if there had been a long drought, and the sky had just determined to make up the deficiency. It fell in sheets, and the wind blew I know not how many

Irish miles an hour. The Frenchman put on a
silk mackintosh with a cape, and was berated by
everybody in the same seat because he stood up
a moment and let the water in under the lap
covers. His umbrella was a dainty *en-tout-cas*
with a mother-of-pearl handle, that had answered
well enough in heavy mist or soft drizzle. His
hat of fine straw was tied with a neat cord to his
buttonhole ; but although that precaution insured
its ultimate safety, it did not prevent its soaring
from his head and descending on Mrs. Shamrock's bonnet. He conscientiously tried holding
it on with one hand, but was then reproved by
both neighbors because his mackintosh dripped
over them.

"How are your spirits, Frenchy ? " asked the
cutler jocosely.

" I am not too greatly sad," said the poor gentleman, " but I will be glad it should be finished ;
far more joyfully would I be at Manchester, triste
as it may be."

Just then a gust of wind blew his cape over his
head, and snapped his parasol.

" It is evidently it has been made in Ireland,"
he sighed, with a desperate attempt at gayety.
" It should have had a grosser stem, and hélas !
it must not be easy to have it mended in these
barbarous veelages."

We stopped at four o'clock at a wayside hostelry, and I had quietly made up my mind to de-

scend from the car, and take rooms for the night, whatever the place might be. Unfortunately, the same idea occurred to three or four of the soaked travelers; and as men could leap down, while ladies must wait for the steps, the chivalrous sex their manners obscured by the circular tour system, secured the rooms, and I was obliged to ascend again, wetter than ever, to my perch beside the driver.

"Can I get the box seat, do you think, if I pay extra for it?" I had asked one of the stablemen, before breakfast.

"You don't need to be payin', miss! Just confront the driver, and you'll get it aisy!" If, by the way, I had confronted him at the end instead of at the beginning of the journey, my charms certainly would not have been all powerful, for my coat had been leaked upon by red and green umbrellas, my hat was a shapeless jelly, and my face imprinted with the spots from a drenched blue vail.

After two hours more of this we reached the Shan Van Vocht Hotel, where we had engaged apartments; but we found to our consternation that it was full, and that we had been put in lodgings a half mile away.

Salemina, whose patience was quite exhausted by the discomforts of the day, groaned aloud when we were deposited at the door of a village shop, and ushered upstairs to our tiny quarters;

but she ceased abruptly when she really took note of our surroundings. Everything was humble, but clean and shining, — glass, crockery, bedding, floor, on the which we were dripping pools of water, while our landlady's daughter tried to make us more comfortable.

"It's a soft night we're havin'," she said, in a dove's voice, "but we'll do right enough if the win' does n't rise up on us."

Left to ourselves, we walked about the wee rooms on ever new and more joyful voyages of discovery. The curtains rolled up and down easily; the windows were propped upon nice clean sticks instead of tennis rackets and hearth brushes; there was a well-washed stone to keep the curtain down on the sill; and just outside were tiny window gardens, in each of which grew three marigolds and three asters, in a box fenced about with little green pickets. There were well-dusted books on the tables, and Francesca wanted to sit down immediately to The Charming Cora, reprinted from The Girl's Own Paper. Salemina meantime had tempted fate by looking under the bed, where she found the floor so exquisitely neat that she patted it affectionately with her hand.

We had scarcely donned our dry clothing when the hotel proprietor sent a jaunting car for our drive to the seven-o'clock table d'hôte dinner. We carefully avoided our traveling companions that night, but learned the next morning that the

Frenchman had slept on four chairs, and rejected
the hotel coffee with the remark that it was not
" *véritable*," — a criticism in which he was quite
justified. Our comparative Englishman had occupied a cot in a room where the tin bathtubs
were kept. He was writing to the Times at the
moment of telling me his woes, and, without seeing the letter, I could divine his impassioned advice never to travel in the west of Ireland in rainy
weather. He remarked (as if quoting from his
own communication) that the scenery was magnificent, but that there was an entirely insufficient
supply of hot water ; that the waiters had the appearance of being low comedians, and their service was of the character one might expect from
that description ; that he had been talking before
breakfast with a German gentleman, who had sat
on a wall opposite the village of Dugort, in the
island of Achill, from six o'clock in the morning
until nine, and in that time he had seen coming
out of an Irish hut three geese, eight goslings,
six hens, fifteen chickens, two pigs, two cows,
two barefooted girls, the master of the house
leading a horse, three small children carrying
cloth bags filled with school-books, and finally
a strapping mother leading a donkey loaded with
peat baskets ; that all this poverty and ignorance
and indolence and filth was spoiling his holiday ;
and finally, that if he should be as greatly disappointed in the fishing as he had been in the hotel

accommodations, — here we almost fainted from suspense, — he should be obliged to go home! And not only that, but he should feel it his duty to warn others of what they might expect.

" Perhaps you are justified," said Francesca sympathetically. " People who are used to the dry, sunny climate and the clear atmosphere of London ought not to expose themselves to Irish rain without due consideration."

He agreed with her, glancing over his spectacles to see if she by any possibility could be amusing herself at his expense, — good old fussy, fault-finding Veritas ; but indeed Francesca's eyes were so soft and lovely and honest that the more he looked at her, the less he could do her the injustice of suspecting her sincerity.

But mind you, although I would never confess it to Veritas, because he sees nothing but flaws on every side, the Irish pig is, to my taste, a trifle too much in the foreground. He pays the rent, no doubt ; but this magnificent achievement could be managed from a sty in the rear, ungrateful as it might seem to immure so useful a personage behind a door or conceal his virtues from the public at large.

XXIV

HUMORS OF THE ROAD

"Cheerful at morn, he wakes from short repose,
Breasts the keen air, and carols as he goes."
Oliver Goldsmith.

IF you drive from Clifden to Oughterard by way of Maam Cross, and then on to Galway, you will pass through the O'Flahertys' country, one of whom, Murrough O'Flaherty, was governor of this county of Iar (western) Connaught. You will like to see the last of the O'Flaherty yews, a thousand years old at least, and the ruins of the castle and banqueting hall. The family glories are enumerated in ancient Irish manuscript, and instead of the butler, footman, chef, coachman, and gardener of to-day we read of the O'Flaherty physician, standard bearer, brehon or judge, master of the revels, and keeper of the bees ; and the moment Himself is rich enough, I intend to add some of these picturesque personages to our staff.

We afterwards learned that there was formerly an inscription over the west gate of Galway : —

"From the fury of the O'Flaherties,
Good Lord, deliver us."

After Richard de Burgo took the town, in 1226, it became a flourishing English colony, and the citizens must have guarded themselves from any intercourse with the native Irish; at least, an old by-law of 1518 enacts that "neither O' nor Mac shalle strutte ne swaggere thro' the streetes of Galway."

We did not go to Galway straight, because we never do anything straight. We seldom get any reliable information, and never any inspiring suggestions, from the natives themselves. They are all patriotically sure that Ireland is the finest counthry in the world, God bless her! but in the matter of seeing that finest counthry in the easiest or best fashion they are all very vague. Indirectly, our own lack of geography, coupled with the ignorance of the people themselves, has been of the greatest service in enlivening our journeys. Francesca says that, in looking back, she finds that our errors of judgment have always resulted in our most charming and unforgettable experiences; but let no one who is traveling with a well-balanced and logical-minded man attempt to follow in our footsteps.

Being as free as air on this occasion (if I except the dread of Benella's scorn, which descends upon us now and then, and moves us to repentance, sometimes even to better behavior), we passed Porridgetown and Cloomore, and ferried across to the opposite side of Lough Corrib. Sal-

emina, of course, had fixed upon Cong as our ob-
jective point, because of its caverns and archæological remains, which Dr. La Touche tells her
not on any account to miss. Francesca and I
said nothing, but we had a very definite idea of
avoiding Cong, and going nearer Tuam, to climb
Knockma, the hill of the fairies, and explore their
ancient haunts and archæological remains, which
are more in our line than the caverns of Cong.

Speaking of Dr. La Touche reminds me that
we have not the smallest notion as to how our
middle-aged romance is progressing. Absence
may, at this juncture, be just as helpful a force
in its development as daily intercourse would be ;
for when one is past thirty, I fancy there is a
deal of " thinking-it-over " to do. Precious little
there is when we are younger ; heart does it all
then, and never asks head's advice ! But in too
much delay there lies no plenty, and there's the
danger. Actually, Francesca and I could be no
more anxious to settle Salemina in life if she were
lame, halt, blind, and homeless, instead of being
attractive, charming, absurdly young for her age,
and not without means. The difficulty is that
she is one of those " continent, persisting, im-
movable persons " whom Emerson describes as
marked out for the blessing of the world. That
quality always makes a man anxious. He fears
that he may only get his rightful share of blessing, and he craves the whole output, so to speak.

We naturally mention Dr. La Touche very
often, since he is always writing to Salemina or
to me, offering counsel and suggestion. Madam
La Touche, the venerable aunt, has written also,
asking us to visit them in Meath ; but this invitation we have declined, principally because the
Colquhouns will be with them, and they would
surely be burdened by the addition of three ladies
and a maid to their family; partly because we
shall be freer in our own house, which will be as
near the La Touche mansion as possible, you
may be sure, if Francesca and I have anything to
do with choosing it.

The La Touche name, then, is often on our
lips, but Salemina offers no intimation that it is
indelibly imprinted on her heart of hearts. It is
a good name to be written anywhere, and we fancied there was the slightest possible hint of pride
and possession in Salemina's voice when she read
to us to-night, from her third volume of Lecky's
History of Ireland in the Eighteenth Century, a
paragraph concerning one David La Touche,
from whom Dr. Gerald is descended : —

" In the last of the Irish Parliaments no less
than five members of the name sat together in
the House of Commons, and his family may claim
what is in truth the highest honor of which an
Irish family can boast, — that during many successive governments and in a period of most lav-
ish corruption it possessed great parliamentary

influence, and yet passed through political life untitled and unstained."

There is just the faintest gleam of hope, by the way, that Himself may join us at the very end of June, and he is sure to be helpful on this sentimental journey ; he aided Ronald and Francesca more than once in their tempestuous love affair, and if his wits are not dulled by marriage, as so often happens, he will be invaluable. It will not be long then, probably, before I assume my natural, my secondary position in the landscape of events. The junior partners are now, so to speak, on their legs, although it is idle to suppose that such brittle appendages will support them for any length of time. As soon as we return in the autumn, I should like to advertise (if Himself will permit me) for a perfectly sound and kind junior partner, — one who has been well broken to harness, and who will neither shy nor balk, no matter what the provocation ; the next step being to urge Himself to relinquish altogether the bondage of business care. There is no need of his continuing in it, since other people's business will always give him ample scope for his energies. He has, since his return to America, dispensed justice and mercy, chiefly mercy, to one embezzler, one honest fellow tempted beyond his strength, one widow, one unfortunate friend of his youth, and two orphans, and it was in no sense an extraordinary season.

To return to notes of travel, our method of pro-
gression, since we deserted the highroad and the
public car, has been strangely varied. I think
there is no manner of steed or vehicle which has
not been used by us, at one time or another, even
to the arch donkey and the low-backed car with
its truss of hay, like that of the immortal Peggy.
I thought at first that " arch " was an unusual ad-
jective to apply to a donkey, but I find after all
that it is abundantly expressive.   Benella, who
disapproves entirely of this casual sort of traveling, far from " answerable roads " and in " back-
wards places " (Irish for "behind the times "), is
yet wonderfully successful in discovering equi-
pages of some sort in unlikely spots.

In towns of any size or pretension, we find by
the Town Cross or near the inn a motley collection of things on wheels, with drivers sometimes
as sober as Father Mathew, sometimes not. Yesterday we had a mare which the driver confessed
he bought without " overcircumspectin' it," and
although you could n't, as he said, " extinguish
her at first sight from a grand throtter, she had
n't rightly the speed you could wish."

" It 's not so powerful young she is, melady ! "
he confessed.   " You 'd be afther lookin' at a
chicken a long time and niver be reminded of
her ; but sure ye might thry her, for belike ye
would n't fancy a horse that would be leppin'
stone walls wid ye, like Dan Ryan's there ! My

little baste 'll get ye to Rossan before night, and
she won't hurt man nor mortial in doin' it."

"Begorra, you're right, nor herself nayther,"
said Dan Ryan; "and if it's leppin' ye mane,
sure she couldn't lep a sod o' turf, that mare
couldn't! God pardon ye, melady, for thrustin'
yerself to that paiceable brindly-colored ould hin,
whin ye might be gettin' a dacint high-steppin'
horse for a shillin' or two more; an' belike I
might contint meself to take less, for I wouldn't
be extortin' ye like Barney O'Mara there!"

Our chosen driver replied to this by saying
that he wouldn't be caught dead at a pig fair
with Dan Ryan's horse, but in the midst of all the
distracting discussions and arguments that followed we held to our original bargain; for we did
not like the look of Dan Ryan's high-stepper, who
was a "thrifle moun*tai*ny," as they say in these
parts, and had a wild eye to boot. We started,
and in a half hour we could still see the chapel
spire of the little village we had just left. It was
for once a beautiful day, but we felt that we must
reach a railway station some time or other, in order to find a place to sleep.

"Can't you make her go a bit faster? Do you
want to keep us on the road all night?" inquired
Francesca.

"I do not, your ladyship's honor, ma'am."

"Is she tired, or doesn't she ever go any better?" urged Salemina.

"She does; it's God's truth I'm tellin' ye, melady, she's that flippant sometimes that I scarcely can hould her, and the car jumps undher her like a spring bed."

"Then what on earth *is* the matter with her?" I inquired, with some fire in my eye.

"Sure I believe she's takin' time to think of the iligant load she's carryin', melady, and small blame to her!" said Mr. Barney O'Mara; and after that we let him drive as best he could, although it did take us four hours to do nine Irish miles. He came, did Mr. Barney, from County Armagh, and he beguiled the way with interesting tales from that section of Ireland, one of which, "The Old Crow and the Young Crow," particularly took our fancies.

"An old crow was teaching a young crow one day, and says to him, 'Now my son,' says he, 'listen to the advice I'm going to give you,' says he. 'If you see a person coming near you and stooping, mind yourself, and be on your keeping; he's stooping for a stone to throw at you,' says he.

"'But tell me,' says the young crow, 'what should I do if he had a stone already down in his pocket?' says he.

"'Musha, go 'long out of that,' says the old crow, 'you've learned enough; the divil another learning I'm able to give you.'"

He was a perfect honey-pot of useless and unreliable information, was Barney O'Mara, and most learned in fairy lore; but for that matter, all the people walking along the road, the drivers, the boatman and guides, the men and women in the cottages where we stop in a shower or to inquire the way, relate stories of phookas, leprehauns, and sprites, banshees and all the various classes of elves and fays, as simply and seriously as they would speak of any other occurrences. Barney told us gravely of the old woman who was in the habit of laying *pishogues* (charms) to break the legs of his neighbor's cattle, because of an ancient grudge she bore him; and also how necessary it is to put a bit of burning turf under the churn to prevent the phookas, or mischievous fairies, from abstracting the butter or spoiling the churning in any way. Irish fays seem to be much interested in dairy matters, for, besides the sprites who delight in distracting the cream and keeping back the butter (I wonder if a lazy up-and-down movement of the dasher invites them at all, at all?), it is well known that many a milkmaid on a May morning has seen fairy cows browsing along the banks of lakes, — cows that vanish into thin mist at the sound of human footfall.

When we were quite cross at missing the noon train from Rossan, quite tired of the car's jolting, somewhat vexed even at the mare's continued enjoyment of her "iligant load," Barney appeased us all by singing, in a delightful mel-

low voice, a fairy song called The Leprehaun.[1]
This personage, you must know, if you have n't
a large acquaintance among Irish fairies, is a
tricksy fellow in a green coat and scarlet cap,
with brave shoe buckles on his wee brogues.
You will catch him sometimes, if the "glamour"
is on you, under a burdock leaf or a thorn bush,
and he is always making or mending a shoe.
He commonly has a little purse about him,
which, if you are quick enough, you can snatch ;
and a wonderful purse it is, for, whatever you
spend, there is always money to be found in
it. Truth to tell, nobody has yet succeeded in
being quicker than Master Leprehaun, though
many have offered to fill his cruiskeen with
"mountain dew," of which Irish fairies are pas-
sionately fond.

> "In a shady nook, one moonlight night,
>   A leprehaun I spied ;
> With scarlet cap and coat of green,
>   A cruiskeen by his side.
> 'T was tick, tack, tick, his hammer went,
>   Upon a weeny shoe ;
> And I laughed to think of his purse of gold ;
>   But the fairy was laughing too !

> "With tip-toe step and beating heart,
>   Quite softly I drew nigh :
> There was mischief in his merry face,
>   A twinkle in his eye.
> He hammered, and sang with tiny voice,
>   And drank his mountain dew ;

[1] By Patrick W. Joyce.

And I laughed to think he was caught at last;
But the fairy was laughing too!

" As quick as thought I seized the elf.
  ' Your fairy purse!' I cried.
' The purse!' he said — ' 't is in her hand —
  That lady at your side.'
I turned to look: the elf was off.
  Then what was I to do?
O, I laughed to think what a fool I 'd been;
  And the fairy was laughing too!"

I cannot communicate any idea of the rollicking gayety and quaint charm Barney gave to the tune, nor the light-hearted, irresistible chuckle with which he rendered the last two lines, giving a snap of his whip as accent to the long "O:" —

" O, I laughed to think what a fool I 'd been;
  And the fairy was laughing too!"

After he had sung it twice through, Benella took my guitar from its case for me, and we sang it after him, again and again; so it was in happy fashion that we at least approached Ballyrossan, where we bade Barney O'Mara a cordial farewell, paying him four shillings over his fare, which was cheap indeed for the song.

As we saw him vanish slowly up the road, ragged himself, the car and harness almost ready to drop to pieces, the mare, I am sure, in the last week of her existence, we were glad that he had his Celtic fancy to enliven his life a bit, — that fancy which seems a providential reaction against the cruel despotisms of fact.

XXV

THE WEE FOLK

" There sings a bonnie linnet
Up the heather glen ;
The voice has magic in it
Too sweet for mortal men !
Sing O, the blooming heather,
O, the heather glen !
Where fairest fairies gather
To lure in mortal men."

CARRIG-A-FOOKA INN, near Knockma,
On the shores of Lough Corrib.

A MODERN Irish poet [1] says something that
Francesca has quoted to Ronald in her letter to-
day, and we await from Scotland his confirmation
or denial. He accuses the Scots of having discovered the fairies to be pagan and wicked, and
of denouncing them from the pulpits, whereas
Irish priests discuss with them the state of their
souls ; or at least they did, until it was decided
that they had none, but would dry up like so
much bright vapor at the last day. It was more
in sadness than in anger that the priests announced this fiat ; for Irish sprites and goblins
do gay, graceful, and humorous things, for the

[1] W. B. Yeats.

most part, tricksy sins, not deserving annihilation, whereas Scottish fays are sometimes malevolent, — or so says the Irish poet.

This is very sad, no doubt, but it does not begin to be as sad as having no fairies at all. There must have been a few in England in Shakespeare's time, or he could never have written The Tempest or the Midsummer Night's Dream; but where have they vanished?

As for us in America, I fear that we never have had any "wee folk." The Indians had their woodland spirits, spirits of rocks, trees, mountains, star and moon maidens; the negroes had their enchanted animals and conjure men; but as for real wee folk, either they were not indigenous to the soil or else we unconsciously drove them away. Yet we had facilities to offer! The columbines, harebells, and fringed gentians would have been just as cosy and secluded places to live in as the Irish foxgloves, which are simply running over with fairies. Perhaps they would n't have liked our cold winters; still it must have been something more than climate, and I am afraid I know the reason well, — we are too sensible; and if there is anything a fairy detests, it is common sense. We are too rich, also; and a second thing that a fairy abhors is the chink of dollars. Perhaps, when I am again enjoying the advantages brought about by sound money, commercial prosperity, and a magnificent system of public education, I shall feel differently about it; but for the moment I am just a bit embarrassed and crestfallen to belong to a nation absolutely shunned by the fairies. If they had only settled among us like other colonists, shaped us to their ends as far as they could, and, when they could n't, conformed themselves to ours, there might have been, by this time, fairy trusts stretching out benign arms all over the continent.

Of course it is an age of incredulity, but Salemina, Francesca, and I have not come to Ireland to scoff, and, whatever we do we shall not go to the length of doubting the fairies; for, as Barney O'Mara says, "they stand to raison."

Glen Ailna is a "gentle" place near Carrig-a-fooka Inn, — that is, one beloved by the *shee-hogues;* and though you may be never so much interested, I may not tell you its exact whereabouts, since no one can ever find it unless he is himself under the glamour. Perhaps you might be a doubter, with no eyes for the "dim kingdom;" perhaps you might gaze forever, and never be able to see a red-capped fiddler, fiddling under a blossoming sloe bush. You might even see him, and then indulge yourself in a fit of common sense or doubt of your own eyes, in which case the wee dancers would never flock to the sound of the fiddle or gather on the fairy ring. This is the reason that I shall never take you to Knockma, to Glen Ailna, or especially to the hy-

acinth wood, which is a little plantation near the
ruin of a fort. Just why the fairies are so fond
of an old *rath* or *lis* I cannot imagine, for you
would never suppose that antiquaries, archæolo-
gists, and wee folk would care for the same
places.

I have no intention of interviewing the grander
personages among the Irish fairies, for they are
known to be haughty, unapproachable, and severe,
as befits the descendants of the great Nature
Gods and the under-deities of flood and fell
and angry sea. It is the lesser folk, the gay,
gracious, little men that I wish to meet; those
who pipe and dance on the fairy ring. The
"ring" is made, you know, by the tiny feet that
have tripped for ages and ages, flying, dancing,
circling, over the tender young grass. Rain cannot wash it away; you may walk over it; you
may even plough up the soil, and replant it ever
so many times; the next season the fairy ring
shines in the grass just the same. It seems
strange that I am blind to it, when an ignorant, dirty spalpeen who lives near the foot of
Knockma has seen it and heard the fairy music
again and again. He took me to the very place
where, last Lammas Eve, he saw plainly — for
there was a beautiful white moon overhead —
the arch king and queen of the fairies, who appear only on state occasions, together with a crowd
of dancers, and more than a dozen pipers piping

melodious music. Not only that, but (lucky little beggar!) he heard distinctly the *fulparnee* and the *folpornee*, the *rap-lay-hoota* and the *roolya-boolya*, — noises indicative of the very jolliest and wildest and most uncommon form of fairy conviviality. Failing a glimpse of these midsummer revels, my next choice would be to see the Elf Horseman galloping round the shores of the Fairy Lough in the cool of the morn.

> " Loughareema, Loughareema,
>   Stars come out and stars are hidin' ;
>   The wather whispers on the stones,
>   The flittherin' moths are free.
> Onest before the mornin' light
>   The Horseman will come ridin'
> Roun' an' roun' the Fairy Lough,
>   An' no one there to see."

But there will be some one there, and that is the aforesaid Jamesy Flanigan! Sometimes I think he is fibbing, but a glance at his soft, dark, far-seeing eyes under their fringe of thick lashes convinces me to the contrary. His field of vision is different from mine, that is all, and he fears that if I accompany him to the shores of the Fairy Lough the Horseman will not ride for him; so I am even taunted with undue common sense by a little Irish gossoon.

I tried to coax Benella to go with me to the hyacinth wood by moonlight. Fairies detest a crowd, and I ought to have gone alone; but, to tell the truth, I hardly dared, for they have a way of kidnapping attractive ladies and keeping them for years in the dim kingdom. I would not trust Himself at Glen Ailna for worlds, for gentlemen are not exempt from danger. Connla of the Golden Hair was lured away by a fairy maiden, and taken, in a "gleaming, straight-gliding, strong crystal canoe," to her domain in the hills; and Oisin, you remember, was transported to the Land of the Ever Youthful by the beautiful Niam. If one could only be sure of coming back! but Oisin, for instance, was detained three hundred years, so one might not be allowed to return, and still worse, one might not wish to; three hundred years of youth would tempt — a woman! My opinion, after reading the Elf Errant, is that one of us has been there, — Moira O'Neill. I should suspect her of being able to wear a fairy cap herself, were it not for the human heart-throb in her verses; but I am sure she has the glamour whenever she desires it, and hears the fairy pipes at will.

Benella is of different stuff; she not only distrusts fairies, but, like the Scotch Presbyterians, she fears that they are wicked. "Still, you say they have n't got immortal souls to save, and I don't suppose they 're responsible for their actions," she allows; "but as for traipsing up to those heathenish haunted woods when all Christian folks are in bed, I don't believe in it, and

neither would Mr. Beresford ; but if you 're set
on it, I shall go with you ! "

"You would n't be of the slightest use," I
answered severely ; "indeed, you 'd be worse
than nobody. The fairies cannot endure doubters ; it makes them fold their wings over their
heads and shrink away into their flower cups.
I should be mortified beyond words if a fairy
should meet me in your company."

Benella seemed hurt and a trifle resentful as
she replied : "That about doubters is just what
Mrs. Kimberly used to say." (Mrs. Kimberly is
the Salem priestess, the originator of the "science.") "She could n't talk a mite if there was
doubters in the hall ; and it 's so with spiritualists
and clairvoyants too, — they 're all of 'em scare-
cats. I guess likely that those that 's so afraid of
being doubted has some good reason for it ! "

Well, I never went to the hyacinth wood by
moonlight, since so many objections were raised,
but I did go once at noonday, the very most unlikely hour of all the twenty-four, and yet —

As I sat there beneath a gnarled thorn, weary
and warm with my climb, I looked into the heart
of a bluebell forest growing under a circle of
gleaming silver birches, and suddenly I heard
fairy music, — at least it was not mortal, — and
many sounds were mingled in it : the sighing of
birches, the carol of a lark, the leap and laugh of
a silvery runnel tumbling down the hillside, the

soft whir of butterflies' wings, and a sweet little
over or under tone, from the over or under world,
that I took to be the opening of a million hyacinth
buds in the sunshine. Then I heard the delicious
sound of a fairy laugh, and, looking under a
swaying branch of meadowsweet, I saw — yes,
I really saw —

You must know that first a wee green door
swung open in the stem of the meadowsweet, and
out of that land where you can buy joy for a
penny came a fairy in the usual red and green.
I had the Elf Errant in my lap, and I think that
in itself made him feel more at home with me, as
well as the fact, perhaps, that for the moment I
was n't a bit sensible and had no money about
me. I was all ready with an Irish salutation, for
the purpose of further disarming his aversion. I
intended to say, as prettily as possible, though,
alas, I cannot manage the brogue, " And what
way do I see you now ? " or " Good-mornin' to
yer honor's honor ! " But I was struck dumb by
my good fortune at seeing him at all. He looked
at me once, and then, flinging up his arms, he
gave a weeny, weeny yawn ! This was disconcerting, for people almost never yawn in my company ; and to make it worse, he kept on yawning,
until, for very sympathy, and not at all in the way
of revenge, I yawned too. Then the green door
swung open again, and a gay rabble of wide-
awake fairies came trooping out : and some of

them kissed the hyacinth bells to open them, and some of them flew to the thorn tree, until every little brancheen was white with flowers, where but a moment ago had been tightly closed buds. The yawning fairy slept meanwhile under the swaying meadowsweet, and the butterflies fanned him with their soft wings; but, alas, it could not have been the hour for dancing on the fairy ring, nor the proper time for the fairy pipers, and long, long, as I looked I saw and heard nothing more than what I have told you. Indeed, I presently lost even that, for a bee buzzed, a white petal dropped from the thorn tree on my face, there was a scraping of tiny claws and the sound of two squirrels barking love to each other in the high branches, and in that moment the glamour that was upon me vanished in a twinkling.

" But I really did see the fairies ! " I exclaimed triumphantly to Benella the doubter, when I returned to Carrig-a-fooka Inn, much too late for luncheon.

" I want to know ! " she exclaimed, in her New England vernacular. " I guess by the looks o' your eyes they didn't turn out to be very lively comp'ny ! "

PART FIFTH
ROYAL MEATH

PART FIFTH. ROYAL MEATH

XXVI

IRELAND'S GOLD

" I sat upon the rustic seat —
   The seat an aged bay-tree crowns —
And saw outspreading from our feet
   The golden glory of the Downs.
The furze-crowned heights, the glorious glen,
   The white-walled chapel glistening near,
The house of God, the homes of men,
   The fragrant hay, the ripening ear."

Denis Florence McCarthy.

THE OLD HALL, DEVORGILLA,
Vale of the Boyne.

WE have now lived in each of Ireland's four provinces: Leinster, Munster, Ulster, and Connaught, but the confines of these provinces, and their number, have changed several times since the beginning of history. In A. D. 130 the Milesian monarchy was restored in the person of Tuathal (Too 'hal) the Legitimate. Over each of the Irish provinces was a *ri* or king, and there was also over all Ireland an Ard-ri or supreme monarch who lived at Tara up to the time of its abandonment in the sixth century. Before Tuathal's day, the Ard-ri had for his land allowance only a small tract around Tara, but Tuathal cut off a portion from each of the four older provinces, at the Great Stone of Divisions in the centre of Ireland, making the fifth province of Royal Meath, which has since disappeared, but which was much larger than the present two counties of Meath and Westmeath. In this once famous, and now most lovely and fertile spot, with the good republican's love of royalty and royal institutions, we have settled ourselves; in the midst of verdant plains watered by the Boyne and the Blackwater, here rippling over shallows, there meandering in slow deep reaches between reedy banks.

The Old Hall, from which I write, is somewhere in the vale of the Boyne, somewhere near Yellow Steeple, not so far from Treadagh, only a few miles from Ballybilly (I hope to be forgiven this irreverence to the glorious memory of his Majesty, William, Prince of Orange !), and within driving distance of Killkienan, Croagh-Patrick, Domteagh, and Tara Hill itself. If you know your Royal Meath, these geographical suggestions will give you some idea of our location ; if not, take your map of Ireland, please (a thing nobody has near him), and find the town of Tuam, where you left us a little time ago. You will see a railway line from Tuam to Athenry, Athlone, and Mullingar. Anybody can visit Mullingar — it is for the million ; but only the elect may go to Devorgilla. It is the captive of our bow and spear ; or, to change the figure, it is a violet by a mossy stone, which we refuse to have plucked from its poetic solitude and worn in the bosom or in the buttonhole of the tourist.

At Mullingar, then, we slip on enchanted garments which conceal us from the casual eye, and disappear into what is, in midsummer, a bower of beauty. There you will find, when you find us, Devorgilla, lovely enough to be Tir-nan-og, that Land of the Ever Youthful well known to the Celts of long ago. Here we have rested our weary bodies and purified our travel-stained minds. Fresh from the poverty-ridden hillsides of Connaught, these rich grazing lands, comfortable houses, magnificent demesnes and castles, are unspeakably grateful to the eye and healing to the spirit. We have not forgotten, shall never forget, our Connemara folk, nor yet Omadhaun Pat and dark Timsy of Lisdara in the north ; but it is good, for a change, to breathe in this sense of general comfort, good cheer, and abundance.

Benella is radiant, for she is near enough to Trim to go there occasionally to seek for traces of her ancestress, Mary Boyce ; and as for Salemina, this bit of country is a Mecca for antiquaries and scholars, and we are fairly surrounded by towers, tumuli, and cairns. "It's mostly ruins they do be wantin', these days," said a wayside

acquaintance. " I built a stone house for my
donkey on the knockaun beyant my cabin jist,
and bedad, there's a crowd round it every Saturday callin' it the risidence of wan of the Danish kings ! An' they are diggin' at Tara now,
ma'am, looking for the Ark of the Covenant !
They do be sayin' the prophet Jeremiah come
over from England and brought it wid him.
Begorra, it's a lucky man he was to git away
wid it."

Added to these advantages of position, we
are within a few miles of Rosnaree, Dr. La
Touche's demesne, to which he comes home from
Dublin to-morrow, bringing with him our dear
Mr. and Mrs. Colquhoun of Ardnagreena. We
have been here ourselves for ten days, and are
flattered to think that we have used the time as
unconventionally as we could well have done.
We made a literary pilgrimage first, but that is
another story, and I will only say that we had
a day in Edgeworthstown and a drive through
Goldsmith's country, where we saw the Deserted
Village, with its mill and brook, the " church
that tops the neighboring hill ; " and even rested
under

> " The hawthorn bush with seats beneath the shade
> For talking age and whispering lovers made."

There are many parts of Ireland where one
could not find a habitable house to rent, but in this

locality they are numerous enough to make it possible to choose. We had driven over perhaps twenty square miles of country, with the view of selecting the most delectable spot that could be found, without going too far from Rosnaree. The chief trouble was that we always desired every dwelling that we saw. I tell you this with a view of lessening the shock when I confess that, before we came to the Old Hall where we are now settled for a month, and which was Salemina's choice, Francesca and I took two different houses, and lived in them for seven days, each in solitary splendor, like the Prince of Coolavin. It was not difficult to agree upon the district, we were of one mind there; the moment that we passed the town and drove along the flowery way that leads to Devorgilla, we knew that it was the road of destiny.

The white thorn is very late this year, and we found ourselves in the full glory of it. It is beautiful in all its stages, from the time when it first opens its buds, to the season when "every spray is white with May, and blooms the eglantine." There is no hint of green leaf visible then, and every tree is "as white as the snow of one night." This is the Gaelic comparison, and the first snow seems especially white and dazzling, I suppose, when one sees it in the morning where were green fields the night before. The sloe, which is the blackthorn, comes still earlier and

has fewer leaves. That is the tree of the old
English song : —

> " From the white-blossomed sloe
>   My dear Chloe requested
>   A sprig her fair breast to adorn.
> ' No, by Heav'ns ! ' I exclaimed, ' may I perish,
>   If ever I plant in that bosom a thorn ! ' "

And it is not only trees, but hedges and bushes
and groves of hawthorn, for a white thorn bush
is seldom if ever cut down here, lest a grieved and
displeased fairy look up from the cloven trunk,
and no Irishman could bear to meet the reproach
of her eyes. Do not imagine, however, that we
are all in white, like a bride : there is the pink
hawthorn, and there are pink and white horse-
chestnuts laden with flowers, yellow laburnums
hanging over whitewashed farm buildings, lilacs,
and, most wonderful of all, the blaze of the yellow gorse. There will be a thorn hedge struggling
with and conquering a gray stone wall ; then a
golden gorse bush struggling with and conquering the thorn ; seeking the sun, it knows no re-
straints, and creeping through the barriers of
green and white and gray, it fairly hurls its yellow
splendors in great blazing patches along the wayside. In dazzling glory, in richness of color,
there is nothing in nature that we can compare
with this loveliest and commonest of all wayside
weeds. The gleaming wealth of the Klondike
would make but a poor showing beside a single

Irish hedgerow; one would think that Mother
Earth had stored in her bosom all the sunniest
gleams of bygone summers, and was now giving
them back to the sun king from whom she bor-
rowed them.

It was at twilight when we first swam this fragrant golden sea, — twilight, and the birds were
singing in every bush ; the thrushes and blackbirds in the blossoming cherry and chestnut
trees were so many and so tuneful that the chorus
was sweet and strong beyond anything I ever
heard. There had been a shower or two, of
course ; showers that looked like shimmering curtains of silver gauze, and whether they lifted or
fell the birds went on singing.

" I did not believe such a thing possible, but it
is lovelier than Pettybaw," said Francesca ; and
just here we came in sight of a pink cottage cud-
dling on the breast of a hill. Pink the cottage
was, as if it had been hewed out of a coral branch
or the heart of a salmon ; pink-washed were the
stone walls and posts ; pink even were the chim-
neys ; a green lattice over the front was the only
leaf in the bouquet. Wallflowers grew against
the pink stone walls, and there is no beautiful
word in any beautiful language that can describe
the effect of that modest rose-hued dwelling
blushing against a background of heather-brown
hills covered solidly with golden gorse bushes in
full bloom. Himself and I have always agreed

to spend our anniversaries with Mrs. Bobby at Comfort Cottage, in England, or at Bide-a-Wee, the "wee theekit hoosie" in the loaning at Petty-baw, for our little love story was begun in the one and carried on in the other; but this, this, I thought instantly, must somehow be crowded into the scheme of red-letter days. And now we suddenly discovered something at once interesting and disconcerting, — an American flag floating from a tree in the background.

"The place is rented, then," said Francesca, "to some enterprising American or some star-spangled Irishman who has succeeded in dis-covering Devorgilla before us. I well understand how the shade of Columbus must feel whenever Amerigo Vespucci's name is mentioned!"

We sent the driver off to await our pleasure, and held a consultation by the wayside.

"I shall call, at any rate," I announced; "any excuse will serve which brings me nearer to that adorable dwelling. I intend to be standing in that pink doorway, with that green lattice over my head, when Himself arrives in Devorgilla. I intend to end my days within those rosy walls, and to begin the process at the earliest possible moment."

Salemina disapproved, of course. Her method is always to stand well in the rear, trembling be-forehand lest I should do something unconven-tional; then, later on, when things romantic begin to transpire, she says delightedly, " Was n't that clever of us ? "

" An American flag," I urged, "is a proclamation ; indeed, it is, in a sense, an invitation ; besides it is my duty to salute it in a foreign land ! "

"Patriotism, how many sins are practiced in thy name ! " said Salemina satirically. " Can't you salute your flag from the highroad ? "

" Not properly, Sally dear, nor satisfactorily. So you and Francesca sit down, timidly and respectably, under the safe shadow of the hedge, while I call upon the blooming family in the darling blooming house. I am an American artist, lured to their door alike by devotion to my country's flag and love of the picturesque." And so saying I ascended the path with some dignity and a false show of assurance.

The circumstances did not chance to be precisely what I had expected. There was a nice girl tidying the kitchen, and I found no difficulty in making friends with her. Her mother owned the cottage, and rented it every season to a Belfast lady, who was coming in a week to take possession, as usual. The American flag had been floating in honor of her mother's brother, who had come over from Milwaukee to make them a little visit, and had just left that afternoon to sail from Liverpool. The rest of the family lived, during the three summer months, in a

smaller house down the road ; but she herself
always stayed at the cottage, to "mind" the Belfast lady's children.

When I looked at the pink floor of the kitchen
and the view from the windows, I would have
given anything in the world to outbid, yes, even
to obliterate the Belfast lady ; but this, unfortunately was not only illegal and immoral, but it
was impossible.   So, calling the mother in from
the stables, I succeeded, after fifteen minutes'
persuasion, in getting permission to occupy the
house for one week, beginning with the next morning, and returned in triumph to my weary consti-
tuents, who thought it an insane idea.

"Of course it is," I responded cheerfully :
"that is why it is going to be so altogether charming.   Don't be envious ; I will find something
mad for you to do, too.   One of us is always
submitting to the will of the majority ; now
let us be as individually silly as we like for a
week, and then take a long farewell of freakish-
ness and freedom.   Let the third volume die
in lurid splendor, since there is never to be a
fourth."

"There is still Wales," suggested Francesca.

"Too small, Fanny dear, and we could never
pronounce the names.   Besides, what sort of
adventures would be possible to three — I mean,
of course, two — persons tied down by marital
responsibilities and family cares ?   Is it the sun-

set or the reflection of the pink house that is shining on your pink face, Salemina?"

"I am extremely warm," she replied haughtily.

"I don't wonder; sitting on the damp grass under a hedge is so stimulating to the circulation!" observed "young Miss Fan."

XXVII

THE THREE CHATELAINES OF DEVORGILLA

" Have you been at Devorgilla,
  Have you seen, at Devorgilla,
Beauty's train trip o 'er the plain, —
  The lovely maids of Devorgilla ? "
Adapted from Edward Lysaght.

THE next morning the Old Hall dropped like a ripe rowan berry into our very laps. The landlord of the Shamrock Inn directed us thither, and within the hour it belonged to us for the rest of the summer. Miss Peabody, inclined to be severe with me for my desertion, took up her residence at once. It had never been rented before ; but Miss Llewellyn-Joyce, the owner, had suddenly determined to visit her sister in London, and was glad to find appreciative and careful tenants. She was taking her own maid with her, and thus only one servant remained, to be rented with the premises, as is frequently the Irish fashion. The Old Hall has not always been managed thus economically, it is easy to see, and Miss Llewellyn-Joyce speaks with the utmost candor of her poverty, as indeed the ruined Irish gentry always do. I well remember taking tea with a family in

West Clare where in default of a spoon, the old squire stirred his cup with the poker, a proceeding apparently so usual that he never thought of apologizing for it as an oddity.

The Hall has a lodge, which is a sort of miniature Round Tower, at the entrance gate, and we see nothing for it but to import a brass-buttoned boy from the nearest metropolis, where we must also send for a second maid.

" That 'll do when you get him," objected Benella, " though boys need a lot of overseeing ; but as nobody can get in or come out o' that gate without help, I shall have to go to the lodge every day now, and set down there with my sewin' from four to six in the afternoon, or whenever the callin' hours is. When I engaged with you, it was n't for any particular kind of work ; it was to make myself useful. I 've been errand boy and courier, golf caddie and footman, beau, cook, land agent, and mother to you all, and I guess I can be a lodge keeper as well as not."

Francesca had her choice of residing either with Salemina or with me, during our week of separation, and drove in my company to Rosaleen Cottage, to make up her mind. While she was standing at my gate, engaged in reflection, she espied a small cabin not far away, and walked toward it on a tour of investigation. It proved to have three tiny rooms, — a bedroom, sitting-room, and kitchen. The rent was only two pounds a month, it is true, but it was in all respects the most unattractive, poverty-stricken, undesirable dwelling I ever saw. It was the small stove in the kitchen that kindled Francesca's imagination, and she made up her mind instantly to become a householder on her own account. I tried to dissuade her; but she is as firm as the Rock of Cashel when once she has set her heart upon anything.

"I shall be almost your next-door neighbor, Penelope," she coaxed, "and of course you will give me Benella. She will sleep in the sitting-room, and I will do the cooking. The landlady says there is no trouble about food. 'What to ate?' she inquired, leaning out sociably over the half-door. 'Sure it'll drive up to your very doore jist.' And here is the 'wee grass,' as she calls it, where 'yous can take your tay' under the Japanese umbrella left by the last tenant. Think how unusual it will be for us to live in three different houses for a week; and 'there's luck in odd numbers, says Rory O'More.' We shall have the advantages of good society, too, when we are living apart, for I foresee entertainment after entertainment. We will give breakfasts, luncheons, teas, and dinners to one another; and meanwhile I shall have learned all the housewifely arts. Think, too, how much better you can paint with me out of your way!"

"Does no thought of your eccentricity blight your young spirit, dear?"

"Why should it when I have simply shaped my course by yours?"

"But I am married, my child."

"And I'm 'going to be married, Aha! Mamma!' as the song says; and what about Salemina, you have n't scolded her?"

"She is living her very last days of single blessedness," I rejoined; "she does not know it, but she is; and I want to give her all the freedom possible. Very well, dear innocent, live in your wee hut, then, if you can persuade Benella to stay with you; but I think there would best be no public visiting between you and those who live in Rosaleen Cottage and the Old Hall, as it might ruin their social position."

Benella confessed that she had not the heart to refuse Francesca anything. "She's too handsome," she said, "and too winnin'. I s'pose she'll cook up some dreadful messes, but I'm willin' to eat 'em, to oblige her, and perhaps it'll save her husband a few spells of dyspepsy at the start; though as far as my experience goes, ministers 'll always eat anything that's set before 'em, and look over their shoulders for more."

We had a heavenly week of silliness, and by dint of concealing our real relations from the general public I fancy we escaped harsh criticism. There is a very large percentage of lunacy anyway in Ireland, as well as great leniency of public opinion, and I fancy there is scarcely a country on the map in which one could be more foolish without being found out. Visit each other we did constantly, and candor obliges me to state that, though each of us secretly prided herself on the perfection of her cuisine, Miss Monroe gave the most successful afternoon tea of all, on the "wee grass," under the Japanese umbrella. How unexpectedly good were her scones, her tea-cakes, and her cress sandwiches, and how pretty and graceful and womanly she was, all flushed with pride at our envy and approbation ! I did a water color sketch of her and sent it to Ronald, receiving in return a letter bubbling over with fond admiration and gratitude. She seems always in tone with the season and the landscape, does Francesca, and she arrives at it unconsciously, too. She glances out of her window at the yellow laburnum tree when she is putting on her white frock, and it suggests to her all her amber trinkets and her drooping hat with the wreath of buttercups. When she came to my hawthorn luncheon at Rosaleen Cottage she did not make the mistake of heaping pink on pink, but wore a cotton gown of palest green, with a bunch of rosy blossoms at her belt. I painted her just as she stood under the hawthorn, with its fluttering petals and singing birds, calling the picture Gráinné Mael : [1] A Vision of Erinn, writing under it the verse : —

[1] Pronounced Graunia Wael, the M being modified. It is one of the endearing names given to Ireland in the Penal Times.

" The thrushes seen in bushes green are singing loud —
   Bid sadness go and gladness glow, — give welcome proud !
The Rover comes, the Lover, whom you long bewail,
O'er sunny seas, with honey breeze, to Gráinné Mael."

Benella, I fancy, never had so varied a week in
her life, and she was in her element. We were
obliged to hire a side car by the day, as two of
our residences were over a mile apart; and the
driver of that vehicle was the only person, I think,
who had any suspicion of our sanity. In the
intervals of teaching Francesca cooking, and eating the results while the cook herself prudently
lunched or dined with her friends, Benella "spring-
cleaned" the lodge at the Old Hall, scrubbed the
gateposts, mended stone walls, weeded garden
beds, made bags for the brooms and dusters and
mattresses, burned coffee and camphor and other
ill-smelling things in all the rooms, and devoted
considerable time to superintending my little
maid, that I might not feel neglected. We were
naturally obliged, meanwhile, to wait upon ourselves and keep our frocks in order ; but as long
as the Derelict was so busy and happy, and so
devoted to the universal good, it would have been
churlish and ungrateful to complain.

On leaving the Wee Hut, as Francesca had,
with ostentatious modesty, named her residence,
she paid her landlady two pounds, and was dis-
comfited when the exuberant and impetuous
woman embraced her in a paroxysm of weeping
gratitude.

"I cannot understand, Penelope, why she was so disproportionately grateful, for I only gave her five shillings over the two pounds rent."

"Yes, dear," I responded dryly; "but you remember that the rent was for the month, and you paid her two pounds five shillings for the week."

All the rest of that day Francesca was angelic. She brought footstools for Salemina, wound wool for her, insisted upon washing my paint brushes, read aloud to us while we were working, and offered to be the one to discharge Benella if the awful moment for that surgical operation should ever come. Finally, just as we were about to separate for the night, she said, with insinuating sweetness, "You won't tell Ronald about my mistake with the rent money, will you, dearest and darlingest girls?"

We are now quite ready to join in all the gayeties that may ensue when Rosnaree welcomes its master and his guests. Our page in buttons at the lodge gives Benella full scope for her administrative ability, which seems to have sprung into being since she entered our service; at least, if I except that evidence of it which she displayed in managing us when first we met. She calls our page "the Button Boy," and makes his life a burden to him by taking him away from his easy duties at the gate, covering his livery with baggy overalls, and setting him to weed the garden. It can never, in the nature of things, be made free from weeds during our brief term of tenancy, but Benella cleverly keeps her slave at work on the beds and the walks that are the most conspicuous to visitors. The Old Hall used simply to be called "Aunt David's house" by the Welsh Joyces, and it was Aunt David herself who made the garden; she who traced the lines of the flower beds with the ivory tip of her parasol; she who planned the quaint stone gateways and arbors and hedge seats; she who devised the interminable stretches of paths, the labyrinthine walks, the mazes, and the hidden flower plots. You walk on and on between high hedges, until, if you have not missed your way, you presently find a little pansy or rose or lily garden. It is quite the most unexpected and piquant method of laying out a place I have ever seen; and the only difficulty about it is that any gardener, unless he were possessed of unusual sense of direction, would be continually astray in it. The Button Boy, obeying the laws of human nature, is lost in two minutes, but requires two hours in which to find himself. Benella suspects that he prefers this wandering to and fro to the more monotonous task of weeding, and it is no uncommon thing for her to pursue the recalcitrant page through the mazes and labyrinths for an hour at a time, and perhaps lose herself in the end. Salemina and I were sitting this morning in the Peacock Walk, where two trees clipped into the shape of long-tailed birds mount guard over the box hedge, and put their beaks together to form an arch. In the dim distance we could see Benella "bagging" the Button Boy, and, after putting the trowel and rake in his reluctant hands, tying the free end of a ball of string to his leg, and sending him to find and weed the pansy garden. We laughed until the echoes rang, to see him depart, dragging his lengthening chain, or his Ariadne thread, behind him, while Benella grimly held the ball, determined that no excuses or apologies should interfere with his work on this occasion.

XXVIII

ROUND TOWERS AND REFLECTIONS

"On Lough Neagh's banks, as the fisherman strays,
    When the cool, calm eve's declining,
He sees the round towers of other days
    Beneath the waters shining."

Thomas Moore.

A DUBLIN car driver told me, one day, that he had just taken a picnic party to the borders of a lake, where they had had tea in a tram car which had been placed there for such purposes. Francesca and I were amused at the idea, but did not think of it again until we drove through the La Touche estate, on one of the first days after our arrival at Devorgilla. We left Salemina at Rosnaree House with Aunt La Touche and the children, and proceeded to explore the grounds, with the view of deciding on certain improvements to be made when the property passes, so to speak, into our hands.

Truth to say, nature has done more for it than we could have done; and if it is a trifle overgrown and rough and rank, it could hardly be more beautiful. At the very farthest confines

of the demesne there is a brook, — large enough,
indeed, to be called a river here, where they have
no Mississippi to dwarf all other streams and
serve as an impossible standard of comparison.
Tall trees droop over the calm water, and on its
margins grow spearwort, opening its big yellow
cups to the sunshine, meadow rue, purple and
yellow loosestrife, bog bean, and sweet flag.
Here and there float upon the surface the round
leaves and delicate white blossoms of the frog-
bit, together with lilies, pondweeds, and water
starworts.

"What an idyllic place to sit and read, or sew,
or have tea!" exclaimed Francesca.

"What a place for a tram tea-house!" I added.
"Do you suppose we could manage it as a surprise to Dr. La Touche, in return for all his kindness?"

"It would cost a pretty penny, I fear," said
Francesca prudently, "though it isn't as if it
were going out of the family. Now that there is
no longer any need for you to sell pictures, I suppose you could dash off one in an hour or two
that would buy a tram; and papa cabled me yesterday, you know, to draw on him freely. I used
to think, whenever he said that, that he would
marry again within the week; but I did him injustice. A tram tea-house by the river, —
wouldn't it be unique? Do let us see what we

can do about it through some of our Dublin acquaintances."

The plan proved unexpectedly easy to carry
out, and not ruinously extravagant, either ; for
our friend the American consul knew the principal director in a tram company, and a dilapidated
and discarded car was sent to us in a few days.
There were certain moments — once when we
saw that it had not been painted for twenty years,
once when the freight bill was handed us, and
again when we contracted for the removal of our
gift from the station to the river bank — when
we regretted the fertility of imagination that had
led us to these lengths ; but when we finally saw
the car by the water side, there was no room left
for regret.   Benella said that, with the assistance
of the Button Boy, she could paint it easily herself ; but we engaged an expert, who put on a
coat of dark green very speedily, and we con-
soled the Derelict with the suggestion that she
cover the cushions and make the interior cosy
and pretty.

All this happened some little time ago.   Dr.
La Touche has been at home for a fortnight, and
we have had to use the greatest ingenuity to keep
people away from that particular spot, which, fortunately for us, is a secluded one.   All is ready
now, however, and the following cards of invitation have been issued : —

*The honor of your presence
is requested at the
Opening of the New Tea Tram
On the River Bank, Rosnaree Desmesne,
Wednesday, June 27th, at 4 p. m.
The ceremony will be performed by
H. R. H. Salemina Peabody.
The Bishop of Ossory in the Chair.*

I have just learned that a certain William Beresford was Bishop of Ossory once on a time, and
I intend to personate this dignitary, clad in Dr.
La Touche's cap and gown.   We spent this sunny
morning by the river bank ; Francesca hemming
the last of the yellow window curtains, and I
making souvenir programmes for the great occasion.   Salemina had gone for the day with the
Colquhouns and Dr. La Touche to lunch with
some people near Kavan and see Donaghmore
Round Tower and the moat.

"Is she in love with Dr. Gerald ? " asked Francesca suddenly, looking up from her work.   " Was
she ever in love with him ?   She must have been,
must n't she ?   I cannot and will not entertain
any other conviction."

"I don't know, my dear," I answered thoughtfully, pausing over an initial letter I was illuminating ; " but I can't imagine what we shall do if
we have to tear down our sweet little romance,
bit by bit, and leave the stupid couple sitting in
the ruins.   They enjoy ruins far too well al-

ready, and it would be just like their obstinacy
to go on sitting in them."

"And they are so incredibly slow about it all,"
Francesca commented. "It took me about two
minutes, at Lady Baird's dinner where I first met
Ronald, to decide that I would marry him as
soon as possible. When a month had gone by,
and he had n't asked me, I thought, like Beatrice,
that I 'd as lief be wooed of a snail."

"I was not quite so expeditious as you," I
confessed, "though I believe Himself says that
his feeling was instantaneous. I never cared for
anything but painting before I met him, so I
never chanced to suffer any of those pangs that
lovelorn maidens are said to feel when the beloved delays his avowals : perhaps that is the
reason I suffer so much now, vicariously."

"The lack of positive information makes one
so impatient," Francesca went on. "I am sure
he is as fond of her as ever ; but if she refused
him when he was young and handsome, with
every prospect of a brilliant career before him,
perhaps he thinks he has even less chance now.
He was the first to forget their romance, and the
one to marry ; his estates have been wasted by
his father's legal warfares, and he has been an
unhappy and a disappointed man. Now he has
to beg her to heal his wounds, as it were, and to
accept the care and responsibility of his children."

"It is very easy to see that we are not the only ones who suspect his sentiments," I said, smiling at my thoughts. "Mrs. Colquhoun told me that she and Salemina stopped at one of the tenants' cabins, the other day, to leave some small comforts that Dr. La Touche had sent to a sick child. The woman thanked Salemina, and Mrs. Colquhoun heard her say, 'When a man will stop, coming in the doore, an' stoop down to give a sthroke and a scratch to the pig's back, depend on it, ma'am, him that's so friendly with a poor fellow crathur will make ye a good husband.'"

"I have given him every opportunity to confide in me," I continued, after a pause, "but he accepts none of them ; and yet I like him a thousand times better now that I have seen him as the master of his own house. He is so courtly, and, in these latter days, so genial and sunny. . . . Salemina's life would not at first be any too easy, I fear ; the aunt is very feeble, and the establishment is so neglected. I went into Dr. Gerald's study the other day to see an old print, and there was a *buzz-buzz-zzzz* when the butler pulled up the blinds. 'Do you mind bees, ma'am?' he asked blandly. 'There's been a swarm of them in one corner of the ceiling for manny years, an' we don't like to disturb them.' . . . Benella said yesterday : 'Of course, when you three separate, I shall stay with the one that needs me most ; but if

Miss Peabody *should* settle over here anywhere, I'd like to take a scrubbing brush an' go through the castle, or whatever she's going to live in, with soap and sand and ammonia, and make it water-sweet before she sets foot in it.' . . . As for the children, however, no one could regard them as a drawback, for they are altogether charming; not well disciplined, of course, but lovable to the last degree. Broona was planning her future life when we were walking together yesterday. Jackeen is to be an 'engineer, by the sea,' so it seems, and Broona is to be a farmer's wife with a tiny red bill-book like Mrs. Colquhoun's. Her little boys and girls will sell the milk, and when Jackeen has his engineering holidays he will come and eat fresh butter and scones and cream and jam at the farm, and when her children have their holidays they will go and play on 'Jackeen's beach.' It is the little people I rely upon chiefly, after all. I wish you could have seen them cataract down the staircase to greet her, this morning. I notice that she tries to make me divert their attention when Dr. Gerald is present; for it is a bit suggestive to a widower to see his children pursue, hang about, and caress a lovely, unmarried lady. Broona, especially, can hardly keep away from Salemina; and she is such a fascinating midget, I should think anybody would be glad to have her included in a marriage contract. 'You have a weeny, weeny line between your eye-

brows, just like my daddy's,' she said to Salemina
the other day. ' It 's such a little one, perhaps I
can kiss it away ; but daddy has too many, and
they are cutted too deep. Sometimes he whispers, "Daddy is sad, Broona ;" and then I say,
"Play up, play up, and play the game ! " and that
makes him smile.' "

"She is a darling," said Francesca, with the
suspicion of a tear in her eye. ' Were you ever in
love, Miss Fancy ? ' she asked me once. ' I was ;
it was long, long ago before I belonged to daddy ;'
and another time when I had been reading to
her, she said, ' I often think that when I get into
the kingdom of heaven the person I 'll be glad-
dest to see will be Marjorie Fleming.' Yes, the
children are sure to help ; they always do in whatever circumstances they chance to be placed. Did
you notice Salemina with them at tea time, yesterday ? It was such a charming scene. The heavy
rain had kept them in, and things had gone wrong
in the nursery. Salemina had glued the hair
on Broona's dolly, and knit up a heart-breaking
wound in her side. Then she mended the legs
of all the animals in the Noah's ark, so that they
stood firm, erect, and proud ; and when, to draw
the children's eyes from the wet window-panes,
she proposed a story, it was pretty to see the grateful youngsters snuggle in her lap and by her
side."

"When does an artist ever fail to see pictures ?
I have loved Salemina always, even when she

used to part her hair in the middle and wear
spectacles; but that is the first time I ever wanted
to paint her, with the firelight shining on the soft
restful grays and violets of her dress, and Broona
in her arms. Of course, if a woman is ever to be
lovely at all, it will be when she is holding a child.
It is the oldest of all old pictures, and the most
beautiful, I believe, in a man's eyes."

"And do you notice that she and the doctor
are beginning to speak more freely of their past
acquaintance?" I went on, looking up at Francesca, who had dropped her work, in her interest.
"It is too amusing! Every hour or two it is:
'Do you remember the day we went to Bunker
Hill?' or, 'Do you recall that charming Mrs.
Andrews, with whom we used to dine occasionally?' or, 'What has become of your cousin Samuel?' and, 'Is your uncle Thomas yet living?'
. . . The other day, at tea, she asked, 'Do you
still take three lumps, Dr. La Touche? You had
always a sweet tooth, I remember.' . . . Then
they ring the changes in this way: 'You were always fond of gray, Miss Peabody.' 'You had a
great fancy for Moore, in the old days, Miss Peabody: have you outgrown him, or does the "Ana-
creontic little chap," as Father Prout called him,
still appeal to you?' . . . 'You used to admire
Boyle O'Reilly, Dr. La Touche. Would you like
to see some of his letters?' . . . 'Are n't these
magnificent rhododendrons, Dr. La Touche, —
even though they are magenta, the color you spe-

cially dislike ? ' And so on.   Did you chance to
look at either of them last evening, Francesca,
when I sang 'Let Erin remember the days of
old ' ? "

"No ; I was thinking of something else.   I
don't know what there is about your singing,
Penny love, that always makes me think of the
past and dream of the future.   Which verse do
you mean ? "

And, still painting, I hummed : —

> "'On Lough Neagh's banks, as the fisherman strays,
>   When the cool calm eve 's declining,
> He sees the round towers of other days
>   Beneath the waters shining.
>
> . . . .
>
> ' Thus shall memory oft, in dreams sublime,
>   Catch a glimpse of the days that are over,
> And, sighing, look thro' the waves of Time,
>   For the long-faded glories they cover.'

"That is what our two dear middle-aged lovers
are constantly doing now, — looking at the round
towers of other days, as they bend over memory's
crystal pool and see them reflected there.   It is
because he fears that the glories are over and gone
that Dr. Gerald is troubled.   Some day he will
realize that he need not live on reflections, and
he will seek realities."

"I hope so," said Francesca philosophically,
as she folded her work ; "but sometimes these
people who go mooning about, and looking
through the waves of Time, tumble in and are
drowned."

XXIX

AUNT DAVID'S GARDEN

> " O wind, O mighty, melancholy wind,
>   Blow through me, blow !
>   Thou blowest forgotten things into my mind,
>   From long ago."
>
> *John Todhunter.*

No one ever had a better opportunity than we, of breathing in, so far as a stranger and a foreigner may, the old Celtic atmosphere, and of relieving the misty years of legend before the dawn of history ; when

> " Long, long ago, beyond the space
>   Of twice two hundred years,
>   In Erin old there lived a race
>   Taller than Roman spears."

Mr. Colquhoun is one of the best Gaelic scholars in Ireland, and Dr. Gerald, though not his equal in knowledge of the language, has " the full of a sack of stories " in his head. According to the Book of Leinster, a professional story-teller was required to know seven times fifty tales, and I believe the doctor could easily pass this test. It is not easy to make a good translation from Irish to English, for they tell us there are no two Aryan languages more opposed to each other in spirit and idiom. We have heard little of the marvelous old tongue until now, but we are reading it a bit under the tutelage of these two inspiring masters, and I fancy it has helped me as much in my understanding of Ireland as my tedious and perplexing worriments over political problems.

After all, how can we know anything of a nation's present or future without some attempt to revivify its past? Just as, without some slender knowledge of its former culture, we must be forever ignorant of its inherited powers and aptitudes. The harp that once through Tara's halls the soul of music shed, now indeed hangs mute on Tara's walls, but for all that its echoes still reverberate in the listening ear.

When we sit together by the river brink, on sunny days, or on the greensward under the yews in our old garden, we are always telling ancient Celtic romances, and planning, even acting, new ones. Francesca's mind and mine are poorly furnished with facts of any sort; but when the kind scholars in our immediate neighborhood furnish necessary information and inspiration, we promptly turn it into dramatic form, and serve it up before their wondering and admiring gaze. It is ever our habit to " make believe " with the children ; and just as we played ballads in Scotland and plotted revels in the Glen at Rowardennan, so we instinctively fall into the habit of thought and speech that surrounds us here.

This delights our grave and reverend signiors, and they give themselves up to our whimsicalities with the most whole-hearted zeal. It is days since we have spoken of one another by those names which were given to us in baptism. Francesca is Finola the Festive. Eveleen Colquhoun is Ethnea. I am the harper, Péarla the Melodious. Miss Peabody is Sheela the Skillful Scribe, who keeps for posterity a record of all our antics, in The Speckled Book of Salemina. Dr. Gerald is Borba the Proud, the Ard-ri or overking. Mr. Colquhoun is really called Dermod, but he would have been far too modest to choose Dermot O'Dyna for his Celtic name, had we not insisted ; for this historic personage was not only noble-minded, generous, of untarnished honor, and the bravest of the brave, but he was as handsome as he was gallant, and so much the idol of the ladies that he was sometimes called Dermat-na-man, or Dermot of the women.

Of course we have a corps of shanachies, or story-tellers, gleemen, gossipreds, leeches, druids, gallowglasses, bards, ollaves, urraghts, and brehons ; but the children can always be shifted from one rôle to another, and Benella and the Button Boy, although they are quite unaware of the honors conferred upon them, are often alluded to in our romances and theatrical productions.

Aunt David's garden is not a half bad substitute for the old Moy-Mell, the plain of pleasure of the ancient Irish, when once you have the key to its treasures. We have made a new and authoritative survey of its geographical features and compiled a list of its legendary landmarks, which, strangely enough, seem to have been absolutely unknown to Miss Llewellyn-Joyce.

In the very centre is the Forradh, or Place of Meeting, and on it is our own Lia Fail, Stone of Destiny. The one in Westminster Abbey, carried away from Scotland by Edward I., is thought by many scholars to be unauthentic, and we hope that ours may prove to have some historical value. The only test of a Stone of Destiny, as I understand it, is that it shall "roar" when an Irish monarch is inaugurated ; and that our Lia Fail was silent when we celebrated this impressive ceremony reflects less upon its own powers, perhaps, than upon the pedigree of our chosen Ard-ri.

The arbor under the mountain ash is the Fairy Palace of the Quicken Tree, and on its walls is suspended the Horn of Foreknowledge, which if any one looks on it in the morning, fasting, he will know in a moment all things that are to happen during that day.

The clump of willows is the Wood of the Many Sallows (a willow tree is familiarly known as a " sally " in Ireland). Do you know Yeats's song, put to a quaint old Irish air ?

" Down by the sally gardens my love and I did meet,
   She passed the sally gardens with little snow white feet.
   She bid me take love easy, as the leaves grow on the tree,
   But I, being young and foolish, with her did not agree."

The summer house is the Greenan ; that is,
grianán, a bright, sunny place. On the arm of a
tree in the Greenan hangs something you might
(if you are dull) mistake for a plaited garland of
rushes hung with pierced pennies ; but it really is
our Chain of Silence, a useful article of bygone
ages, which the lord of a mansion shook when he
wished an attentive hearing, and which deserved
a better fate and a longer survival than it has met.
Jackeen's Irish terrier is Bran, — though she does
not closely resemble the great Finn's sweet-voiced,
gracefully-shaped, long-snouted hound ; the coracle lying on the shore of the little lough — the
coracle made of skin, like the old Irish boats —
is the Wave-Sweeper ; and the faithful mare that
we hire by the day is, by your leave, Enbarr of
the Flowing Mane. No warrior was ever killed
on the back of this famous steed, for she was as
swift as the clear, cold wind of spring, traveling
with equal ease and speed on land and sea, an'
may the divil fly away wid me if that same 's not
true.

We no longer find any difficulty in remembering all this nomenclature, for we are "under
gesa" to use no other. When you are put under
gesa to reveal or to conceal, to defend or to

avenge, it is a sort of charm or spell; also an obligation of honor. Finola is under gesa not to write to Alba more than six times a week and twice on Sundays; Sheela is bound by the same charm to give us muffins for afternoon tea; I am vowed to forget my husband when I am relating romances, and allude to myself, for dramatic purposes, as a maiden princess, or a maiden of enchanting and all-conquering beauty. And if we fail to abide by all these laws of the modern Dedannans of Devorgilla, which are written in The Speckled Book of Salemina, we are to pay eric-fine. These fines are collected with all possible solemnity, and the children delight in them to such an extent that occasionally they break the law for the joy of the penalty. If you have ever read The Fate of the Children of Turenn, you remember that they were to pay to Luga the following eric-fine for the slaying of their father, Kian: two steeds and a chariot, seven pigs, a hound whelp, a cooking spit, and three shouts on a hill. This does not at first seem excessive, if Kian were a good father, and sincerely mourned; but when Luga began to explain the hidden snares that lay in the pathway, it is small wonder that the sons of Turenn felt doubt of ever being able to pay it, and that when, after surmounting all the previous obstacles, they at last raised three feeble shouts on Midkena's Hill, they immediately gave up the ghost.

The story told yesterday by Sheela the Scribe was The Magic Thread-Clue, or The Pursuit of the Gilla Dacker, Benella and the Button Boy being the chief characters ; Finola's was The Voyage of the Children of Corr the Swift-Footed (the Ard-ri's pseudonym for American travelers); while mine, to be told to-morrow, is called The Quest of the Fair Strangers, or The Fairy Quicken Tree of Devorgilla.

<h1 style="text-align:center">XXX</h1>

THE QUEST OF THE FAIR STRANGERS, OR THE FAIRY QUICKEN TREE OF DEVORGILLA [1]

> " Before the King
> The bards will sing,
> And there recall the stories all
> That give renown to Ireland."
> *Eighteenth Century Song,*
> *Englished by George Sigerson.*

PEARLA'S STORY

THREE maidens once dwelt in a castle in that part of the Isle of Weeping known as the cantred of Devorgilla, or Devorgilla of the Green Hill Slopes ; and they were baptized according to druidical rites as Sheela the Scribe, Finola the Festive, and Péarla the Melodious, though by the dwellers in that land they were called the

---

[1] It seems probable that this tale records a real incident which took place in Aunt David's garden. Penelope has apparently listened with such attention to the old Celtic romances as told by the Ard-ri and Dermot O'Dyna that she has, consciously or unconsciously, reproduced something of their atmosphere and phraseology. The delightful surprise at the end must have been contrived by Salemina, when she, in her character of Sheela the Scribe, gazed into the Horn of Foreknowledge and learned the events that were to happen that day. — K. D. W.

Fair Strangers, or the Children of Corr the Swift-Footed.

This cantred of Devorgilla they acquired by paying rent and tribute to the Wise Woman of Wales, who granted them to fish in its crystal streams and to hunt over the green-sided hills, to roam through the woods of yew trees and to pluck the flowers of every hue that were laughing all over the plains.

Thus were they circumstanced: Their palace of abode was never without three shouts in it, — the shout of the maidens brewing tea, the shout of the guests drinking it, and the shout of the assembled multitude playing at their games. The same house was never without three measures, — a measure of magic malt for raising the spirits, a measure of Attic salt for the seasoning of tales, and a measure of poppy leaves to induce sleep when the tales were dull.

And the manner of their lives was this: In the cool of the morning they gathered nuts and arbutus apples and scarlet quicken berries to take back with them to Tir-thar-toinn, the Country beyond the Wave; for this was the land of their birth. When the sun was high in the east they went forth to the chase; sometimes it was to hunt the Ard-ri, and at others it was in pursuit of Dermot of the Bright Face. Then, after resting awhile on their couches of soft rushes, they would perform champion feats, or play on their harps, or fish in their clear-flowing streams that were swimming with salmon.

The manner of their fishing was this: to cut a long, straight sallow-tree rod, and having fastened a hook and one of Finola's hairs upon it, to put a quicken-tree berry upon the hook, and stand on the brink of the swift-flowing river, whence they drew out the shining-skinned, silver-sided salmon. These they would straightway broil over a little fire of birch boughs; and they needed with them no other food but the magical loaf made by Toma, one of their house servants. The witch hag that dwelt on that hillside of Rosnaree called Fan-na-carpat, or the Slope of the Chariots, had cast a druidical spell over Toma, by which she was able to knead a loaf that would last twenty days and twenty nights, and one mouthful of which would satisfy hunger for that length of time.[1]

Not far from the mayden castle was a certain royal palace, with a glittering roof, and the name of the palace was Rosnaree. And upon the level green in front of the regal abode, or in the banqueting halls, might always be seen noble companies of knights and ladies bright, — some feasting, some playing at the chess, some giving ear to the music of their own harps, some continually shaking the Chain of Silence, and some listening to the poems and tales of heroes of the olden

[1] Fact.

time that were told by the king's bards and shanachies.

Now all went happily with the Fair Strangers until the crimson berries were ripening on the quicken tree near the Fairy Palace. For the berries possessed secret virtues known only to a man of the Dedannans, and learned from him by Sheela the Scribe, who put him under gesa not to reveal the charm to any one else. Whosoever ate of the honey-sweet, scarlet-glowing fruit felt a cheerful flow of spirits, as if he had tasted wine or mead, and whosoever ate a sufficient number of them was almost certain to grow younger. These things were written in The Speckled Book of Salemina, but in druidical ink, undecipherable to all eyes but those of the Scribe herself.

So, wishing that none should possess the secret but themselves, the Fair Strangers set the Gilla Dacker [1] to watch the fruit (putting him first under gesa to eat none of the berries himself, since he was already too cheerful and too young to be of much service); and thus, in their absence the magical tree was never left alone.

Nevertheless, when Finola the Festive went forth to the chase one day, she found a quicken berry glowing like a ruby in the highroad, and Sheela plucked a second from under a gnarled thorn on the Slope of the Chariots, and Péarla discovered a third in the curiously-compounded,

[1] Could be freely translated as the Slothful Button Boy.

swiftly-satisfying loaf of Toma. Then the Fair
Strangers became very angry, and sent out their
trusty, fleet-footed couriers to scour the land for
invaders ; for they knew that none of the Dedannans would take the berries, being under gesa
not to do so. But the couriers returned, and
though they were men able to trace the trail of
a fox through nine glens and nine rivers, they
could discover no proof of the presence of a foreign foe in the mayden cantred of Devorgilla.

Then the hearts of the Fair Strangers were
filled with grief and gall, for they distrusted the
couriers, and having consulted the Ard-ri, they
set forth themselves to find and conquer the invader ; for the king told them that there was one
other quicken tree, more beautiful and more
magical than that growing by the Fairy Palace,
and that it was set in another part of the bright-
blooming, sweet-scented old garden, — namely, in
the heart of the labyrinthine maze of the Wise
Woman of Wales ; but as no one of them, neither
the Gilla Dacker nor those who pursued him, had
ever, even with the aid of the Magic Thread-
Clue, reached the heart of the maze, there was
no knowledge among them of the second quicken
tree. The king also told Sheela the Scribe, secretly, that one of his knights had found a money-
piece and a breviary in the forest of Rosnaree ;
and the silver was unlike any ever used in the
country of the Dedannans, and the breviary could

belong only to a pious Gael known as Loskenn of the Bare Knees.

Now Sheela the Scribe, having fasted from midnight until dawn, gazed upon the Horn of Foreknowledge, and read there that it was wiser for her to remain on guard at the Fairy Palace, while her sisters explored the secret fastnesses of the labyrinth.

When Finola was appareled to set forth upon her quest, Péarla thought her the loveliest maiden upon the ridge of the world, and wondered whether she meant to conquer the invader by force of arms or by the power of beauty.

The rose and the lily were fighting together in her face, and one could not tell which of them got the victory. Her arms and hands were like the lime, her mouth was as red as a ripe strawberry, her foot as small and as light as another one's hand, her form smooth and slender, and her hair falling down from her head under combs of gold.[1] One could not look at her without being " all over in love with her," as Oisin said at his first meeting with Niam of the Golden Hair. And as for Péarla, the rose on her cheeks was heightened by her rage against the invader, the delicate blossom of the sloe was not whiter than her neck, and her glossy chestnut ringlets fell to her waist.

Then the Gilla Dacker unleashed Bran, the

[1] Description of the Princess in Guleesh na Guss Dhu.

keen-scented terrier hound, and put a pearl-embroidered pillion on Enbarr of the Flowing Mane, and the two dauntless maidens leaped upon her back, each bearing a broad shield and a long, polished, death-dealing spear. When Enbarr had been given a free rein she set out for the labyrinth, trailing the Magic Thread-Clue behind her, cleaving the air with long, active strides ; and if you know what the speed of a swallow is, flying across a mountain side, or the dry wind of a March day sweeping over the plains, then you can understand nothing of the swiftness of this steed of the flowing mane, acquired by the day by the maydens of Devorgilla.

Many were the dangers that beset the path of these two noble champions on their quest for the Fairy Quicken Tree. Here they met an enormous wild stoat, but this was slain by the intrepid Bran, and they buried its bleeding corse and raised a cairn over it, with the name " Stoat " graven on it in Ogam ; there a druidical fairy mist sprang up in their path to hide the way, but they pierced it with a note of their far-reaching, clarion-toned voices, — an art learned in their native land beyond the wave.

Now the dog Bran, being anhungered, and refusing to eat of Toma's loaf, as all did who were ignorant of its druidical purpose, fell upon the Magic Thread-Clue and tore it in twain. This so greatly affrighted the champions that they sounded the Dord-Fian slowly and plaintively, hoping that the war cry might bring Sheela to their rescue. This availing nothing, Finola was forced to slay Bran with her straight-sided, silver-shining spear; but this she felt he would not mind if he could know that he would share the splendid fate of the stoat, and speedily have a cairn raised over him, with the word "Bran" graven upon it in Ogam, — since this is the consolation offered by the victorious living to all dead Celtic heroes; and if it be a poor substitute for life, it is at least better than nothing.

It was now many hours after noon, and though, to the Fair Strangers, it seemed they had traveled more than forty or a hundred miles, they were apparently no nearer than ever to the heart of the labyrinth: and this from the first had been the pestiferous peculiarity of that malignantly meandering maze. So they dismounted, and tied Enbarr to the branch of a tree, while they refreshed themselves with a mouthful of Toma's loaf; and Finola now put her thumb under her "tooth of knowledge," for she wished new guidance and inspiration, and, being more than common modest, she said: "Inasmuch as we are fairer than all the other maydens in this labyrinth, why, since we cannot find the heart of the maze, do we not entice the invaders from their hiding place by the quicken tree; and when we see from what direction they advance, fall upon and slay

them; and after raising the usual cairn to their
memory, and carving their names over it in the
customary Ogam, run to the enchanted tree and
gather all the berries that are left? For this is
the hour when Sheela brews the tea, and the
knights and the ladies quaff it from our golden
cups; and truly I am weary of this quest, and far
rather would I be there than here."

So Péarla the Melodious took her timpan,[1] and
chanted a Gaelic song that she had learned in the
country of the Dedannans; and presently a round-
polished, red-gleaming quicken berry dropped
into her lap, and another into Finola's, and, looking up, they saw naught save only a cloud of
quicken berries falling through the air one after
the other. And this caused them to wonder, for
it seemed like unto a snare set for them; but
Péarla said, "There is naught remaining for us
but to meet the danger."

"It is well," replied Finola, shaking down the
mantle of her ebon locks, and setting the golden
combs more firmly in them; "only, if I perish, I
prithee let there be no cairns or Ogams. Let
me fall, as a beauty should, face upward; and if
it be but a swoon, and the invader be a handsome prince, see that he wakens me in his own
good way."

"To arms, then!" cried Péarla, and, taking

[1] An ancient Irish instrument; not to be confounded with tin
pan.

up their spears and shields, the Fair Strangers dashed blindly in the direction whence the berries fell.

"To arms indeed, but to yours or ours?" called two voices from the heart of the labyrinth; and there, in an instant, the two brave champions, Finola and Péarla, found the Fairy Tree hanging thick with scarlet berries, and under its branches, fit fruit indeed to raise the spirits or bring eternal youth, were, in the language of the Dedannans, Loskenn of the Bare Knees and the Bishop of Ossory,— known to the children of Corr the Swift-Footed as Ronald Macdonald and Himself!

And the hours ran on; and Sheela the Scribe brewed and brewed and brewed and brewed the tea at her table in the Peacock Walk, and the knights and ladies quaffed it from the golden cups belonging to the Wise Woman of Wales; but Finola the Festive and Péarla the Melodious lingered in the labyrinth with Loskenn of the Bare Knees and the Bishop of Ossory. And they said to one another, "Surely, if it were so great a task to find the heart of this maze, we should be mad to stir from the spot, lest we lose it again."

And Péarla murmured, "That plan were wise indeed, save that the place seemeth all too small for so many."

Then Finola drew herself up proudly, and replied, "It is no smaller for one than for another;

but come, Loskenn, let us see if haply we can lose ourselves in some path of our own finding."

And this they did; and the content of them that departed was no greater than the content of them that were left behind, and the sun hid himself for very shame because the brightness of their joy was so much more dazzling than the glory of his own face.   And nothing more is told of what befell them till they reached the threshold of the Old Hall; and it was not the sun, but the moon that shone upon their meeting with Sheela the Scribe.

XXXI

GOOD-BY, DARK ROSALEEN!

" When the poor exiles, every pleasure past,
    Hung round the bowers, and fondly looked their last,
    And took a long farewell, and wished in vain
    For seats like these beyond the western main,
    And shuddering still to face the distant deep,
    Returned and wept, and still returned to weep."
                                    Oliver Goldsmith.

It is almost over, our Irish holiday, so full of delicious, fruitful experiences ; of pleasures we have made and shared, and of other people's miseries and hardships we could not relieve. Almost over! Soon we shall all be in Dublin, and then on to London to meet Francesca's father ; soon be deciding whether she will be married at the house of their friend the American ambassador, or in her own country, where she has really had no home since the death of her mother.

The ceremony over, Mr. Monroe will start again for Cairo or Constantinople, Stockholm or St. Petersburg ; for he is of late years a determined wanderer, whose fatherly affection is chiefly shown in liberal allowances, in pride of his daughter's beauty and many conquests, in conscientious letter-writing, and in frequent calls

upon her between his long journeys. It is because of these paternal predilections that we are
so glad Francesca's heart has resisted all the shot
and shell directed against it from the batteries
of a dozen gay worldlings and yielded so quietly
and so completely to Ronald Macdonald's loyal
and tender affection.

At tea time day before yesterday, Salemina suggested that Francesca and I find the heart of
Aunt David's labyrinth, the which she had discovered in a less than ten minutes' search that
morning, leaving her Gaelic primer behind her
that we might bring it back as a proof of our suc-
cess. You have heard in Péarla's Celtic fairy
tale the outcome of this little expedition, and
now know that Ronald Macdonald and Himself
planned the joyful surprise for us, and by means
of Salemina's aid carried it out triumphantly.

Ronald crossing to Ireland from Glasgow, and
Himself from Liverpool, had met in Dublin, and
traveled posthaste to the Shamrock Inn in Devorgilla, where they communicated with Salemina
and begged her assistance in their plot.

I was looking forward to my husband's arrival
within a week, but Ronald had said not a word
of his intended visit; so that Salemina was properly nervous lest some one of us should collapse
out of sheer joy at the unexpected meeting.

I have been both quietly and wildly happy
many times in my life, but I think yesterday was

the most perfect day in all my chain of years.
Not that in this long separation I have been dull,
or sad, or lonely. How could I be? Dull, with
two dear, bright, sunny letters every week, letters
throbbing with manly tenderness, letters breathing the sure, steadfast, protecting care that a
strong man gives to the woman he has chosen!
Sad, with my heart brimming over with sweet
memories and sweeter prophecies, and all its tiny
crevices so filled with love that discontent can
find no entrance there! Lonely, when the vision
of the beloved is so poignantly real in absence
that his bodily presence adds only a final touch
to joy! Dull, or sad, when in these soft days of
spring and early summer I have harbored a new
feeling of companionship and oneness with Nature, a fresh joy in all her bounteous resource
and plenitude of life, a renewed sense of kinship
with her mysterious awakenings! The heavenly
greenness and promise of the outer world seem
but a reflection of the hopes and dreams that ir-
radiate my own inner consciousness.

My art, dearly as I loved it, dearly as I love it
still, never gave me these strange, unspeakable
joys with their delicate margin of pain. Where
are my ambitions, my visions of lonely triumphs,
my imperative need of self-expression, my enno-
bling glimpses of the unattainable, my companionship with the shadows in which an artist's life
is so rich? Are they vanished altogether? I

think not; only changed in the twinkling of an eye, merged in something higher still, carried over, linked on, transformed, transmuted, by Love the alchemist, who, not content with joys already bestowed, whispers secret promises of raptures yet to come.

The green isle looked its fairest for our wanderers. Just as a woman adorns herself with all her jewels when she wishes to startle or enthrall, wishes to make a lover of a friend, so Devorgilla arrayed herself to conquer these two pairs of fresh eyes, and command their instant allegiance.

It was a tender, silvery day, fair, mild, pensive, with light shadows and a capricious sun. There had been a storm of rain the night before, and it was as if Nature had repented of her wildness, and sought forgiveness by all sorts of winsome arts, insinuating invitations, soft caresses, and melting coquetries of demeanor.

Broona and Jackeen had lunched with us at the Old Hall, and, inebriated by broiled chicken, green peas, and a half holiday, flitted like fireflies through Aunt David's garden, showing all its treasures to the two new friends, already high in favor.

Benella, it is unnecessary to say, had confided her entire past life to Himself after a few hours' acquaintance, while both he and Ronald, concealing in the most craven manner their original objections to the part she proposed to play in our triangular alliance, thanked her, with tears in their eyes, for her devotion to their sovereign ladies.

We had tea in the Italian garden at Rosnaree, and Dr. Gerald, arm in arm with Himself, walked between its formal flower borders, along its paths of golden gravel, and among its spirelike cypresses and fountains, where balustrades and statues, yellowed and stained with age (stains which Benella longs to scrub away), make the brilliant turf even greener by contrast.

Tea was to have been followed in due course by dinner, but we all agreed that nothing should induce us to go indoors on such a beautiful evening; so baskets were packed, and we went in rowboats to a picnic supper on Illanroe, a wee island in Lough Beg.

I can close my eyes to-day and see the picture, — the lonely little lake, as blue in the sunshine as the sky above it, but in the twilight first brown and cool, then flushed with the sunset. The distant hills, the rocks, the heather, wore tints I never saw them wear before. The singing wavelets " spilled their crowns of white upon the beach " across the lake, and the wild flowers in the clear shallows near us grew so close to the brink that they threw their delicate reflections in the water, looking up at us again framed in red-brown grasses.

By and by the moon rose out of the pearl grays

and ambers in the east, bevies of black rooks flew
homeward, and stillness settled over the face of
the brown lake. Darkness shut us out from Devorgilla ; and though we could still see the glim-
mer of the village lights, it seemed as if we were
in a little world of our own.

It was useless for Salemina to deny herself to
the children, for was she not going to leave them
on the morrow ? She sat under the shadow of a
thorn bush, and the two mites, tired with play,
cuddled themselves by her side, unreproved.
She looked tenderly, delectably feminine. The
moon shone full upon her face ; but there are no
ugly lines to hide, for there are no parched and
arid places in her nature. Dews of sympathy,
sweet spring floods of love and compassion, have
kept all fresh, serene, and young.

We had been gay, but silence fell upon us as it
had fallen upon the lake. There would be only
a day or two in Dublin, whither Dr. Gerald was
going with us, that he might have the last word
and hand clasp before we sailed away from Irish
shores ; and so near was the parting that we were
all, in our hearts, bidding farewell to the Emerald
Isle.

Good-by, Silk of the Kine! I was saying to
myself, calling the friendly spot by one of the
endearing names given her by her lovers in the
sad old days. Good-by, Little Black Rose, growing on the stern Atlantic shore ! Good-by, Rose

of the World, with your jewels of emerald and amethyst, the green of your fields and the misty purple of your hills! Good-by, Shan Van Vocht, Poor Little Old Woman! We are going back, Himself and I, to the Oileán Ur, as you used to call our new island, — going back to the hurly-burly of affairs, to prosperity and opportunity; but we shall not forget the lovely Lady of Sorrows looking out to the west with the pain of a thousand years in her ever youthful eyes. Good-by, my Dark Rosaleen, good-by!

XXXII

"AS THE SUNFLOWER TURNS"

"No, the heart that has truly lov'd never forgets,
    But as truly loves on to the close,
As the sunflower turns on her god, when he sets,
    The same look which she turn'd when he rose."
                                        Thomas Moore.

HERE we all are at O'Carolan's Hotel in Dublin, — all but the Colquhouns, who bade us adieu at the station, and the dear children, whose tears are probably dried by now, although they flowed freely enough at parting.   Broona flung her arms tempestuously around Salemina's neck, exclaiming between her sobs, "Good-by, my thousand, thousand blessings !" — an expression so Irish that we laughed and cried in one breath at the sound of it.

Here we are in the midst of life once more, though to be sure it is Irish life, which moves less dizzily than our own.   We ourselves feel thoroughly at home, nor are we wholly forgotten by the public ; for on beckoning to a driver on the cab stand to approach with his side car, he responded with alacrity, calling to his neighbor, "Here's me sixpenny darlin' again !" and I recognized him immediately as a man who had once remonstrated with me eloquently on the subject of a fee, making such a fire of Hibernian jokes over my sixpence that I heartily wished it had been a half sovereign.

Cables and telegrams are arriving every hour, and a rich American lady writes to Salemina, asking her if she can purchase the Book of Kells for her, as she wishes to give it to a favorite nephew who is a bibliomaniac. I am begging the shocked Miss Peabody to explain that the volume in question is not for sale, and to ask at the same time if her correspondent wishes to purchase the Lakes of Killarney or the Giant's Causeway in its stead. Francesca, in a whirl of excitement, is buying cobweb linens, harp brooches, creamy poplins with golden shamrocks woven into their lustrous surfaces; and as for laces, we spend hours in the shops, when our respective squires wish us to show them the sights of Dublin.

Benella is in her element, nursing Salemina, who sprained her ankle just as we were leaving Devorgilla. At the last moment our side cars were so crowded with passengers and packages that she accepted a seat in Dr. Gerald's carriage, and drove to the station with him. She had a few last farewells to say in the village, and a few modest remembrances to leave with some of the poor old women; and I afterward learned that the drive was not without its embarrassments. The butch-

er's wife said fervently, " May you long be spared
to each other ! " The old weaver exclaimed,
" 'T would be an ojus pity to spoil two houses
wid ye ! " While the woman who sells apples at
the station capped all by wishing the couple " a
long life and a happy death together." No wonder poor Salemina slipped and twisted her ankle,
as she alighted from the carriage ! Though walking without help is still an impossibility, twenty-
four hours of rubbing and bathing and bandaging
have made it possible for her to limp discreetly,
and we all went to St. Patrick's Cathedral together this morning.

We had been in the quiet churchyard, where a
soft misty rain was falling on the yellow acacias
and the pink hawthorns. We had stood under
the willow tree in the deanery garden, — the tree
that marks the site of the house from which Dean
Swift watched the movements of the torches in
the cathedral at the midnight burial of Stella.
They are lying side by side at the foot of a col-
umn in the south side of the nave, and a brass
plate in the pavement announces : —

" Here lies Mrs. Hester Johnson, better known
to the world by the name of Stella, under which
she is celebrated in the writings of Dr. Jonathan
Swift, Dean of this Cathedral."

Poor Stella, at rest for a century and a half
beside the man who caused her such pangs of
love and grief, — who does not mourn her ?

The nave of the cathedral was dim, and empty of all sight-seers save our own group. There was a caretaker who went about in sloppy rubber shoes, scrubbing marbles and polishing brasses, and behind a high screen or temporary partition some one was playing softly on an organ.

We stood in a quiet circle by Stella's resting place, and Dr. Gerald, who never forgets anything, apparently, was reminding us of Thackeray's gracious and pathetic tribute : —

" Fair and tender creature, pure and affectionate heart ! Boots it to you now that the whole world loves you and deplores you ? Scarce any man ever thought of your grave that did not cast a flower of pity on it, and write over it a sweet epitaph. Gentle lady ! so lovely, so loving, so unhappy. You have had countless champions, millions of manly hearts mourning for you. From generation to generation we take up the fond tradition of your beauty ; we watch and follow your story, your bright morning love and purity, your constancy, your grief, your sweet martyrdom. We know your legend by heart. You are one of the saints of English story."

As Dr. Gerald's voice died away, the strains of Love's Young Dream floated out from the distant end of the building.

" The organist must be practicing for a wedding," said Francesca, very much alive to anything of that sort.

" ' Oh, there 's nothing half so sweet in life,' "

she hummed. "Is n't it charming?"

"You ought to know," Dr. Gerald answered, looking at her affectionately, though somewhat too sadly for my taste; "but an old fellow like me must take refuge in the days of 'milder, calmer beam,' of which the poet speaks."

Ronald and Himself, guide-books in hand, walked away to talk about The Burial of Sir John Moore, and look for Wolfe's tablet, and I stole behind the great screen which had been thrown up while repairs of some sort were being made or a new organ built. A young man was evidently taking a lesson, for the old organist was sitting on the bench beside him, pulling out the stops, and indicating the time with his hand. There was to be a wedding, — that was certain; for Love's Young Dream was taken off the music rack, at that moment, while "Believe me, if all those endearing young charms" was put in its place, and the melody came singing out to us on the vox humana stop.

> " Thou wouldst still be adored, as this moment thou art,
>   Let thy loveliness fade as it will,
> And around the dear ruin each wish of my heart
>   Would entwine itself verdantly still."

Francesca joined me just then, and a tear was in her eye. "Penny dear, when all is said, ' Believe me ' is the dearer song of the two. Anybody can sing, feel, live, the first, which is but a

youthful dream, after all ; but the other has in it
the proved fidelity of the years. The first song
belongs to me, I know, and it is all I am fit for
now ; but I want to grow toward and deserve the
second."

"You are right; but while Love's Young
Dream is yours and Ronald's, dear, take all the
joy that it holds for you. The other song is for
Salemina and Dr. Gerald, and I only hope they
are realizing it at this moment, — secretive, pro-
voking creatures that they are ! "

The old organist left his pupil just then, and
disappeared through a little door in the rear.

"Have you The Wedding March there ? " I
asked the pupil who had been practicing the
love songs.

"Oh yes, madam, though I am afraid I cannot
do it justice," he replied modestly. "Are you
interested in organ music ? "

" I am very much interested in yours, and I am
still more interested in a romance that has been
dragging its weary length along for twenty years,
and is trying to bring itself to a crisis just on the
other side of that screen. You can help me precipitate it, if you only will ! "

Well, he was young and he was an Irishman,
which is equivalent to being a born lover, and he
had been brought up on Tommy Moore and music,
— all of which I had known from the moment I
saw him, else I should not have made the pro-

position. I peeped from behind the screen. Ronald and Himself were walking toward us; Salemina and Dr. Gerald were sitting together in one of the front pews. I beckoned to my husband.

"Will you and Ronald go quietly out one of the side doors," I asked, "take your own car, and go back to the hotel, allowing us to follow you a little later?"

It takes more than one year of marriage for even the cleverest Benedict to uproot those weeds of stupidity, denseness, and non-comprehension that seem to grow so riotously in the mental garden of the bachelor; so, said Himself, "We came all together; why should n't we go home all together?" (So like a man! Always reasoning from analogy; always so to speak, "lugging in" logic!)

"Desperate situations demand desperate remedies," I replied mysteriously, though I hope patiently. "If you go home at once without any questions, you will be virtuous, and it is more than likely that you will also be happy; and if you are not, somebody else will be."

Having seen the backs of our two cavaliers disappearing meekly into the rain, I stationed Francesca at a point of vantage, and went out to my victims in the front pew.

"The others went on ahead," I explained, with elaborate carelessness, — "they wanted to